P9-DBY-810

Alfred A. Knopf
New York

APR 2 2 2021

FADE
AWAY

E. B. Vickers

THIS IS A BORZOI BOOK PUBLISHED BY ALFRED A. KNOPF

This is a work of fiction. Names, characters, places, and incidents either are the product of the author's imagination or are used fictitiously. Any resemblance to actual persons, living or dead, events, or locales is entirely coincidental.

Visit us on the Web! GetUnderlined.com

Educators and librarians, for a variety of teaching tools, visit us at RHTeachersLibrarians.com

Library of Congress Cataloging-in-Publication Data is available upon request.
ISBN 978-0-593-18019-8 (trade) — ISBN 978-0-593-18020-4 (lib. bdg.) — ISBN 0-593-18021-1 (ebook)

The text of this book is set in 11-point Georgia Regular.
Interior design by Andrea Lau

Printed in the United States of America
March 2021
10 9 8 7 6 5 4 3 2 1

First Edition

for
my dad, my first and best coach
my husband, unparalleled teammate and soulmate
my son, for whom the sky's the limit

and for anyone who has ever faced
the monster of Not Enough

Countdown

Kolt

After

Here's how I remember that night:

At 8:53 p.m., there were thousands of people watching my best friend. Me and Seth and Coach and Daphne and Luke and every other person in that gym. Jake brought the ball down the court for one last shot as the clock ticked down to that row of zeros, and the crowd chanted along: *"Three . . . two . . . one . . ."*

There's always been something pure about the way Jake plays, like some wild animal doing exactly what it was born to do. A mountain lion, maybe—sturdy and silent, and when it's coming for you, you might as well piss your pants as try to stop it. In the final seconds, he drove hard to the hoop, then pulled back for a fadeaway with more finesse than Van freaking Gogh.

When the shot went up, I was ready to grab the board, even though I knew he wouldn't need it. Even though the buzzer was already blaring in my ears. You practice something that many times—the shot goes up and you seal your guy off—that you do it without even thinking. That's probably why even now I look for Jake when I get out of world history. Why I expect it to be him every time my phone vibrates.

With one perfect flick of his wrist, the rock's through the rim, and the state title is ours. Then it's all cheering and chest bumps, and half the guys are crying, and the whole crowd's got their phones out, trying to catch this moment so they can put it in their pocket and pull it out anytime, like they're witnessing their own little moment of world history.

There's more I remember about that night. The satisfying snip of cutting down the net, the roar of the crowd when we brought the trophy straight over to the student section. But none of it's as important as this: at 8:53 p.m., there were thousands of people watching my best friend. Hundreds of cameras snapping and shooting his every move.

But when the show's over, we all look away.

So nobody saw it happen. Nobody knows how or why or even exactly when he disappeared.

All we know is that by the next morning, Jake was gone.

Pain or Poison

After

It's dark down here. Dark and cold.

His breathing is slow, his lips are blue.

"Sit up," a voice demands.

He hears it faintly, like it's coming through a thick wall, even though they're in the same room.

"Sit up." Louder this time, and he feels the hot breath on his ear. His head throbs, but he lifts it a few inches and hopes it's enough that the voice will stop yelling.

"Take this," the voice says, and something small and round is shoved between his lips. He hopes it's something for the pain, because every muscle burns and aches. He feels himself choking on the water being poured into his mouth to chase it down.

The pill is still there, swimming against his tongue. He

wants to swallow it so badly, but his head is foggy and he's not sure he should.

Is it for the pain? Or is it poison?

Poison, he remembers. *They're all poison.*

He turns toward the sound of the voice and draws air into his nose, ready to spit the poison right back in the person's face.

That's assuming the voice has a face and a person to go with it. Sometimes, down here, they don't.

"Swallow it," says the voice, grabbing a handful of his hair and yanking his head backward.

And because, really, that's what he wanted to do all along, he swallows it.

"Good," says the voice, and then Jake lets his head fall back to the pile of rags, already soaked with his sweat and snot and tears.

Police Statement:
Kolt Martin

When was the last time you saw Jake Foster?

In the locker room, after the game.

Did he do or say anything unusual?

He didn't do or say much, so maybe that was unusual. But he played the entire game. Dude had to be exhausted.

And after that? Who did you leave the game with?

My whole family. Well, except my brother Kade. You probably remember him, huh? Kade Martin? Goes by Kmart? Don't worry, he's the Flagstaff PD's problem now.

So you went home for a while. Did you go to the party at Coach Cooper's house after that?

Yeah. Everybody did.

Everybody except Jake.

That's true.

Did Jake party?

No.

Did he drink at all?

No. He never smoked anything, either, if that's your next question. He's clean for pretty much the same reason I am, and I already told you mine.

Is there anybody else you think we should talk to? Anybody on the team who didn't like Jake?

Seth Cooper, I guess.

Why is that?

Dude was always weird about Jake. Told him he hated him before the game.

We'll look into that. So, the last time you saw Jake was back in the Ashland locker room, after the game. Is that the last time you heard from him at all?

Yes, sir.

And how long have you known him? How long have you two been best friends?

Both questions, same answer: since the summer before sixth grade.

Where It Begins

Kolt

The Summer Before Sixth Grade

Even though we were from the same part of town—the wrong part—Jake and I went to different elementary schools. The boundary cut right between our run-down houses like an imaginary line to keep us from being friends.

Until we were old enough for Junior Warriors Basketball Camp the summer before sixth grade, anyway.

You could already tell how good Jake was going to be, even as a skinny almost-sixth-grader. Watching him back then was like that feeling when a burp's built up inside you and you know it's going to be huge. (Jake wouldn't even mind me saying that. He has sick burping skills.)

But in this case, everybody could tell something big was coming *except* Jake. He worked harder than anybody—

finishing first on conditioning and still running an extra lap, always looking around during drills to make sure he was doing stuff right. Didn't even notice the rest of us trying not to stare at him because the way he did things was the definition of right. I was already a show-off and a punk by then, but even I was too intimidated to say a word to him.

On the last day of camp, Coach Cooper sat us all down in the locker room, and somehow I wound up smashed on that too-small bench right next to Jake himself.

"I know this feels like the end, boys," Coach said, "but this is actually where it begins. Sixth grade for you, first year as head coach for me. It might take some time to build the program up to where I want it to be, but by the time you boys are seniors"—he waved a finger down the line at all of us, stopping on his own kid, Seth—"we're going to be state champions. I'm making that promise to all of you today, and I will do whatever it takes to keep it."

We'd all seen the trophies in the case outside the gym and the banners hanging from the rafters like flags from some battlefield. We knew that all the old guys around town asked "When did you play?" and if you said one of *those* years, you got your soda paid for or an extra token for the car wash.

But we were all too young to actually remember the last time the Warriors had won it. We just knew it was back before the last guy, Coach Braithwaite, had lost his edge. Those were his boxes piled in the corner. He was so old he should have been retiring anyway, but the rumor was that the boosters and the school district had pushed him out the door after what happened that season.

Which was why Coach Cooper was the one trying to give us the pep talk as we sat there, still sweating from a full day of drills and scrimmages. "Winning isn't everything," he said, and this deep, disturbing V wrinkle took over his forehead. "It's the only thing."

There was so much fire in his eyes and spit at the corners of his mouth I didn't dare tell him that didn't really make sense. But Jake, he was drinking it in like Gatorade after suicides.

Then we heard a soft knock on the locker-room door, and there he was. Coach Braithwaite: the man, the legend, the dinosaur.

"Sorry to interrupt your speech," he said. "You always were a fine leader, Seth." That confused me for a second, until I realized that Coach Cooper and his kid must both be named Seth, and maybe that was why the new head varsity coach was willing to run the sixth-grade camp. I wondered if having the same name as your dad would be annoying (because if somebody says "Seth" in your house, how do you know they're talking to you and not the other one?) or really nice (because if there's one last Sprite and somebody wrote "Seth" on the bottle, you could be like, "Well, it has my name on it . . .").

Coach B smiled at us, all the way down the bench, like we were his grandkids here for a visit or something. "Well, look at you boys," he said. "Marvelous, every one of you." Then he gave a little nod like that made it true.

"Mind if I grab these?" he asked, waving a hand at the boxes in the corner.

"Sure, sure, of course," said Coach C. Even he seemed softer around the old man.

"Would you like me to take this too?" Coach B asked, pointing to a sign in the corner I hadn't even noticed. "You shouldn't be saddled with my old philosophy." Three words had been spelled out on the sign in bold lettering:

HEAD

HANDS

HEART

Coach C reached up and ran his finger along the edge. I think he forgot we were there, to be honest. It was like that sign took him straight back to his own days of sitting on this butt-numbing bench, feeling the sweat dry on his skin. "You can leave it," he said. "If that's okay. I might need a reminder someday."

"Of course, son." Coach B looked over us boys on the

bench. His knees crackled like firewood as he bent to pick up one of the boxes in the corner.

"Boys, help Coach B with those. We're finished here anyway. Good work today."

Jake and me were on the end of the bench, so we got the other two boxes. We followed Coach B out to his car, if you could even call it a car. Really, it was more like one of those Jeeps you see in old war movies. We slid the boxes in the back and slammed the hatch shut.

"Thank you, boys," Coach B said, and he reached out to shake our hands. It was all so formal. I hoped, hoped, *hoped* he wouldn't ask us our full names. Even though I was only a sixth grader, I didn't want him to recognize me and realize it was my waste of a brother who'd cost him the championship last season—and probably his job.

So of course that was when Kmart pulled up. He stumbled out of his truck, high as Everest.

"Kade Martin," Coach B said. "I've been hoping I'd see you again." He stuck out the same hand to Kmart as he had to us—and gave him the same smile too.

My brother spat at his feet.

"Get in the truck, Kolt," he said. "Before he ruins your life too."

He didn't ruin your life. You did this to yourself. I wanted to scream it, to spit right back at him. *And look what you did to him.*

But instead I froze, like the weak-ass baby I was.

Coach B took a step toward Kmart. "Now, son . . ."

"I'm not your son. I'm the kid whose future you trashed because you expect everybody to be perfect like you." Kmart's voice got louder with every word, and he struck the passenger-side door with a hollow *bang, bang, bang,* right in rhythm. "Get in the truck, Kolt. Get in the damn truck."

People were looking now, watching the show from the safety of their cars.

"He can't," Jake said, stepping between me and Kmart. "We have to help with the rest of the boxes. My mom is taking him home."

Everybody knew there were no more boxes—except Kmart. He stared Jake down for what felt like forever, but Jake didn't look away, even though Kmart was twice his size and ten kinds of unpredictable.

"Waste of my time," Kmart finally muttered. He stumbled back to his truck, brushing past Jake's shoulder hard enough to knock him off balance.

"Maybe you shouldn't be driving," somebody said, but Kmart just gave the whole parking lot the one-finger salute before slamming the door and swerving away.

"Where's your mom?" I asked, feeling ready for that ride and too grateful to actually say thanks.

Jake looked toward Dollar Depot. "She's at work," he

said. "Sorry. I don't usually lie, I just . . . I think we're walking."

"Nonsense," Coach B said. "I'll take you as far as my place if you'll help me get these boxes into the house."

So that's how we ended up at Coach B's house the first time. That old Jeep had a motor so loud it was almost impossible to hear anything else, but I knew I had to say what I had to say before I lost the guts to say it.

"Thanks," I told Jake. "My brother's the worst."

"Your brother reminds me of my dad," he said. We had to practically shout to hear each other as we rattled down the road, but something about that felt right. Like the words hurt less when you didn't have to whisper them.

"Your dad's addicted too?" I asked.

"Was," Jake corrected, and I wondered for half a second if he'd gotten clean, until I looked at Jake's face and realized what he meant by "was."

"Just alcohol," he said, then corrected himself. "Well, not *just*."

After that, there wasn't anything else we needed to say about either of them. Not even when Kmart got caught selling and had to go to jail, or when he moved away without a word the day he got out.

We loved them and we hated them and we were never, ever going to be like them.

Everything Hurts

After

Jake is awake more of the time now, but he wishes he weren't. All he wants is sleep.

His stomach cramps and clenches. He runs for the toilet in the corner, but not fast enough, and vomit splatters the floor, splashes his bare feet and the cuffs of his pants. The stains around the toilet tell him this has happened before, but he barely has time to register that fact before he's throwing up again, leaning so far into the bowl that it spatters back in his face.

Afterward, he rinses the taste out with water from the faucet and wipes his mouth with the back of his arm. The wave has passed, but something—a premonition, maybe, or a hazy memory—tells him it won't be long until the next one comes. His body gives one great shudder, and suddenly his skin crawls with goosebumps and his limbs begin to shake.

It hurts. Everything hurts.

The only light comes from one small window and one bare bulb, but the window is high and has bars over it, and the bulb buzzes in a way that makes him want to pull his ears off.

And what is there to see down here, anyway? A small, dirty cot and an old blanket. A folding chair. The toilet and sink and shell of a shower in the corner, all rimmed brown, and the remnants of studs and Sheetrock that tell him it must have been an actual bathroom once, before this place fell apart.

Jake worked construction last summer. He's pretty sure, anyway. It's hard to think about anything but the thing he misses most.

"Hey!" he shouts into the locked door, his heart racing. "Where's my poison?"

But he's alone.

For now.

Police Statement: Daphne Sharp

Tell me how you know Jake Foster.

We're friends.

Only friends?

We were together for two years—beginning of sophomore basketball to the beginning of the season this year—but we're not together anymore.

Did you talk to him Saturday night?

We ran into each other in the training room before the game. I went to get ice for my ankle, and he was in there, looking for a trainer to help with his knee. I didn't even know it was bothering him again, but there he was.

Did he seem nervous?

He's been nervous all season, and the whole town's

hopes were riding on that one game. Of course he was nervous.

Have you heard from Jake since then?

No. Wait—why? Where is he? Is he okay?

That's what we're trying to find out, Ms. Sharp.

Seth checked on him Saturday night after the party. I think Jake was with Kolt. Have you talked to Kolt yet?

We have.

What about Jake's mom? What about Luke? Are you saying nobody has seen him since Saturday night?

We're still working on that part too. Did Jake ever talk about hurting himself?

No. Never. Jake wouldn't do that.

Did he ever talk about running away?

No. Why would he run away right after they won state? Jake wouldn't run, and he wouldn't hurt himself. . . . But where would he be? You don't think something happened to him, do you?

At this point, we're investigating all those possibilities.

I'm sorry for asking so many questions. I know that's your job. This is just . . .

Hey, that's okay. Keep asking questions—around school, with your friends—and let me know if you hear anything, okay? Oh, and say hi to your dad for me.

Tomorrow's Going to Hurt

Daphne

Sophomore Year

The first time I ever saw Jake, he was sitting in my dad's courtroom in a collared shirt and khakis, trying to blend in. I just looked over, and there he was, this guy from my English class, sneaking in right before the hearing on some drug case where the defendant didn't even show.

"What are you doing here?" he whispered.

"That's my dad," I said, nodding toward the bench. (Dad came to enough of my games and recitals that I liked to return the favor once in a while, so sometimes I'd go watch court and just be there for him while he did his thing.) "What are *you* doing here?"

Jake sighed. "Racketeering, money laundering, making moonshine in my bathtub."

His face was so bright and clean that nobody would

have bought it, even if we'd been in juvenile court. I tried to swallow my laugh, but enough escaped that Dad gave me the Look from the bench.

By then I'd realized that no guy would ever be good enough for Dad, but I didn't blame him. (Not yet, anyway.) It would be hard to see the best in people if you spent your days passing judgment on a parade of broken laws and lives.

From the moment the bailiff called "All rise" in Dad's courtroom, there was no question how you were supposed to behave or who was in charge. In the few weeks we'd been in town, he'd already had to take the whole "Your Honor" business up a level, thanks to a slow but steady flow of defendants (and one idiotic attorney) who thought his being new somehow gave him less authority and tried to push the limits.

Dad definitely didn't need his own daughter disrupting things. So once I got the Look, I didn't even dare ask what Jake was really doing there. I snapped to attention, and by the time I had the guts to glance back over a few minutes later, he was gone.

But after that, I noticed Jake everywhere. Messing around in the parking lot with friends. At the grocery store with his little brother. In the weight room every Thursday.

I definitely noticed him there. Not because he looked hot (although, yeah, he looked hot), but because he was so different from his friends. He never lifted in front of the mirror, like Seth; he didn't make fart sounds when people did squats, like Kolt. He actually wiped his sweat off the equipment before moving along. Sometimes he sang PBS Kids songs while he benched plates.

(Note: I was very careful not to let him notice all my noticing.)

Once sophomore football was over, Jake started coming to open gym too. The girls took one gym and the boys took the other, playing pickup games until the coaches left and Mr. Caruso, the creepy custodian, kicked us out. There was no official roll, and the coaches weren't even allowed to talk to us until tryouts, but we knew they were taking note and taking names. Something inside me did the same thing with Jake, wanting to look out onto the court and find him there before losing myself in a game of my own.

During those weeks, we didn't play just because of who was watching. We played because we wanted to. We wanted that spot on the roster, sure, but we wanted little things just as much: the sting on our palms of a chest pass fired fast, the rush when a three goes through the hoop with that satisfying snap of ball on net. Those little hits of adrenaline, better than any drug. Or that's what Jenna told me, anyway.

"I've sampled it all," she said on the first day of tryouts.

We were leaned over, nearly puking after running twelve suicides. "And none of it makes you feel this good." She was grinning so hard I had to believe her.

Even though tryouts had me feeling high too, my shot had been off all day. So after everybody else had packed up, I rolled the rack back out and started shooting threes, one after another. When I'd shot them all, I reloaded the rack and moved to a new spot. No way would I go home until I made it all the way around the arc, until it felt natural and they started falling.

"It's going to take forever if you do it like that."

I spun around to find the source of the voice, and there he was, leaning against the doorway. Hair a mess, a deep V of sweat down his T-shirt, holding a beat-up ball against his hip. Everything inside me prickled alive.

"Plus, it's not the same motion as in a game," he said.

I rolled my eyes. "Thanks for mansplaining that. I hadn't realized they don't push these metal racks around during the game."

"Well, back in the old days, they did," he said, dribbling as he walked toward me. "When the baskets were peach buckets and the jerseys were still made of wool."

"Wow," I said. "I'm so lucky to have you here to teach me all this." I grabbed a ball from the rack and drained a three. Thank goodness.

Jake caught it with his free hand before it even had a

chance to hit the ground. I expected him to make some showboat shot of his own, but he fired it back at me, and there was the sting in my palms again.

"Come on," he said. "I'll feed you. But you gotta stay on the move."

I sent the rack and the rest of the balls rolling for the bleachers, then dribbled toward the baseline, pulled up, and took the shot—totally aware that his eyes were on me.

Air ball, straight over the rim.

He didn't laugh, though. Just grabbed the ball and gave it back with a quick bounce pass. Not to where I was, though—to the next spot on the arc.

Keep moving, I reminded myself.

Another miss, but closer this time.

"Use your legs," he said.

"I thought we talked about the mansplaining," I shot back.

"Holy crap, Sharp," he said, putting a little more heat on his next pass. "It's not because you're a girl. It's because you know how your shot *feels*, but I know how it *looks*. We're switching, by the way, once you get to the baseline. And you can give me all the feedback you want."

So I did. We did. We alternated between three-pointers and ten-footers (jump shots for me, fadeaways for Jake) until Mr. Caruso came and turned off the lights.

"Looking good out there, Foster," he said.

Jake gave him an up-nod but kept his eyes on me.

"You're going to make the team, you know. They'd be crazy to cut you." He stood there, dribbling between his legs and behind his back so naturally that I wasn't even sure he realized he was doing it.

"Can I tell you a secret?" I asked. I hadn't said the words out loud, even to my dad, but it felt safer to say now that the bright lights were gone and I could only see Jake's silhouette in the glow of the one small bulb by the door.

He picked up his dribble and stepped toward me, close enough I could have touched the soft hem of his T-shirt. "Spill it, Sharp," he said.

"I don't want to make the sophomore team," I confessed. "I want to make varsity."

He stepped even closer, and suddenly we were face to face, his arms around me, holding the ball as it curved into the small of my back. He leaned in to whisper into my right ear.

"Secret number one: me too. That's half the reason I stayed after."

And then into my left.

"Secret number two: you will."

Then he walked away, putting the ball in the rack and wheeling it back to the equipment room for me. "Get some rest, Sharp," he called over his shoulder. "Tomorrow's going to hurt."

He was right. The next day at tryouts, every muscle

in me screamed, "Didn't we do this yesterday?" But my shots fell, again and again, and I saw the head coach point at me as the assistant scribbled something on her clipboard. And by the end of the week, when the rosters were posted, our secrets had turned into promises kept.

I made varsity.

And so did he.

I was the only sophomore on the girls' varsity roster, but Jake wasn't the only boy. Seth and Kolt got called up too. Everybody knew exactly what Coach Cooper was doing: giving the sophomores varsity experience, going all in on a chance at a championship his son's senior year. And Jake was as smart a bet as you could make on the basketball court.

The lists were posted together, boys and girls, on the bulletin board outside the gym. I wandered back for one more look before I headed home, just to make sure I hadn't imagined it.

Jake was there, bag slung over his shoulder, staring at it too.

"Congratulations," I said.

"Hey, you too," he said. "It was probably all that extra shooting practice, huh?"

"Oh, yeah," I agreed. "You would've been cut otherwise."

He laughed, and I felt something slide into place inside me, like two magnets finally close enough to click together. He'd made me laugh the very first time he'd spoken to me, back in the courtroom, and now I'd finally returned the favor. It was an easy, low laugh, and already I wanted to hear it again.

I shifted my gym bag to the other shoulder, and as my free hand fell back, Jake locked a finger around my pinkie.

"We should probably keep staying after, then," he said, swinging my hand back and forth the littlest bit. "So I don't lose my edge."

"Probably," I agreed, spidering my fingers along his until they were all interlocked.

He looked down at our hands, then up at me with a shy, sideways grin. "Okay," he said. "Get some rest, Sharp."

"Because tomorrow's going to hurt?" I asked.

"No," he said, squeezing my hand as he leaned over to kiss me on the cheek. "Because you earned it."

Taking a Bet

Daphne

After

Seth is waiting outside the school counselor's office when I come out of my interview with the police. He folds me into his arms as I bury my head in his chest.

"He's gone," I say. What else is there?

I guess that's the question the cops are trying to answer too.

We stand there, totally silent, until I can feel the damp circle my tears have made on his shirt.

The door opens, and somebody comes out.

"Seth Cooper?" Officer Vega asks. Like he didn't just walk in with us. Like he doesn't know exactly who Seth is.

Seth squeezes me even tighter, then lets Vega lead him into the room. I'm alone in the reception area, my mind looping between replaying the interview and my last conversation with Jake in the training room before the game.

The things we said and didn't say. The ache in his words. The moment I still can't tell Seth about.

If the police had asked me what happened in the training room, I would have told them. But even as I think that, I'm not sure it's true.

And now the interview's over and Jake's gone and I'm here, totally helpless.

No. Not totally helpless. I will not be the crying girl who waits around for things to happen. Even though everything fell to pieces between Jake and me months ago, even though he turned into someone I hardly recognized by the time we broke up, I have to do *something*. Because there's no doubt in my mind he would be the first one to start searching if anything ever happened to me.

I pull my phone from my pocket and dial him for only the second time in months, knowing he won't pick up but hoping for it anyway.

"This is Jake. Leave a message."

"Call me," I say. "Please." It's all I've got, and when I hang up, I know I don't want to do this alone. I need Jenna.

I don't know if she reached out to me that day at sophomore tryouts because she felt like an outsider too, but we've been tight ever since. She's my person now—and pretty much the perfect partner in crime (fighting) to call up in this moment anyway. She's a lot smarter than her GPA suggests and is especially good at getting information out of people. I shoot her a text.

Jake is missing.

I wonder whether I should add something more, but then the dots on my screen tell me she's already writing back. When the words come through, they confirm that she was the right person to pull in.

Holy freak. Like MISSING missing?

And seconds later:

What's our move?

I'm still searching for the answer when Seth comes out, looking so focused that I have to ask the same question to get his attention.

"What's our move?"

Confusion wrinkles his brow. "Our move?"

"Jake is missing. What's our move?"

"We made our move. Go in there, answer questions, let the police do their job. They said they'd let us know if they need to organize a search party, but it seems like they're thinking he ran."

This surprises me. "They barely mentioned that in my interview. They think he ran . . . based on what?"

Seth puts his hands up helplessly. "Based on the fact that his backpack was missing from his house and some of his clothes were gone."

I feel a spike of anger that they told Seth this and not me, but even more that everybody seems to be accepting it when Jake could be hurt somewhere—or worse.

"He probably had it packed from the tournament. He could have left it at the arena. His stuff could be anywhere. Why are we even worried about his stuff, though, when the actual person is missing?"

Seth drops his hands. He can't even look at me now.

"What did you tell them?"

"The truth," he says, his voice tensing. "I told them Jake never came to the party on Saturday and I saw him take off with Kolt. I told them he'd talked about getting out of Ashland after the season was over."

My tone tenses to match his. "Everybody talks about getting out of Ashland. All. The. Time. Not running away, though. Not without telling anybody. Do you even want them to look for him?"

"Of course I do."

But before his words, there's a hesitation so brief I wonder if I imagine it. Is this a stupid jealousy thing? Or is there something more here? I fold my arms and look him straight in the eye. "But you don't want to help."

Seth shrugs. Actually shrugs. "I don't think there's anything I can do."

I stare at him, feel my jaw tighten. "You're probably right. *You've* done everything you can. But I haven't."

Seth trails behind me as I head for the exit, and I push the door open so hard my palms sting.

"Don't go," he says. "I'm sorry. It's just . . . My dad does this too. Last year he took off for a couple of days after the season ended. This feels like that to me. I bet he'll be back by the end of the week."

I stop and spin to face him. The wind blows cold between us. "This is different. Your mom probably knew where he was, and also your dad's an adult. And there's a difference between taking off and disappearing. I know Jake better than anybody," I say, not caring that the words may hurt him. "Something's wrong. I can feel it."

And I do feel it. There's a panic growing inside me, scratching at my rib cage, throbbing in my head.

"Don't you think . . . ," he starts.

I wait, assuming he actually has something important to say. But whatever it was, he swallows it. "Don't you need a ride?" he asks.

"Nope," I say. "I'm walking to Jenna's. We're going to find him. Or at least we're going to try." I don't add "unlike you." I don't have to.

Jake doesn't answer any of the five times I call or the three times I text on my way to Jenna's. If the police won't do it, I might have to assemble a search party myself. Who else will care as much as I do?

Kolt.

I stop to make the call before I go inside Jenna's house.

Kolt answers without a hello. "Your boyfriend's an ass-hole," he says.

Your boyfriend. It takes me a second to realize he's referring to Seth, not Jake.

"What are you talking about?"

"The police are on their way over. They have 'a few more questions' for me and decided to 'stop by' on their way back to the station. I told them everything already. What did Seth say?"

I think about Seth: the weird look on his face, the hesitation, the words he swallowed. "I don't know," I tell Kolt. "But Seth wouldn't lie. He wouldn't try to hurt anybody. I'm sure it's just a misunderstanding."

"The police are coming to my house, Daphne. Do you know what this will do to my parents? After all the shit my brother put them through?"

He's right. Kolt pushes every limit he can, but he never breaks the law. Not after his brother.

"I know. And I'm sorry. But here's what I called to say: I'm going to try to find Jake. Let me know if you want to help."

My phone buzzes with another call, and my heart jolts. Is it him?

"I gotta go," I tell Kolt, already pulling the phone from my ear.

But it's not Jake. It's Dad.

"Hello?" I say, letting a little annoyance sneak into my tone.

"Where are you?" he asks. "You okay?"

He knows about Jake. Of course he does.

"I'm fine, Dad. Just busy."

"Did the police talk to you already? You know you're allowed to have a lawyer present, don't you?"

"Yes, Dad. And you know you're not allowed to give legal advice, don't you?"

He doesn't laugh. "I'm allowed to do anything to keep my daughter safe. That's why I called. Don't think this is your problem to solve."

Dammit. He knows me too well.

But I'm not giving in that easily. "If I can help, I'm going to."

"Of course," he says. "But no boyfriend is worth your health and safety, honey."

I pace the sidewalk. "Dad. I know you never liked him, but give him a little credit. It's not like anything to do with Jake automatically puts me in danger. And he's not my boyfriend, remember? We broke up months ago."

"Are you sure about that?" he asks. "I saw the way you were looking at him during the game. Kind of wondered if you two might be getting back together."

"Dad. No." I try to sound calm and sure, to tamp down

the panic that wants to surface. What exactly did he see? And how exactly *was* I looking at Jake?

"Okay. I believe you. Just promise me you'll let the police do their job. Promise me you'll be smart."

I sigh. "I will, Dad."

I climb the steps and knock on Jenna's door, feeling a little thrill of triumph. In the end, all I promised was to let the police do their job. He didn't say I couldn't try to do their job too. And to be smart—which is exactly what I intend to do.

Jenna swings the door open. She's wearing a tank top and a pair of running shorts, even though it's technically still winter. March is never warm in Ashland, but so far this one's colder than most.

"What's our move?" I ask her.

She breaks into a grin. "I was starting to wonder if you'd chickened out. Let's go."

"Where?" I ask.

She tosses a knot of clothes at me. "Running, dummy. Well, driving too, if we need to. But if we happen to end up on private property, it'll look less suspicious if we're out for a run. We still have a couple of hours of daylight left."

I'm still baffled, so I ask the question again. "Yeah, but . . . where?"

"Wherever Jake would have gone. I mean, he would

have driven from the school to his house after the bus dropped him off, so definitely that stretch. We'll figure the rest out as we go. Talk to people who know him that the police might not think of. Stuff like that."

It's better than anything I've got, and my head is often clearest when I run, so I give in and go to Jenna's room to change. The leggings are elastic enough that they fit great, and the shoes are okay too once I have a couple of pairs of socks on. The T-shirt says MIKE'S AUTO BODY on the front, and it's not until I catch my reflection in the mirror that I realize it says I'VE GOT ALL THE RIGHT PARTS in giant letters across the back. Only Jenna.

We wind through town, down a path Jake and I have run on together before, up to the water tank, where sometimes people mess around late at night. The rhythm and the movement lift my heart and clear my mind enough that this feels like the right thing to do—a feeling that's confirmed when we pass a newer neighborhood next to the trail.

"Hang on," I say, slowing to a walk. There's a house under construction, with guys coming in and out and climbing on the roof. It's like an anthill over there. But the thing that catches my attention is an old pickup parked out front with TIM'S TOP-OF-THE-LINE ROOFING written on the door.

"Jake works for them. Or worked." I'm pretty sure

he quit after his accident, but he didn't like to talk about what happened that day.

"Let's go," Jenna says. And before I can stop her, she's bounding up to the house and shouting at the guys on the roof.

"Hey! Is one of you Tim?"

A super-built guy in a gray henley looks down at her. Okay, they all look at her because that's what guys do. But Gray Henley steps forward.

"Yup. What can I do for you?"

"How about you hop down from there and talk to us?"

Gray Henley—Tim, I guess—descends the ladder and comes over to us.

"You haven't seen Jake Foster, have you?"

Tim tucks his thumbs in his pockets. "Sorry, ladies. Jake hasn't worked for me since his accident. Why are you asking?"

I'm not sure the police want it public, but Jenna barges ahead. "Because he's missing. Gone since the championship game." She puts her hands on her hips, cocks her head. "Wait—he hasn't worked for you since his accident? You didn't fire him, did you? Because that would be pretty cold."

Tim backs up, holds his hands out. "Hey, now. It was his choice, and I helped out with his medical bills. Jake said we were cool." He takes off his hat and scratches his head. "He's missing? You serious?"

"Yeah," Jenna says. "But don't worry. He'll turn up. Jake's the kind of kid whose face will look good on a missing-person poster. He's a white male who happens to be good at sports. The whole town will care." She stares him down. "We'll find him." She might not be trying to sound threatening, but Tim gives her a nervous nod and hurries back to the job, and I'm glad to be on her side.

I want her to be right about this. Still, I worry. Besides me and Kolt and Jake's family, will anybody care long enough to bring him home?

We stop at Jenna's dad's pharmacy for a drink. While I grab a Gatorade from the cooler (Glacier Cherry; there is no other worthy flavor), her dad comes out from behind the counter and gives her a hug. Even though it's cold outside, we're too sweaty to stay inside with the paying customers, so we go to the bench behind the store to sit while we hydrate, dodging the guys who are working on remodeling the offices upstairs.

"You want Tim to take care of the roof for you?" I ask.

Jenna takes a swig of her (inferior) Glacier Freeze. "Tim can kiss my asphalt. I take it he seemed sketchy to you too?"

I twist the cap on my bottle. "I guess."

Jenna chugs the last of her Gatorade and makes a

perfect eight-footer into the recycling bin. "It's too loud to think with the construction here. Let's get back at it. We just haven't been to the right place yet or asked the right questions. Time to retrace his steps."

So we run past the high school, then follow the route Jake would have taken in his truck after the bus dropped him off Saturday night. There's nothing that stands out to me, other than the fact that I feel totally useless and have no idea what I'm looking for.

When we're about to turn the corner onto Jake's street, I stop. "We're not really going to his house, are we? They don't need us bothering them right now."

I picture Jake's mom, still in her sweater and slacks from teaching all day. But she wouldn't have gone to school, would she? Will Luke be home? What do you do the day after your life shatters?

Jenna's already looking around the corner. "Jake's truck is there, but that's it. No cops."

"No blue Civic?" I ask.

"Nope," Jenna says.

Then Jake's mom isn't home. Maybe nobody is.

"Okay," I concede. "Maybe we can look around. For a minute."

We run down the street, then slow when we get to the house. I'm stunned, stuck. I can't stop staring at the house, the truck. How many times have I walked through the front door? Or sat in the passenger seat and lifted up on the handle so the door shuts right? There's a hollow ache inside me. Things will never be the same between me and Jake. I may never do either of those things again.

"It's weird that the truck is here," Jenna says. "I mean, if he was running away, wouldn't he have taken it?" She reaches over and gives my hand a squeeze, then strides to the front door to knock. I'm terrified someone will answer, and terrified they won't.

Nobody answers.

She tries the knob, and I'm almost relieved when it's locked. After a quick peek through the mail slot, she just shrugs and smiles. "I guess we'll have to try the truck."

I'm rooted in the sparse grass along the curb. "Are you sure we should be touching anything?" I ask. "What if they're considering it a potential crime scene?"

Jenna waves the questions away. "They'd have it taped off. Plus, you said they think he ran. I thought you wanted to do something about this, Sharp."

I do. But the truck's locked too—and Jake never locks his truck. He even leaves a key in the ashtray in case Kolt ever needs to borrow it. (When I asked Kolt why he doesn't just keep the key, he said, "Because usually when I need to borrow Jake's truck, it's because I can't find my keys." Which makes perfect sense in the way only Jake and Kolt ever could.)

"Any ideas?" Jenna asks, pulling on the driver-side handle.

"Maybe . . . ," I say, heading for the passenger side. If whoever opened it last wasn't me, if they didn't know about the whole lift-the-handle thing, maybe the latch hasn't quite caught.

Sure enough, with a strong lift and a little counterintuitive push, the door almost comes open.

"Try it again," Jenna says. "I'll grab the edge when it pops out."

I'm not sure how this will change anything other than possibly breaking Jenna's fingers, but Jenna's stronger than I am, and she's already getting herself in position. "Ready?"

"One . . . two . . . three . . ."

I yank and push the top while Jenna pulls the bottom, and somehow the door swings open.

And that is when the police cruiser drives up.

We spin to face the street, and the officer leans out of the window enough to shout, "Step away from the vehicle, please!" Then he cuts the engine and starts typing something into his computer. After a minute, he turns away from the computer, and I brace myself for a very uncomfortable conversation. But no, he just starts talking to somebody over the radio.

We stepped away from the vehicle like he asked, but

now it's like he's forgotten we're here. The officers and bailiffs are always friendly enough in my dad's courtroom, but mostly they ignore me.

Am I lucky enough for that to be what's happening now?

"Can we go?" I whisper to Jenna. "Is he even here for us?"

Jenna looks at me like I'm an idiot. "Honey, you don't leave when the cops pull up. Even if you're Daphne Sharp."

Yeah, okay.

Finally he finishes talking and climbs out of the car.

And it's Officer Vega. The same guy from earlier.

"Ladies," he says, giving us a nod. "Ms. Sharp, I told you to keep asking questions, not to try breaking and entering."

I'm panicked, sick, but Jenna is cool as Glacier Cherry. "Just trying to help, Officer."

"Have you been in the house?" he asks.

"No, sir. It's locked."

"So was the truck."

He has a point.

Jenna frowns. "Was the truck locked when you were here earlier today?"

He hesitates, which makes me wonder if it wasn't. If maybe somebody's trying to keep somebody else out.

Maybe Jake's mom, keeping things secure, but maybe not.

Officer Vega clears his throat. Whatever he's thinking, he's not about to share it with us.

"Anything I should be concerned about here, besides the fact that you were breaking and entering? Did you remove anything from the premises?"

"No, sir."

He looks at us for a few long seconds. "Okay, then. Why don't you let me take it from here?"

"Of course," Jenna says. "Let us know if there's anything we can do to help. There's going to be a search party, right? Amber Alert? Flyers? We could help with flyers."

"We'll be sure to let you know," he says. "Thanks for the offer."

"You're so welcome," Jenna says. "We'll go finish our run. Have a nice day."

Apparently now is the time when it's okay to walk away from the officer.

Or maybe not.

Officer Vega gives her half a smile. "Oh, I'd say you've finished your run. I've arranged for a ride for you girls."

What does that mean? A ride in his cruiser? The possibility makes my stomach churn, but when another car pulls up and the driver gets out, it's every bit as bad.

"Hi, Dad."

He doesn't even answer. Just comes around and opens the back door, and Jenna jumps in without a word. I think about sliding in next to her, but that would feel like climbing into a cop car, and I am not a prisoner or a suspect here. I don't exactly want to sit next to Dad, but I want to stand up to him even more. So I step around him and sink into the passenger seat, realizing too late that I've shown him the crude message on the back of my shirt.

He'll blame Jake for all of this. He's always blamed Jake for things that weren't his fault.

Once Jenna's dropped off at home, he lays into me, with a "directly disobeyed" and a few rounds of "so disappointed." I didn't technically break my promise, but still, I know better than to argue with him when he's in hyperparanoid-judge mode. So I don't say a word, just stare out the window and nod at the appropriate times. Even though I'm probably in more trouble than I've ever been in in my life, it feels better than when I was standing there, feeling helpless, after the police interview.

"You're not going anywhere but school for a very long time."

Those are the last words he says to me before he pulls into the garage and climbs out of the car. The verdict has been delivered; details of the sentencing to be determined.

———

Alone in my room, I get back to work.

Jenna was right. A lot of people care about Jake, even if it's just because he won us a state championship. A lot of people pay attention to him. Adults with badges and government paychecks aren't the only ones who can solve this, and maybe they're not even the best candidates for the job.

I pull out my phone and open up Jake's profile on social media—and there he is, inches away, with his messed-up hair and sleepy smile. Tears prick my eyes as I wonder where he is now; I won't let myself think about the possibility that I won't see him again. *You will see him,* I remind myself. *If you can find him.*

As I scroll, something catches my attention: a post from two hours ago that already has forty-eight comments.

We're taking a bet, Jake. Where you at? NBA or NCAA?

It takes me a minute to process it. Darius Ruckert, the punk junior point guard who never could decide if he idolized Jake or wanted to take him out to steal his starting spot, is wagering whether Jake ran away to play pro ball or college ball.

I hear Jenna's voice in my head: "First rule of life: never read the comments."

And then I ignore it.

I bet he's meeting with agents right now.

Nah, my man's smart. Probably college recruiters.

We in a time machine here? Junior year Foster was headed somewhere. Senior year? Not so much.

The second one's from Kolt, and I wonder if he's writing what he wants to believe or trying to spin this to protect Jake the best he can. Or maybe both.

And below that:

Your just mad you lost your best customer

Customer for what?

Down the list, there's one that makes my heart stop.

The real question is, NBA or OD?

It makes no sense. Jake's never even tried pot, never had a drop to drink. And how can you say that when somebody's gone missing? The comment below it is even worse.

He's either in a ditch or in a freezer. Depends on if they found him yet.

I scan the names and profile pictures, the faces my age but unfamiliar. Who are these people? My eyes swim, my whole body paralyzed by this cruel image painted by those I thought might be able to help.

But I blink back the tears. I won't let them win. I won't let them turn this into a place to hurt somebody I care about. I text Kolt, tell him to hack into Jake's account and shut the post down. Then I start a new page of my own.

Title: Missing Person: Jake Foster

Category: Community

I upload a photo of Jake in his basketball uniform for the profile picture and a full-court shot for the cover photo. It feels cheap, but Jenna's right: people care about Jake Foster, MVP. And if that will get us more visibility, more eyes on the lookout, it's worth it. I add a quick description of the page:

Let's do everything we can to bring Jake home safe. Please post any information you have on the whereabouts of Jake Foster.

But it can't be a place for wild, depressing speculation. The information will need to be monitored and moderated, but I don't know if I've got the guts to sift through all the content. So I send Jenna the link and an invitation to be the admin.

Here's our next move. Can you help?

Five seconds later, she accepts the invitation, and something inside me uncoils.

After that, I share the link across social media and send it to anybody I can think of. Teammates, friends, *everybody*—except the asswipes on Ruckert's post. When I click back to my new page, there are already two posts, nearly identical and nearly useless.

Kolt Martin: Thanks for starting this Sharp. Hope it helps.

Seth Cooper: Good idea, Daph. Help us out, everybody.

I'm annoyed at the "us." Now that I've done something, he wants to claim part of it? Where was that concern this afternoon?

Seth and Kolt. I look at the two names next to each other and think back to that night. If the police felt the need to question Kolt again, their stories must not have lined up.

46

I know them both, trust them both. So why is one of them not telling the whole truth when Jake's life could be on the line?

The memory of the cruel comment makes me shudder. *He's either in a ditch or in a freezer. Depends on if they found him yet.*

I won't believe that Jake is dead. I can't.

But where the hell is he?

Burning Up

After

Still dark down here. Still cold. Jake feels both in his bones as he's startled from sleep, the cot shaking beneath him.

"What did you tell them?"

The voice is angry, the words sharp. They rattle inside Jake's skull. He squeezes his eyes shut, but strong hands grab greedy fistfuls of his shirt.

"Sit up. Look at me when I'm talking to you."

Jake sits up, tries to open his eyes. Is he home? Why is his dad here?

"You didn't tell them anything, did you?"

But no. His dad is dead. Isn't he?

"Holy shit. Can't you even follow instructions?"

Those are his dad's words, though. They all are.

If his dad is dead and his dad is here, is Jake dead too?

Then, footsteps. Pacing. Like the man is getting ready to walk away.

"This isn't how any of this was supposed to go down. You shot my plan to hell—you know that?"

Jake feels a sob in his throat. "I'm sorry, Dad. I'll do better. Please don't go." Maybe this time Jake can get it right. Be enough.

A muttered curse and a hand against his forehead. "You're burning up. Get in the shower. Cold water. I'll get you some shorts. Your clothes are drenched."

Jake wants to obey, but his body is a wet sack of sand. The man watches him, sighs, lifts him by the armpits, and guides him to the shower. "You'd better be able to take it from here. I'm not your nurse."

I know you're not a nurse. You're a mechanic. Or you were.

I know you.

Jake thinks he says the words out loud, but the man either doesn't hear or doesn't care. He snaps on the light and turns on the water, and then he's gone.

Alone again, Jake realizes he *is* burning up. That he does want a shower. A line from an old kindergarten song floats into his mind: *Soap and bubbles wash your troubles away.*

Yes. He repeats the line in his mind, again and again, like an anchor from his past to figure out his present.

Finally the room comes into focus. Jake recognizes

himself now, slick with soap, the pain in his body too raw and real for him to believe any longer that he's dead. He's still in the dark, run-down basement, but whether it's two blocks or a hundred miles from home, he doesn't know.

When the man comes back, tossing the shorts onto the cot, Jake can see it's not his dad. Too young, too wiry. Too *wired*. And, of course, too alive.

"Did you tell them where you were going?" the man, pacing again, asks once Jake is dressed. "Did you leave a note or something? Anything? Think, Jake. Did you tell anybody you saw me?"

So many questions, and Jake can't seem to form the words to answer any of them. He's afraid if he doesn't say something soon, the questions will just keep coming. So he thinks hard, makes sure to say the words aloud when he tries again with a question of his own.

"Are you going to kill me?"

The man laughs, harsh and sharp. "Well, I hadn't planned on it, but that was before you got the cops looking for us."

Jake studies the man, tries to tell if he's joking. But who would joke in a moment like this? He remembers another of the man's questions and attempts to answer it.

"How could I tell anybody I saw you if I don't even know who you are?"

"You know who I am, Jake." The man scratches the back of his neck, and there's something familiar about the gesture. "But don't think about me right now. And for God's sake, stop thinking about your dad. If you're going to think about somebody, think about your mom and your little brother."

Their faces come back to him in a rush, and he has to sit down.

Mom, her hair pulled into a knot on top of her head, looking up from chopping peppers to smile when he comes through the door.

And Luke, writing notes and poems and stats in that old notebook and hiding it where Jake can't help but find it.

"You want to see them again, right? You don't want them to hurt anymore?"

"Yes. No."

The room starts to spin. Since he's been down here, he's become so weak that already those clear images of the people he loves are getting fuzzy, and he can't seem to hold on.

"Then you've got to learn to follow instructions. Do we understand each other?"

Jake will do anything to make all this stop. To see them again.

"Yes," he says as the room swirls around him.

"Good," says the man, and the last thing Jake hears is the sound of retreating footsteps before everything is dark again.

Police Statement: Luke Foster

How old are you, Luke?

Eleven.

And Jake is eighteen.

And a half.

Do you like your brother?

I love my brother.

Sometimes it's hard to have a brother who's that much bigger, even if you love him.

[*Pause.*]

That wasn't a question. Do you have another question?

Did Jake ever talk about running away?

Only for an adventure. And only together.

Where were you two going to go?

Springfield.

Excuse me?

Springfield, Massachusetts. The Basketball Hall of Fame.

Tell me about the night he disappeared. Jake usually threw his warm-up jersey to you in the stands when they announced the starting lineup. Is that right?

Yes.

And did he do that the night of the championship game?

No.

Do you know why not?

No.

Did you talk to him that night?

I told him good luck before the game.

And what did he say?

[*Shifts in his chair.*] He didn't say anything.

Was that normal?

No . . . Maybe . . . Normal sometimes changes.

I understand, Luke, and I know these are hard questions, but we need to ask them so we can understand what happened. Was Jake ever mean to you? Did you ever fight?

He was never mean to anybody. He never fought with anybody.

What about Kolt Martin or Seth Cooper? Did he fight with them sometimes?

[Picks at a stain on the table.]

Luke? Did Jake fight with his friends?

No.

Were you ever afraid of him?

I'm afraid now that he's gone. Can we talk about something else?

Okay. I like your Space Jam *shirt.*

Thanks. Jake gave it to me.

Space and basketball. Those are your favorite things, right?

Actually, can we be done talking?

Big Bang: Part 1

Luke

After

Once upon a time there was
Nothing
and then there was
Something.

No, that's not totally true.
Once upon a time
there was a very small, very dense, very hot
Something.
It wasn't Nothing, but it didn't look like much.
At least, I don't think it did, but who knows?
There was no light to see it by.
And there was nobody to look at it.
Unless you believe in God.

Unless God was there before the
Nothing
that became
Something.

I believe in God.
I think.

But anyway, that very small, dense, hot
Something
E X P A N D E D
with a bang
(yeah, a BIG one)
and then there was a
Universe.

At first it was just
light
energy
gas
(not that kind)
and only the smallest, simplest atoms.

But after a while
(if you can call billions of years a while)
there were
galaxies

planets
oceans
mountains
grass and trees
seasons
whales
birds
cows
spiders
people.

And it was good.

Mostly.

Because as soon as there were people,
they could hurt themselves.
They could hurt each other.
And they did.
And it hasn't stopped.

That's what happened to my brother
when he disappeared.

Somebody took him in the night
when it was dark and the world felt small
    and secret

and nobody saw it coming,
except maybe God.

Now nobody knows where he is
    on heaven?
    or earth?
Nobody knows,
except maybe God.

So where is He?
And where is he?

Fadeaway

The opposite of a big bang is a fadeaway.
Disappearing instead of
appearing.

Jake taught me to shoot a fadeaway two summers ago.
"My signature move," he said.
"Impossible to defend without getting in my face,
in my space,
and the stripes call that foul
every
single
time."

He was already falling backward
as the ball

       rolled

           off

               his

                     fingertips,
and as beautiful as they were together,
the sight of them coming apart,
of Jake catching himself
as the ball whispered through the net—
it was so perfect I stopped breathing for a second.

"Try it," he said.
"Make a hundred, and I'll level you up to
Beginner."

So I tried
and I failed,
but with my brother beside me
I tried again.
Again.
Again.
By the time I made a hundred,
my arms were spaghetti.

The night he disappeared,
Jake made twelve of his famous fadeaways,

including the
game-winning shot.
Thirty-four points, fifteen boards,
twelve assists.
That triple-double
took the ball to the rim
and his team to the state title.
I felt so lucky to be his brother,
even though he didn't throw me his warm-up
or give me a salute in the stands
like he had for
every
single
game
since freshman year.

Instead, he looked up
at a shady, shadowy person in the back
during every timeout,
after every shot.
Who was he?
There was something familiar about the face
or the way he moved
or just
Something
that told me
I'd seen him before.

The Book of Luke and Jake:
Part 1

I usually like writing
more than talking,
and that is one reason why
I like
The Book of Luke and Jake.

The Book of Luke and Jake
sounds fancy, but it's not.
It's just a notebook
from the dollar store
and the title is written in Sharpie,
not gold.

It started that time
when Jake lost his biology notebook
and borrowed one of mine.

When he gave it back,
there was a joke inside
in his dark, spiky lowercase.

Why did Cinderella stink at basketball?
Because she kept running away from the ball.

After that, we started passing it
        back
            and forth,
writing
jokes, memories, and things to look forward to
(that's Jake),
poems, basketball statistics, and science facts
(that's me).

When you're done writing,
you slide it under the other person's pillow
and wait for him to find it
and wait for it to appear
under your pillow one night
with a new message on the next page.

It's like getting a letter in the mailbox but
so
much
better.

Why else did Cinderella stink at basketball?
Because her coach was a pumpkin.

The record is eighty-seven days between
     messages,
but it is not the kind of record
you want to break
or even have in the first place.

Eighty-seven days means
almost three months of nothing last fall,
and I'm afraid it happened because of what
     I saw
     that time on the roof
     when I couldn't stop him
     and I didn't save him.
     Because I wasn't brave enough.

I kept waiting for him to write me back and tell me
why
he did it.
But eighty-seven days is enough
to make you
wonder if you saw
what you thought you saw
or if you saw
anything at all.

Enough to make you wonder
    if the notebook will ever be under your pillow again,
       if the mail for Jake
          you're stacking on his desk
             from colleges that don't know he's missing
                will touch the ceiling
                   or topple over.

When the detective asked me if we ever fought,
I wanted to scream,
"Of course we fought! We're brothers!"
But I knew that was the wrong answer.

We're like Luke Skywalker and Han Solo
(good thing my mom didn't name him Han).
We argue about pretty much everything.
But we've always got each other's backs.

I know how this sounds,
I KNOW,
but the night after he disappeared
I dreamed I saw him
frozen in carbonite.

Dreamed I saved him with
a princess and
a Wookiee.

I told you, I know.
It was just a dream.

I open the book and almost write it down because
it would make him laugh.

But when I put the pen to the paper,
I think a thought that knocks my breath away.

What if I'm supposed to save him this time?
And what if I can't?

Rise and Shine

After

The man kicks the empty tray from last night's dinner.

"Rise and shine, Jake."

Jake waits with his eyes closed. Even though his heart pounds, he slows his breathing so it will look like he's sleeping.

He hears the footsteps coming closer, but he just waits.

Keeps waiting as the man blocks the blood-red light coming through Jake's eyelids.

He hears the pop and crack of somebody else's bad knee as the man kneels next to the cot. "I said, rise and—"

Jake strikes, bare knuckles full force against the man's jaw. He jumps up as the man staggers back. Knocks the man's legs out from under him with one swift, sweeping kick.

In the very next heartbeat, Jake is running for the door, but the man is already up, racing him to it. Jake's knees nearly buckle as the man jumps onto his back. The man wraps his arms around Jake, slapping his right hand over Jake's mouth.

If he's trying to keep me quiet, there might be somebody nearby. Jake opens his mouth to shout.

But really, that was what the man wanted, and Jake realizes his mistake when he feels a pill at the back of his throat. The man's hand still covers his mouth, so Jake bites down, hard, and there's a satisfying taste of blood on his tongue as the man roars and pulls his hand away.

Jake spits out the blood and the pill, but he's weak. Why is he so weak? He is Jake freaking Foster. MV-freaking-P.

He spins to find the man again, which is another mistake, because the room keeps spinning, even after he's stopped. But finally he sees the man kneeling behind an old metal box, messing with the lock.

Jake hasn't noticed the box before, and for a moment he hesitates, wondering what could be in there. Drugs? Guns?

Whatever it is, he doesn't want to wait for the man to use it on him. Jake charges toward the man as the key turns and the lid swings open. The man reaches inside right before Jake tackles him, pinning him to the ground.

"I'm leaving, and you can't stop me," Jake spits at the man. "You're lucky I'm not going to kill you first."

But then there's a sharp pain in his thigh. Jake looks down to see a syringe, its needle sunk cleanly through his basketball shorts, its plunger already down, only a few drops remaining of its pale blue dose.

Jake feels the anger and the energy drain from him. Maybe this is it. His last dose of poison.

"You're not ready to leave," the man says, easily pushing Jake off him as all of Jake's muscles release and his senses dull. The man drags Jake to the cot, and Jake is grateful to lie down. He's suddenly so, so sleepy.

"Don't you dare try that again, or I'll give you another blue-light special. This whole thing was your idea, remember?"

Jake shakes his head, trying to clear it, as he tells the man no.

That can't be right.

The last thing Jake sees before his eyes close is the man's face; the last thing he hears, the man's voice. And he wonders if maybe he's seen the face and heard the voice before. He even wonders if he has wondered this before, but it's all a blur, it's all going in circles, circling the drain, he's so drained . . .

When he wakes up, the man is gone, and so is the metal box.

And Jake's left hand is cuffed to a pipe on the wall.

Police Statement: Sabrina Foster

Thank you for coming in, Mrs. Foster. We'll just ask you a few questions, and then you can get back to your son.

Sons. I have two.

Yes, ma'am.

I'm sorry. I know you're doing everything you can. And I'll do whatever I can to help you.

Right now we're trying to figure out the timeline. And Jake's frame of mind. How was he earlier in the day? Did you see him after the game? Had anything changed?

I didn't see him during the day. He left with the team before I got home. I texted him before warm-ups to tell him good luck, but that was it. That makes me sound like a terrible mother, doesn't it?

No, ma'am. Teenagers are hard to connect with. Did he respond to your text?

He did. Something like "Thanks, Mom" and that was it. I thought he must have been nervous.

Did he get nervous a lot? Have you noticed any changes in his behavior?

His senior year has been hard. It's been tough recovering from his injuries. If I'm honest, he's been more withdrawn this year, and I can't help but feel like it's partly my fault. Jake had to grow up too quickly, especially after his dad died. He was always trying to make me happy, make sure I was okay. He did the same thing with the team, and especially with Coach. There's probably some psychoanalysis in that: trying to earn the love and respect from a father figure that he never got from his own dad.

Are we talking about Coach B or Coach C?

Both, I guess. But I was thinking of Coach Cooper. He's more like Jake's dad, in a way. Coach B is more . . . like a saint.

And it didn't worry you when he didn't come home?

I was asleep. The rule is that he comes in and tells me when he gets home, but to be honest, I sleep through that sometimes. And when I woke up, his truck was there.

Is that why you didn't call the police until almost noon the next day?

Yes. Another thing that makes me a terrible mother.

Now, there's nobody who thinks that.

I do.

Invisible

Sabrina

After the Game

Luke and I are already hoarse from cheering, but when Jake bows as the MVP medal is placed around his neck, we're too joyful to hold anything in.

It takes him a moment to stand back up, but then there he is: my son, who worked so hard and sacrificed so much. Who has grown more distant and combative all year as he struggled through school and health problems and heartache, chasing this dream. There he is, back to himself, practically glowing in this moment he's fought for so fiercely, and for all these years. It's not until I see that pure, true smile that I realize how long it's been since I've seen it.

Luke and I watch as the crowd files out. The longer we wait, the more I dread the drive home on the dark, icy highway when I'm already worn down and there's more snow in the forecast.

Finally there's Jake, running toward us from the parking lot instead of from the locker room. Maybe the celebrations have already started. I stand, ready to deliver a whole speech about how proud I am of him and how I hope he'll take a moment to soak it all in so he'll always remember this night.

But Jake has no time for any of it. "Bus is leaving," he says, dropping an arm across my shoulders and knocking knuckles with Luke.

"Okay," I say. "I love you."

He bounds down the bleachers so fast I'm not sure he heard me.

He definitely isn't there to hear his little brother, reliving every play for the whole ninety-minute drive home.

Luke's knees bounce as the memories bubble over. "Remember when Jake stole the ball and actually swatted it through that defender's legs?"

"Maybe," I say, frustrated that I don't. That even my best efforts at supporting my sons are not really enough for either of them. A semi pulls up behind me, following too close, then swerves into the passing lane at the last second. The trailer fishtails, swinging near us as the wheels spray snow across our windshield.

"Did you notice how they switched their whole

defense at halftime to try to stop Jake, and it still didn't work?"

Did you notice that I'm driving through a blizzard? I bite back the question just in time for Luke to ask another.

"Which happened first: the three-pointer that almost rolled out or the one that rattled around the rim?"

"I don't know," I snap. The tires lose traction, and all at once we are sliding, not driving. The treads regain their grip before I have time to react, but the slip leaves me breathless, heart racing.

"But you were there," Luke says. "Weren't you watching?"

"Of course I was watching," I say, eyes still on the road, trying to keep my voice even. One son I spend my life watching, and the other I spend my life listening to. But sometimes I wonder if either of them even sees me. Hears me. "I just don't understand the game like you do. I can't remember every single play. I have other things to think about."

Luke gets quiet, and for a minute that's a relief. We reach a few miles of dry road, and my grip loosens on the steering wheel; my jaw relaxes. I realize the radio is on and start to hum along. But then I look over at my incredible son, who is now afraid to speak. I reach to scratch his arm with my free hand, just the way he likes.

"I'm sorry, Luke. I do have other things to think about. That's why I need you to pay attention to the details for me," I say. "You're a lot better at it than I am. What would I do without you here to tell me the stuff I miss?"

But he answers his own question instead of mine. "The one that almost rolled out happened first," he says. "I remembered while I was being quiet."

"Oh, good," I say. "I'm glad you remembered."

After I've gotten Luke to bed, I stand at the bathroom sink, troubled by something floating right below my consciousness that I can't quite grab hold of. I swallow my blood-pressure medication, then lift a smaller bottle from the shelf. I shake one sleeping pill into my palm, then another.

It'll be fine, I assure myself.

Two is reasonable after a night like tonight.

I probably won't even need one tomorrow, and then I'll be right back on schedule.

The sleeping pills are new. It used to be caffeine to keep me awake, back when I was working at the Dollar Depot while I finished my teaching degree. But this year, there's no danger of my mind slowing down, even when I want it to. So if I want to fall asleep instead of worrying about my sons or my students all night, I need a little help.

"A glass of wine would do the same thing as a pill," Mrs. Cooper said once when I told her I had trouble sleeping. "Relaxes your mind, signals to your body that it's time to go to sleep. Are you sure you don't drink?" She said it with a smile, and I didn't take offense, but I also didn't tell her that I wouldn't drink even if my religion allowed it. Not a drop. Not after my husband.

Still, on a night like tonight, it would be nice. Not just to relax, but to celebrate and commemorate. It truly is the end of an era.

Since Jake was small, our lives have run in seasons dictated by sports. Football, basketball, baseball, repeat. But Jake has already announced he won't be playing baseball, and even though he'll play college basketball, it won't be the same. His uniforms won't be washed in our machine, and games will require more travel—more expense, more time off work—than we can afford. So no more rides with Luke. No more watching the way even opposing fans sigh at the perfection of Jake's fadeaway.

Before Jake was born, I didn't know what a fadeaway was. But when you love somebody, you learn to find the beauty in the things they love as you see the world through their eyes. Or you try, anyway. You do the best you can.

I swallow both pills.

As I pull my hair back and close the medicine cabinet,

the staccato of a knock sounds at the front door. I pad toward the entry, wondering if Jake has lost his key.

Coach Braithwaite's wife. Gentle and smiling and holding a platter with a small cake on top, coconut flakes sprinkled across its whorls of icing.

I push open the screen door, searching my memory for her first name, heavy with guilt at the way I immediately identify her only in relation to him.

"Come in, come in," I say, hoping repetition and a warm tone will somehow compensate for the lack of a first name.

"I can't stay," she says. "It's far past my bedtime. I just wanted to drop by and offer congratulations."

She holds out the platter, and I take it from her, smiling and grateful and certainly not about to tell her that Jake hates coconut. "Thank you," I say. "He's not back yet, but I'll make sure he gets it."

"Oh, no," she says, her eyes wide with surprise. "The cake is for you. You deserve to celebrate tonight. I'll be quite pleased if you don't share a bit. It's only big enough for one, and that's not by accident." She pulls her coat tighter around herself. "I know what it's like to wear yourself out making someone else's dreams come true. You've been the support staff for the town hero. And, my dear, you have always done it with remarkable patience and grace."

I am struck nearly speechless. I never realized how

invisible I'd become until this tiny old woman stood before me and actually saw me.

"Thank you," I say again, knowing there are no other words that will be close to enough.

I stay at the door until her taillights disappear around the turn. Then I sit at the kitchen table with one fork, one glass of milk, and the whole cake on its beautiful platter. If I have carried the stress of all those seasons, maybe a small part of the celebration does belong to me too.

Soon I find myself scrolling through the photographs on my phone and watching the video clips I've recorded, marveling at the beauty of this boy of mine playing the game he loves.

It hurts to see the worry on his face in so many of the shots. No denying it's been a rough year. Slipping grades, inconsistent on the court, tired and irritable at home. There have been days when I barely recognize him. I study the screen, wishing I could wipe that worry away, waiting for the moment when he will come through the door and we can celebrate this together and maybe even have something of a fresh start. He may not like coconut, but there's chocolate–peanut butter ice cream—his favorite—in the freezer.

But the whole team was invited to a party at Seth's, and all the parents agreed there's no curfew for state champions—especially if they're safe at the coach's house.

So I wrap the other half of the cake to save for tomorrow and leave a note on the counter for him.

So proud of you. I hope you had fun tonight, because you deserve it. Wake me up when you get home, okay?

Love,
Mom

I stop by Luke's room and snap off his lamp but not before noticing what he'd been reading until he grew too tired to turn off the lamp himself: *Astrophysics for People in a Hurry.*

I smile to myself. Luke is a good athlete, but he will likely never receive the same kind of recognition Jake got tonight. He may never excel in an exceedingly public arena. But he too is bright and beautiful, and in that moment it is okay with me if I'm the only one to see it.

There are few nights I can fall asleep without the nagging presence of tasks left undone or the lingering worry that as a teacher or a parent I could have done more. But tonight, I fall hard and fast into a truly deep sleep, undisturbed by dreams in the wake of the one that has come true.

———

By the next morning, though, the glow of victory has given way to the forgotten relics of reality: the sooty remnants of melted street snow from the bottoms of our shoes, a sink full of dishes, and an inexplicable sheaf of blank notebook paper strewn across the table.

Of course Luke is up, mouthing along with an episode of *The Clone Wars* he's watched so many times that even I can recite half the lines.

"Luke," I bark. "Come clean up this paper and start on the dishes. I've got to mop the floor."

"It's not my mess," he says, not even looking away from the screen.

"Doesn't matter," I say. "I asked you to clean it up, so come clean it up."

He turns off the TV and starts gathering the papers in a neat pile, grumbling about Jake owing him.

"You worry about you, and I'll worry about Jake," I say, even though I'm not the least bit worried about Jake. The presence of his truck in the driveway tells me he came home during the night, and he's earned the right to sleep in.

But by ten I wonder enough to crack open his door.

The bed hasn't been slept in.

I check my phone for a text saying he spent the night at Kolt's. That must be what happened, even though I'm not sure why he'd bring his truck home first.

Still, he must be with Kolt. Maybe he typed up a message and was so busy celebrating that he forgot to hit Send.

There's a buzz of irritation at the back of my skull as I text him: **Time to come home or at least check in. Even MVPs have to report to their moms.**

By the time I've cleaned the floors and finished the dishes Luke left half done and sent Jake three more unanswered texts, the irritation has been joined by a small seed of worry. Is he okay? Surely I would have heard by now if something had happened to him.

I pull up Coach Cooper's number but hesitate. It was handy to have in the seasons before Jake had his own phone. But it's been years since I used it, and I've never taken him up on his offer to "ask about anything, anytime." I had no real cause to suspect that he was so warm to me for any reason other than that I was his star player's mom, but I'd always wondered if there was something not quite right in the offer. If there might have been an element of it that stemmed from the fact that I was his star player's *single* mom, since he lowered his voice and glanced at his wife whenever he made the offer.

So I keep my text to Coach Cooper formal and brief.

Hi, Coach. This is Sabrina Foster. Is Jake still at your house by any chance?

I've barely had time to set the phone down when it chimes with the reply.

> **We never did see Jake last night. I kept**
> **hoping he'd come. And I hope you know you**
> **would have been welcome too.**

My chest feels like it's caving in. I type the words "Are you sure he was never there?" and erase them, three times. Of course he's sure. For all his faults and border-line flirtations, no one could question that Coach C always knows exactly where his players are and what they're up to. Sometimes better than even their parents do.

I scroll through my contacts until I find the one person who might have been able to convince Jake to skip the team party. When they were together, I saw enough signs—hasty ponytails for her, shirt buttons missed for him—that I knew they weren't saints, but they'd never spent the night together.

Now I find myself hoping, hard, that they have.

> **Hi, Daphne. You haven't seen Jake, have you?**

This time, the reply takes longer, and I let myself imagine that she's with him now. Maybe they've gotten back together and are trying to find the way to cover some indiscretion, not realizing that all that matters to me in this moment is knowing that my son is safe.

Finally the answer comes.

> **I haven't seen him since before the game. I'm**
> **sorry. Do you have Kolt's number?**

She sends the number along, but it doesn't help. Kolt hasn't seen Jake, either.

"He's missing, isn't he?"

Luke appears at my shoulder as I stare at my phone, tears stinging my eyes.

"The first twenty-four hours are the most critical in missing-person cases," he says. It's a far cry from *The Clone Wars,* but he's clearly quoting something.

"What should I do now?" I ask, as much to God as to myself.

But it's Luke who answers. "Call the police."

So I do.

Second Police Statement: Kolt Martin

Thanks for talking with us again, Kolt. We've received some new information that raises additional questions.

Okay.

When was the last time you saw Jake Foster?

In the locker room, after the game.

Are you sure? Think hard, son. Because we have a witness who says they saw you pick him up from his house around midnight.

No, sir. That witness is mistaken, or messing with you. I can promise you I haven't seen Jake or heard a word from him since the locker room. Is Seth Cooper your witness? Because I already told you, he's the one you should be questioning again.

Is there anybody who can vouch for your whereabouts at midnight that night?

Sure. My parents. Like I said, I went to the party earlier that night—everybody did—but I was home before midnight and didn't leave the house again.

If everybody was at this party, weren't you worried that Jake wasn't there?

I wasn't worried then. Jake doesn't always come out after games. But I'm worried now. Where's my best friend? That's the only question that matters.

Did you and Jake ever fight?

Nope. This is pointless. Quit talking to me and go find him. Where's my best friend?

Did he ever get angry at you? Were you ever afraid of him?

Nope. Where's my best friend?

Were you jealous of Jake? His athletic ability, his relationship with the coaches, anything like that?

Jealous? Are you kidding me? He's my best friend. Where's my best friend?

Were things different between you and Jake after his injury last summer?

Where's my best friend?

I think we're done here. Let us know if you remember anything, okay?

Close One

Kolt

After

When the police leave my house, my parents just sit there on the couch. I slouch across from them, hands in my pockets, pinching the soda-can tab I picked up yesterday at Jake's house until it cuts into my thumb.

Maybe I should show it to my parents.

Maybe I should have shown it to the police.

Maybe no matter who I show it to, they'll tell me it doesn't mean anything.

Not maybe. That's *exactly* what will happen.

Maybe I'm an idiot for picking it up in the first place.

The second I saw it there, I could picture what might have gone down the night Jake disappeared. But what evidence did I have? A piece of garbage that's tied to a memory and a conversation that didn't even happen?

I pull my hands out of my pockets. Lean forward to scratch the back of my neck as I rest my elbows on my knees. My parents and I stare at each other until I can't stand it anymore.

"Well, that was a close one," I joke. "They almost discovered my heroin stash."

"Kolt," my dad warns. He always comes home with his tie loose and his top button open. Not today.

"I didn't do anything wrong! Effing Seth Cooper and his effing lies. He's the one they should be questioning again."

Mom twists the dish towel she was holding when the cops showed up. "Watch your language," she says.

I wonder if she remembers that Kmart used to scream the actual word right in her face.

It had to be Seth who sent the cops over here. I want to hate him, but the idiot probably pissed his pants right there in the office and said the first thing that popped into his brain. Probably wasn't trying to get me in trouble so much as get an attaboy out of them. To hell with the truth, I guess, and who cares if my parents end up shizzing their shorts when the police show up to visit their "good" son?

"You really don't have any idea where he might have gone?" Mom asks.

I slump back in the chair and cover my face with my hands. "I thought the questioning was over."

"It is," Dad says. "It is. We're just trying to help. The sooner he's found, the sooner your life goes back to normal too."

Like finding Jake for Jake's sake isn't enough to make it worthwhile.

Up in my room, my phone's all lit up with notifications from Daphne. We used to be closer, back when she was dating Jake, and I still miss her sometimes. It's not like I cut her out or blamed her for what happened. Jake got all drama since last summer and probably deserved to be dumped on his ass. But still, it feels better not to have Jake between us, messed up as that sounds.

So I do what she asks and jump on social media to log in as Jake. (She obviously doesn't know his password is still *daphne32* or she would have hacked into his account herself.) I shut down the garbage thread she asked me to. Then I log back into my account and comment on her "Find Jake" page, even though I don't think it'll do any good, since all of social media is a garbage thread. Gotta respect the girl for giving it a shot, though.

Speaking of garbage, I stand over mine and make myself drop the soda-can tab.

I didn't lie to the police, but I didn't tell them everything, either.

Show Me a Sign

The Summer Before Senior Year

Just because somebody's your best friend doesn't mean they can't be an asshat sometimes too. Case in point: our first summer-ball tournament before senior year.

Coach was usually a little less intense for summer ball, but not this time. When we got to the locker room for our first game of the tournament, he sat us down and unzipped the bag he'd lugged from Ashland. We'd all been speculating about what might be in there—new there. New uniforms? Personalized water bottles? A metric ton of junk food?

The second I saw what it actually was, I froze.

One beat-up old sign, three words:

HEAD

HANDS

HEART

"Isn't it bad luck to take that out of the locker room?" I asked, backing away, just in case. "Like when you tell an actor to break their leg or something?"

Seth and Jake both laughed at me.

"That's *good* luck, idiot," Seth said. "And there's no superstition about the sign. Nothing bad is going to happen."

Coach Cooper held it up for us. "Do you remember six years ago, when you first came to Junior Warriors camp? Remember how we sat in the locker room on our last day of camp and Coach B asked if I wanted to keep this?"

We nodded. There were a few new guys and younger guys, but most of us had been in the room that day. This was the team Coach had been building all along, and the season he'd been building it for.

"This sign has hung in that locker room since I played at Ashland. But I never really took the time to think about it, to understand it, until that day. Here's what it means to me, boys.

"You play with your head. Run every play like we practiced it. See the court. See each other. Be smarter than your opponent during every single second the clock's running. That's the part I can help you with most, but still, it's the five on the floor who have to make it happen.

"You play with your hands. Hard passes, soft touch on the shot, your hand in their face or at the waist or wherever it needs to be to stop them on defense.

"And you play with your heart. That's the part you boys have shown me for six years now, at every single practice, in every single game. This is our season. I promised you it would be. Today is the day we begin to keep that promise."

We stood and shouted, gathered in the center of the room by the speech and the adrenaline and all those years of working toward this moment. As we piled our hands in the circle, nobody even had to tell us what the chant would be.

"Head, hands, heart!" All our voices came together as one, and for a second I almost felt sorry for the team that had to face us that day.

But then Jake looked over at me with this weird panic in his eyes. No way he'd play the way we needed him to if he was in his head that bad. Time to lighten it up a little.

"Break a leg, gentlemen!" I shouted. "Break them both, if you're an overachiever like Foster!"

Everybody laughed but Jake.

He pulled me aside as we headed out to the court. "Be serious," he said. "We can't mess around this year."

"Jake, I love you, man, but you're wound tighter than a two-dollar watch. We're a team, you know. It's not all on you. Lighten up."

"What would Arizona State say if I lightened up?"

There it was again. Jake had a verbal agreement to play for the school he'd been dreaming of since sixth grade, and he wouldn't let anybody forget it.

"They'd say, 'Congratulations on being less of an up-tight ass.'"

"Shut up, Kolt. Verbal agreements don't mean shit, and you know it. Until I sign on the dotted line, they can walk away."

It was so dumb I had to laugh. "Dude, they've been recruiting you since eighth grade. They'd be gold-plating your toilet seat if the NCAA would let them. They're not walking away. Just go out there and play your game. That's all they want."

Jake walked away, muttering about how I'd never get it.

"Yeah, maybe I won't. What I really don't get is why you changed."

He didn't even turn back, like I wasn't worth an answer. We'd disagreed with each other about five thousand times before, but this time felt different somehow. Deeper.

Whatever was off between us, we carried it onto the court: missing each other's passes, not quite anticipating each other's cuts, not calling the switch on the screen in time to prevent a score. Jake's nothing special in the classroom, but he usually reads the court like a damn novel. Not that day, though. And okay, maybe I missed a few key rebounds myself.

We still had a pretty solid lead in the third quarter. When Jake swatted the ball from his guy, I took off, ready for the easy layup at the other end of the court. I looked back just as Jake fired a pass to me—and then watched it sail right over my outstretched fingers.

"Next time," I said as we jogged back down to play D.

"Would have been *this* time if you hadn't let yourself get so slow in the off-season."

Jake and I had been trash-talking each other for six years straight, but this had an edge to it I hadn't heard before.

The kid guarding me snickered.

"Dude, shut up," I said. "You're down by twenty."

"Whatever, Assland."

I slapped him on the back, just hard enough. "Congratulations, man. That is literally the first time I've ever heard that joke."

After that, he slunk off like the idiot he was. But still. I didn't like getting laughed at by some punk kid who was stealing my material and belonged in the JV bracket. In spite of the scoreboard, we still had something to prove.

So when Seth put up a shot that clanged off the back of the rim like a back-alley trash can, I crashed the boards hard, determined to grab the rebound. Unfortunately, so did Jake—which meant I smashed straight into his back while he was in the air.

He slammed down sideways, right on top of me. We

hit the hardwood together, and the impact was brutal against my back and chest. I rolled out from under him and popped back up, ready for the next play, expecting him to do the same. But he just lay there, bent and buckled, grabbing his knee and rolling on the floor and making these long, low sounds like a wounded animal.

"Martin!" Coach barked at me. "What the hell was that?"

I didn't argue that Jake shouldn't have even been in there—that he should have hung back to play defense. That he wouldn't have gotten hurt if he hadn't come flying in, trying to do my job. You didn't argue with Coach—especially not about Jake.

Coach shoved me aside to get to Jake. "You'd better hope he's not out for the rest of the game."

I didn't mean to hurt him. Of course I didn't. Yeah, something was off between us, but he was still my best friend—and I wouldn't even take out my worst enemy like that. The way Jake's face had gone all tight and white had me pretty shook.

Two athletic trainers rushed out and helped him to his feet. The scattered crowd cheered as Jake limped out, arms slung around the trainers' necks, eyes shut tight against the pain. I tried to follow them, but Coach yanked me back.

"We've got a game to finish, Kolt," he said. "And you'd

better make damn sure we still win it after that stunt you just pulled."

We won, even with some new kid named Ruckert playing like crap at point. But it didn't feel like it was supposed to. Everybody's eyes kept flicking toward the locker room, hoping to see Jake running or, hell, even hobbling back out. As soon as the buzzer went off, we fived the other team and filed down into the locker room to check on him.

But he wasn't there.

"They took him to the hospital," the trainers told us. "His knee was messed up pretty good."

So we piled into cars to head over there, still in our uniforms. Everybody was too quiet, too stiff, too worried. Something had to change before we walked into that room and stressed Jake out even worse. Dude hated anything medical. My guess: it had something to do with his dad. But you can bet we never talked about it.

"Maybe you should have showered first," I said to Seth as the hospital door slid open for us. "Pretty sure making people puke is the opposite of what they're trying to do here."

Seth stared me down. "Don't you ever know when to turn that crap off?" he asked, and he'd never looked as much like Coach as he did right then.

It took a while, but they finally let us see him. Not gonna lie, it was weird. Jake had barely been to the doctor since I'd known him, and now here he was in a hospital bed.

"My boys!" He threw his arms out and nearly knocked over his IV stand. "You came."

Whatever they'd given him for the pain had definitely done some unwinding on him.

"He has to go for some tests soon," said Luke, looking proud to be the eleven-year-old with the information the whole varsity team was waiting for. "But you can stay until they take him."

So we stayed until the nurse came. It was nice to see Jake finally laughing and joking with the guys. Maybe this would turn out to be a good thing.

But that night, when Seth and I went back to the hospital to check on Jake and give him the stats of the game, he didn't exactly throw his arms open.

"'Break a leg,'" he said as his eyes drilled into me. "That's what you said before the game."

"Come on, bro. Even you're not superstitious enough to believe in that crap," I said. "Besides, you didn't break your leg. It's not like I said 'Tear an ACL, boys.'"

Jake smacked his hand on the hospital tray, and the whole thing shook like it wanted to shatter. "I'm in the hospital, and you can't even take this seriously."

"I'm serious as a heart attack." I slapped my hands to my face. "Oh, shit, now you're probably going to have a heart attack, and it's all my fault."

"This is my season. My future. Can you stop joking for once in your life?" He sat forward and gripped the side rails of the hospital bed. "Can you just say sorry and admit this is your fault?"

"I'm not joking. I'm straight-up telling you that this isn't my fault. It's your fault. You should have hung back to play D instead of trying to save the day with your crap rebounding skills. You want me to be serious? How's this: stop trying to blame your problems on everybody else. Oh, and it's not just *your* season. Did you even realize you said that?"

Jake looked like he might climb out of the bed and stab me in the face with his IV needle. Seth stepped between us, one hand on my chest and the other out toward Jake.

"Jake, I think we'd better let you get some rest," he said. "We'd rather win that tournament *with* you, but we'll go out there and win it *for* you instead."

The crazy thing was, we did. We won that trophy two days later and delivered it to Jake the night before his surgery.

"Thanks, guys," he told us, wearing the same goofy, drugged-up grin he'd had when we'd first seen him in the hospital. "I'll see if I can smuggle it in under my gown." He shoved it under his blanket, making it tent up in exactly the wrong place.

Jake laughed like he'd lost it. He was so proud of the joke, even though it wasn't that funny, and I was sort of proud of him for letting go enough to joke about stuff as serious to him as basketball *and* surgery.

"Yeah," he sighed. "This thing is definitely good luck."

Good luck, bad luck. I'm still not sure I believe in either. But the next time we met in our own locker room, when we looked up at the rectangle on the wall where the paint hadn't faded quite so much and realized Coach had left the HEAD HEART HANDS sign at the tournament a state away, you didn't even have to be that superstitious to get the feeling our season was headed in the wrong direction.

Shrapnel

The Summer Before Senior Year

Coach Braithwaite knew the hospital well. The official form always showed his full name, but even here nobody called him anything but Coach B.

He had never been in a hospital before the war, had counted himself too strong and healthy for any of that. But there was still shrapnel—even in his face—that nobody dared take out, so here he came every time he woke up with blood on his pillow to visit his friends in the ENT clinic and get his wounds cauterized before things opened up too wide.

Coach B had made peace with the nosebleeds and frequent visits. He'd even made peace with the shrapnel. There were certainly worse ways to carry the war with you for the rest of your life. He'd lost friends to some of them. To PTSD, most of all, and the ways people tried to silence it.

This day, though, he turned away from the ENT clinic and headed toward Med/Surg, where he'd visited friends and players recovering from all sorts of things. He carried a jar of daisies his wife had cut for Jake and, as he always did on one of these visits, a small envelope.

"Thanks," Jake said, looking grateful even though he clearly wasn't sure what to do with the flowers. "And tell Mrs. Braithwaite thanks too." But his smile was dim, even under the fluorescent lights of the hospital room.

Maybe it's the medication, Coach B thought. *And there's a mental trauma that goes along with an injury that's every bit as great as the physical. Sometimes greater for a kid like Jake, who carries the weight of the world—or the team, at least—on his shoulders.*

"How are you feeling?" he asked, knowing the answer, but also knowing the value of Jake putting his truth into his own words.

"Fine, sir. Really good. It was all pretty minor."

Unfortunately, none of this was the truth.

In fifty-one years at the same school, Coach B had gotten to know a lot of young people. They graduated. They left town, or they stayed, or they left and then made their way back. They found true love or something like it, built careers, had kids. In a few cases, he'd even gotten to coach those kids. He'd had no regrets about walking away when the time came.

But, oh, he would have loved to coach Jake Foster. Not because of his ability to read the opponent or his accuracy and consistency as a shooter or even his sheer will to win, although those were the sorts of things you could build a championship team around. The boy was grateful and teachable and just plain hungry. He reminded Coach B of himself when he was younger, and Coach B had been around enough to know that today's teenagers were on a battlefield of their own. That some of them were sustaining wounds they'd be tending to for the rest of their lives.

Coach B held out the envelope, wishing it were more. Surely the medical bills would bury Jake and his mother. But his own bank account was nearly empty; his own medical bills felt like a precarious slope before a landslide.

No, there was no money in the envelope.

"I wrote you a poem."

Jake had seen Coach B, sitting at his kitchen window, writing poem after poem for friends, former players, journalists—anybody whose path he had crossed who came upon a hard time. But he had never been on this side of the tradition, had never even read one of the poems.

"Thank you," Jake said. "This means a lot to me."

And now, Coach B knew, he was telling the truth.

"You can read it later," he said. "While I'm here, let's talk."

Jake struggled to sit up in bed. "Who's going to mow your lawn while I'm out?"

Coach B waved the question away, even though he didn't have an answer for it. "I'll find someone, or the grass will grow. You deserve a break after six summers, anyway. What will you do with this chance to slow down? That's what I'd like to know."

"Probably write poetry," Jake said, laughing.

But Coach B didn't laugh. "Summer is a good time to write poetry. You could do exactly that, if you wanted."

Jake's brow contracted a little, just like it did on the court. "I'm going to smash every record for rehab and physical therapy. Even before that, I've got a whole lineup of old games to watch on YouTube. And they never said I couldn't lift with my upper body."

"Or," Coach B said, "you could write poetry. Or learn to play the clarinet. Or take up painting. You could let yourself heal and come back stronger. How about that?"

Jake shook his head. "I have to get back out there. Without that ball in my hands, I'm nothing. Nobody."

Before Coach B could tell Jake how wrong he was, a nurse came into the room, handed Jake a small cup with three pills inside, and watched as he swallowed them. Coach B watched too, thinking how he'd spent too many years taking too many pills and not asking enough questions about them. Even though it seemed true of so many his age, he hated that the body he'd always been able to depend on had become so dependent on chemicals.

But this visit was about Jake's problems, not his. When they were alone again, Coach B tried to remember what he'd wanted to say before the nurse interrupted. It was harder to remember here—too sterile, too many distractions. He wished they were in the shade of his backyard. Or at his kitchen table, where the words came most easily. Still, he had to try.

"You are somebody, Jake. Please believe that."

Jake shrugged. "Maybe. But without basketball, I'll never be enough."

"'Enough' doesn't come on the court, son. 'Enough' comes from here," Coach B said, tapping the tips of his stiff fingers on Jake's chest. "And in there, your cup runneth over."

Jake turned away.

He didn't believe it, but Coach B could see in his eyes how badly he wanted to.

"Thank you for the poem," Jake said, and Coach B hoped the words in the envelope would reach him better than the ones he had spoken today.

"You're welcome. And Jake? Give yourself time to heal."

"I will. And I'll send somebody over to mow your lawn."

For the rest of the summer, the boys on the team took turns at the task. Each time Coach B looked out the kitchen window and thought the grass was getting a little long, someone new showed up and made quick work of it, building muscle and character under the hot summer sun.

Even from a hospital bed, Coach B thought, *Jake Foster is a leader.*

Last to come for mowing duty was Kolt Martin, headphones on and dancing at every turn. Coach B shook his head, smiled, turned back to the blank sheet of paper before him, hoping he could make something beautiful of it. Perhaps another poem for Jake.

A single drop of blood fell to the clean white sheet.

It was time to go to the hospital again.

Fog and Fever

After

Jake's been cooperating, but not because he wants to. Everything just hurts too much to even think about fighting back. He noticed this morning that the handcuffs were gone, and he's too grateful to risk messing that up.

Still, there's something else he's got to do. Something important enough to cut through this fog and fever, and he'll be sick until he knows it's done.

"Please," he begs. "Just let me tell them I'm okay."

The man scoffs at this. "Are you?"

"I want them to think I am."

"And how long have you been playing that game?"

When Jake doesn't answer, the man reaches into his back pocket and pulls out a phone, metallic red with the AHS logo.

Jake's phone.

"Fine," he says. "We wouldn't want anybody to be worried." He turns on the phone and points it at Jake. "Smile," the man says, and the flash is so bright after all the darkness that Jake is blind for a moment. He does smile, though. At least, he pulls his mouth up in the way he remembers from before.

"Now for your message," the man says. "I'll give you four words, one for every day you've been here. And because I'm so nice, I'll let you send them to four people."

Has it only been four days? That can't be right. The man is lying. He has to be.

Jake will think through that later, if he can keep his eyes open. For now, he needs to focus on the message.

"Let me type it," he begs. He actually falls to his knees, but sharp pains shoot through them both, and he can't stay there. Each of his knees has endured a trauma that might never fully heal.

The man rolls his eyes at Jake's weakness and at his words. "Are you kidding me? I'm not sending it from here. What if they trace the signal?"

Jake is confused. "Can they do that?"

The man lets out an impatient breath. "I'd rather not find out. I've already had to disable the location encryption on your pictures." He dangles the phone in front of Jake's face, taunting him. "So. Your message. What'll it be? 'Don't worry, I'm alive' or 'Getting my shit together'? I swear, Foster, I won't type 'I love you all.' You've got to give me something better than that."

Jake thinks it over. Four words, four people. When they get the message and the picture from his phone, they'll know he's alive, so "I'm alive" would be a waste of half his words. What is it he wants to say most?

Then he knows. He gives the man the names of the four people he wants the message sent to, and then come the words.

"It's not your fault."

The man drives to a lonely hill, covered in sage and bitterbrush that cling to the dry dirt, struggling to survive. He finds the four contacts Jake gave him and sends the four words to each of them.

Because in spite of it all, he is not a monster. He too is only trying to survive.

It's not your fault.
It's not your fault.
It's not your fault.
It's not your fault.

He tells himself the words are true for him too.

Then he climbs into the truck and gets the hell out of there.

It's Not Your Fault

After

Daphne scrolls the "Find Jake" page, searching for anything that seems even the smallest bit credible or helpful. Nothing ever does.

Kolt stands by the window, spinning a soda-can tab between his thumb and finger. Drops the tab, tells himself it's nothing.

Luke opens Jake's nightstand drawer. The little first-aid tin is gone, just like his brother. But nothing in that kit could have fixed much of anything, anyway.

Then four phones light up with the words *It's not your fault* and a photo, blurry and washed out, of Jake wearing a pained smile.

They each try to call him then, three shaking hands holding phones to three eager ears, but of course it goes straight to the voicemail message they've been hearing since he disappeared.

Daphne, Kolt, and Luke recognize each other's numbers, but none of them are sure who the fourth number belongs to. When they call it (and they all do), they hear only the automated recording that came with the phone, repeating the number back to them, even though it's the only piece of information they already know.

Still, none of them call each other.

Each of them sits, alone and wrecked, and reads the words again: *It's not your fault.*

Not one of them believes it.

Any New Symptoms?

Daphne

The Summer Before Senior Year

Sometimes I wonder if my defining characteristic is my obsession with drugs.

When I was little, I dreamed of being a doctor. I'd give all my relatives checkups with my plastic kit and boxes of Band-Aids. (When Dad told me I could pick out a treat at the store, I'd pick Band-Aids every time.)

Somewhere along the line, though, I realized it usually wasn't the doctor who fixed you.

It was the medicine.

Even my seven-year-old self could see that. You go to the doctor, they take your temperature and look down your throat or whatever, and you leave feeling exactly the same. It's the five milliliters of grape-flavored goodness your dad pours (or your mom, I guess, if she stuck around) that actually make the difference.

Why would you want to be a doctor, I wondered, when you could be a pharmacist? The person who actually delivers the goods?

So when Jake came home after a couple of days in the hospital postsurgery, I put myself in charge of managing his meds. It turned out that was an easy job compared with trying to keep him off his feet. Jake was ready to get back onto the court, and it took all four of us—Kolt, Luke, Jake's mom, and me—tag-teaming him to keep him occupied enough that he wouldn't try anything stupid.

Since there's no off-season for college prep, I tried to figure out things Jake and I could do that were entertaining but still required brain activity, even if it was a stretch. That's how we ended up playing so many card games and watching entire seasons of *Grey's Anatomy*.

"You could be Derek Shepherd someday," I told him one night as Meredith's voice-over began against the Seattle skyline. Jake's injured leg ran the length of the couch behind me, but it was still so comfortable, leaning back against his chest, him resting his chin on top of my head. "You'd be out there saving lives, filling out the scrubs."

He couldn't have sat up faster if the couch had caught on fire, launching me to the other end.

"No way," he said. "I hate doctors and hospitals and blood. I hate all of it."

I stared at him. "Jake, we're on season three. You've watched fifty episodes of doctors and hospitals and blood in the last week. Why did you sit through fifty episodes of everything you hate?"

He shrugged. "Because I love you."

He'd never said it before, and I'm still not sure he meant to say it then, but he didn't backpedal. He just pulled me close and kissed me, maybe partly so I wouldn't feel any pressure to say it back.

"Speaking of medicine," I said, even though that was definitely not the last thing we'd been speaking of, "it's time for your pain meds." Jake's mom had thanked me for keeping on top of it, since he'd been known to try to skip a dose or two.

Jake groaned. "They make me all loopy and nauseous."

"Nauseated," I corrected him. "'Nauseous' isn't incorrect, but it can also mean you're causing nausea, and I can confirm that's definitely not the case. I actually feel quite great when I'm around you."

He nodded. "Right. So calling a grown-ass man 'McDreamy' is nauseous because it makes me nauseated. Is that correct?"

I shook a pill from the bottle and handed it to him, along with his water bottle. "Very funny. And the doctor said you'll heal faster if you stay on top of the pain."

"Okay, fine," he said, tossing the pill back with a swallow of water. "But I can't guarantee what my digestive system's going to do if I keep taking these things."

We spent the next few hours playing cards, with college

basketball reruns on ESPN Classic giving us just enough noise in the background. As the medication kicked in, Jake turned back into the kid I'd first met at the courthouse—joking, laughing, laid-back. Maybe this was what he was like when he got a little break from competitive sports.

I thought of the three words he'd spoken earlier—*the three words*—and wondered if the pills gave him confidence too. He seemed more sure of himself than I'd ever seen him off the court.

We'd just hit halftime on a John Wooden championship game when Jake's phone rang.

"Kolt," he said, setting the phone to speaker so he could use both hands to shift himself on the couch. "How's it going?"

"J-Money," Kolt said. "We've got to get you out of that house."

"Nah," Jake said. "I'm good."

"You haven't left that couch in way too long. I will drive you to Disneyland tomorrow, dude. Just say the word."

Jake played a card—a good one—and waggled his eyebrows at me. "Neither one of us can afford Disneyland. And you just want to take me there because my crutches get you to the front of the line."

"That cuts me real deep, Jake. But I'll forgive you if you get out of your freaking house. How about I take you to the lake?"

"Daphne's over. We're playing cards."

"Please tell me you're at least playing strip poker."

I leaned over the phone. "Hey, Kolt. You're on speaker."

"Ah, good. Daph, as much as Jake needs a win right now, I think you'd better waste him at this one. Get my boy down to his skivvies and then beat him at one more hand and rip that brace right off him. Then we can actually go somewhere."

I smiled at Jake and shook my head. "We're not playing strip poker, Kolt. And the brace stays on four more weeks if you want him to heal right and be healthy for basketball season."

"Okay, okay. Well, lucky for you, Jake, I know this other game you two can play, where you're this injured war hero and Daphne is the sexy nurse and—"

"I'm hanging up now, Kolt," Jake said. "We'll call you if we need any more ideas." He blushed pretty bad, and it made the heat rise to my cheeks too.

I watched Jake as he hung up the phone, and I realized Kolt was right. Jake was trying to be happy, probably for my sake, but it was hard for him to be stuck on the couch.

"Should we go to my house?"

Jake dealt us another hand. "Your dad hates me."

"No, he doesn't," I said, but neither of us totally believed it. Not after a year and a half of Dad encouraging me to go out with other guys—sometimes in front of

Jake—because nobody could possibly be good enough for his little girl.

"We can stay here, but Kolt's right. We've got to do something." I stood up. "I'll be right back," I told him, ducking into Luke's room to look for something fun to do. We'd never done Legos together before, but maybe that would at least get Jake's hands and brain working?

Then my gaze landed on something else: Luke's Red Cross T-shirt, lying right there on his bed. *Maybe it's not a terrible idea,* I admitted. *I mean, considering it came from Kolt.* I picked it up and put it on, trying to channel my inner Jenna. The shirt fit a little tight across the chest and left a sliver of skin showing above the waistband of my jeans, which meant it was probably exactly what Kolt had in mind.

"Good evening, Mr. Foster," I said, strutting back into the living room. I felt the heat in my cheeks as I straightened his prescription bottles and adjusted the pillows under his knee. "I'm the on-call nurse tonight. Any new symptoms to report?"

Jake sat up straighter. He tried to think of an answer, but I'm pretty sure he was distracted by my "uniform," which gave me a flush of confidence.

"Um, yeah. My shoulders are a little tight," he said. As awkward as I was at this game, we'd definitely gotten his mind off his injury.

I sat behind him on the arm of the sofa. "Yes, you're right," I said as I began to knead his shoulders and neck. I leaned around and kissed him on the temple, and again on his earlobe. "What else?" I whispered.

"Rapid heartbeat."

I slid my hand under the collar of his T-shirt and rested it against the smooth muscles of his chest. "Hmm. Yes. Rapid indeed. Let me check that from another angle."

Jake moved to the back of the couch and pulled me on top of him. I ran my thumbs across his jaw, stopping just below to feel the throbbing pulse in his neck. "Tight shoulders. Rapid heartbeat. Anything else I should know about?" I traced my fingers back until they tangled in his hair, and we locked eyes for a long moment.

"Yes," he said, and swallowed hard. "I think I mentioned the thing about the digestive system." Then he let out a long fart that shook the couch.

A laugh burst out of me before I could stop it. Meanwhile, Jake looked like he wanted to laugh and cry and hide in a hole all at once. "I am so sorry," he said. "I swore I was never going to do that in front of you, and I made it a year and a half. But I told you these pain meds are messing me up."

I fell against him, laughing so hard my shoulders shook. I guess that gave him all the permission he needed to laugh too. We were pressed so tight together on the couch we could feel each other laughing, which made it funnier somehow, which shook another huge fart loose inside him.

"Feeling better?" I asked.

"So good. I'm done. I promise." He let his head fall back against the cushion. "No, that's not true. I can't promise anything."

"This is the sexiest game ever," I said, tugging at the Red Cross T-shirt where it looked like Luke had wiped some nacho cheese.

"You do make a great nurse, Daph," he said, reaching to tuck my hair behind my ear. "At least, you would, if you weren't destined to be a brilliant pharmacist instead."

I studied his face, wondering how somebody could make me burn with want and shake with laughter and swell with gratitude, all in the space of a few minutes. And then it all swirled into one feeling inside me, and there was no keeping it in, even if I'd wanted to.

"Jake," I said as the corner of my mouth crept up into a smile. "I love you too."

"Then I'm the luckiest man alive," he whispered, and then he kissed me.

Winter Quiet

Kolt

Senior Year

We crushed the competition all summer. Nobody expected it after Jake's injury, including us. But the wins kept coming, and the team kept jelling. And even though Jake was mostly on the sidelines with Coach, it still felt like he was the leader we needed.

But as time went on, things got weird. For example:

Jake quit football to keep roofing, but even with all the extra money he was making in the preseason, he was always asking me to spot him at Best Burger.

Then the night of the first football game (a big L), the team was literally sitting there talking about what a difference Jake would have made on defense when we got the word he was back in the hospital after another accident. I swear, the first thing I thought was that I hoped he was okay. But the second was that I hoped he'd be fully recovered before basketball season.

And he is, I guess. I mean, he stopped cracking jokes, and he's even worse about taking them, which I didn't think was possible. But even though he hasn't been as consistent on the court as he was junior year, there are still moments when he belongs on the *SportsCenter* highlight reel, and even whole games when you see all those buckets of promise inside him poured out on the court.

Basketball season—*our* season—is going strong, but I miss him sometimes, even when he's standing right in front of me. And that doesn't make sense, until one day it does. Until the day I see Jake and Coach together in the locker room after Jake's worst practice of the season. He's acting like it's the end of the world, even though he still smoked the rest of us.

"It's my knees," he tells Coach. "I can play through the pain, and I'll keep doing it, but it's hard to be at the top of my game. It's like the harder I play, the more it hurts, you know?"

I keep behind the corner of the lockers so they won't see me, but I still have a clear enough shot of them to see the way Jake's biting his tongue but trying to hide it.

He's not telling the truth about something.

Coach nods. "I know. Let's get you to the athletic

trainer. I want you alternating ice and heat, every night. We'll get those knees back where they belong."

"It felt a lot better before I ran out of oxys—"

Jake hasn't finished the sentence before Coach is in his face, shoving Jake's chin up with his clipboard. "We're not fixing one problem with another. And trust me, pills *are* a problem. Heat, ice, PT, tape or braces, if you need them. That's what we're going to do about this. Ibuprofen, if you have to have it. Understand?"

Jake nods, hangs his head. But when Coach walks back into the office, Jake's eyes follow him, still begging.

We swore we wouldn't use any of that stuff, I want to say. *Did you forget? Or did you lose that part of you too?*

Because it wasn't just one promise on that first day, in the back of Coach B's Jeep. We promised again when my brother got so high that he missed his own hearing and again the day he went to prison for selling. We promised every year on the anniversary of the day Jake's dad drove his truck into the ravine.

I want to grab him and shake his shoulders. Hell, I want to punch him in the face. I must have made a sound, because he looks up, and suddenly the smile is back.

"Hey, there you are. Want to go spotlighting?"

"Sure." I scratch the back of my neck and tell myself I imagined it. The begging, the hunger, the supposed-to-be-smooth cover-up when there's no promise of scoring what you want. Because this chill guy in front of me is my best friend, and even superstar Jake Foster can't go coast to coast that fast.

It's dark so early now that we grab the spotlights and some Best Burger and head out right then. Once we're surrounded by sagebrush, Jake turns on the spotlight while I drive. We find all kinds of animals: deer, pronghorn, a couple of foxes that dart away so fast I wonder if I imagined them too. But the others stay still and let us get a good look, so blinded by the light that they can't turn away. Sometimes we climb out of the truck and see how close they'll let us come, neither of us really sure what we'd do if they decided on fight over flight.

"We should have brought Luke," Jake says when we find a doe and fawn, bedded down under a juniper. We get out of the truck, but this time we don't walk any closer.

"Nah. He'd just give us some lecture on nocturnal versus crepuscular or the anatomy of the eyeball in the presence of bright light."

Jake laughs. "You're probably right. How did he turn out so good with such a crap male role model?"

"Are you kidding?" I ask. "He's got you."

Jake picks the dirt from under his fingernails. "Yeah. Right."

"You're going to play college hoops. You're every kid's hero. ASU send your letter yet?"

"Nah, not yet."

I can tell it's bugging him. The county paper already ran a story about the big shot from Cedar Hills signing with Gonzaga.

"It's coming. They're probably just fighting over who gets to hand-deliver it."

He tries to smile.

"And hey," I add, "you're a better big brother than I ever had."

Jake looks up. "I heard Kmart got clean and he's living in Flagstaff."

I shrug. "Wouldn't know. He hasn't come home in years. But I doubt it. My parents always have an address to forward stuff to, but he made us promise not to come find him. Easiest promise I've ever kept."

I turn the spotlight off, and when her eyes adjust, the doe leads the fawn deeper into the trees, somewhere safe from pain-in-the-ass teenage boys.

We lean back against the tailgate, and it's quiet for a minute. Not summer quiet, either, with the bugs and frogs in the background. Winter quiet, when everything's gone to sleep.

Jake and I don't do so well with quiet. Never have. So we both blurt something out at the same time.

I say, "Do you think God can make a spotlight so bright that even He can't look into it?"

And at that exact moment, Jake says, "I think I might have a problem."

At least, I think that's what he says. But my voice is louder, and my conversation is easier, so that's the road we roll.

Later that night, after I've showered all the sweat and grit from my skin, I still can't shed the memory of that moment. And I realize I'll never know what was down that other path, because it's way too late to talk about it now.

Four Elements

Luke

After

carbon
hydrogen
nitrogen
oxygen

96 percent of your body is made
of those four elements.
One time
Daphne explained it to me with Legos,
even though I am smart enough to understand it
    without them.
96 percent of a person is built
with just those four bricks.

It matters how you connect them.
N_2 is most of what we breathe

with every single breath.
In and out,
like waves on a shore.

H_2O is water, and you can't live without it.
H_2O_2 is hydrogen peroxide, and it will kill you.
$C_6H_{12}O_6$ is glucose—plant sugar—if you connect it
    one way,
but
there are about a hundred other ways
to combine those same Legos,
and some of them are poisonous.

I build another molecule in my mind sometimes:
The one I looked up after the roof.
The one I'm most afraid of.

$C_{18}H_{21}NO_4$

And then I break it apart
turn it into
water
sugar
air
so it can't hurt anybody
it's supposed to be helping.

carbon
hydrogen
nitrogen
oxygen

Four elements. Four words.
The ingredients
to make
or wreck
your world,
even if somebody tells you:

It's not your fault.

Four Words

It's not your fault.

When I see the text,
I rush it to Mom,
who rushes it to the police,
who track the text location
to an empty hill in the middle of nowhere.

The good news: fresh tire tracks.
The bad news: tires so old and bald
they don't tell us anything.

It's not your fault.

I hear her talking on the phone,
but it isn't the police.

It's the pharmacy, with four words
I hear on speaker
that make her worry lines even deeper:
"Too soon to fill."

"But I'm out. I took them exactly like you said,
and I'm already out."
"But I need them, especially with all that's going on."
"Yes, I understand. Two weeks. I'll call back."

She doesn't understand,
because she doesn't know
what I know.

She sits on the couch and buries her head in her
      hands,
so I sit down beside her
gentle like snow
and ask the question gently too.

"Mom, are there pills missing?"

"They counted wrong at the pharmacy.
And it's not the first time.

I love Ashland Drug, but I'm transferring
     somewhere else.
It's just too many mistakes."

It's not their fault, I want to tell her.
It's not a mistake.
Is there a way to make her see without hurting her
     more?

"Painkillers?" I ask,
but not because of the pain in her face.

"No," she says, shaken awake.
"I haven't needed painkillers since my surgery.
Just my blood-pressure pills
and my sleeping pills."

And I breathe a little easier because
maybe it *was* the pharmacy's mistake.

But pills are pills are
carbon
hydrogen
nitrogen
oxygen
and I should probably tell her

what I saw
and what I know.

It's not your fault.

That's what Jake's text said.
Except he's wrong.
It *is* my fault.
Because I saw
and I knew
and I said nothing.

Still, I say nothing.

A Jake joke
from *The Book of Luke and Jake:*

> *A chemist walks into a bar and says,*
>   *"I'll have a glass of H_2O."*
> *His buddy says, "I'll have a glass of H_2O too."*
> *Then he died.*

The Book of Luke and Jake: Part 2

The Summer Before Senior Year

Jake promised himself that once the last refill from his surgery ran out, that would be it. No prescriptions, so no pills.

It almost worked too. He'd been toughing it out for nearly two weeks before one of the punks on the JV team left his locker open and Jake saw an orange prescription bottle on the top shelf.

It was Darius Ruckert's locker. Jake recognized the Lakers sticker on the door. He laid a hand on the locker and nearly shut it before he remembered that Ruckert wasn't injured—and saw that it wasn't even his name on the bottle. He wasn't doping, was he? That stuff would mess you up in a hurry.

Jake's mind flashed back to the previous basketball season, when Ruckert had almost made varsity as a sophomore and Coach had asked Jake to take him under his wing. Hadn't Jake promised to help Ruckert any way he could?

Now it was time to make good on that promise. Jake snagged the bottle and shut the locker. Ruckert might be a punk, but if Jake could save him from going down a dangerous path, he'd do it in a heartbeat.

He was going to flush them right there in the locker room. He really was. But Kolt came in just then, so Jake tucked the bottle away in his bag. Better to take care of it at home. But when he got home, Luke and his mom were ready for dinner, and by the time dinner was over, it made more sense to flush them after everybody else had gone to bed. Just to be safe.

That night, Jake sat in his room and spread his math homework across his desk to get his mind off the bottle in his bag. He used to be so good at math, and now here he was, retaking the second semester of junior math in summer school. He used to love it, because back then, it made sense. Even algebra had been okay in seventh grade, when it was a matter of solving one equation for one variable. For $7x + 3 = 59$, Jake didn't even have to write anything down to tell you that $x = 8$. But then there were two variables, which meant you needed two equations to solve it, and the more things you didn't know, the harder it was to learn any of them.

Now he didn't even know where to start. He looked up, and there was Daphne in his favorite picture from last season, her hair a little messy from the game but her smile bright. Daphne was the only reason he'd passed math sophomore year. He could call her. She'd be here in a heartbeat, and she'd know exactly how to do every one of these problems.

But he couldn't let her see him struggling like this. Not when she was so strong, so smart. Even after a year and a half, there were still moments when he worried she'd wake up and realize how much better she could do.

He shook it off and got back to work, solving for the first variable, and then somehow it circled back around to where his first answer couldn't possibly be correct. Square root of a negative number, and he wasn't looking for imaginary solutions here. He wasn't sure what that really meant, but it struck him as a metaphor anyway. Too bad those were helpful in English, not math.

The lead on his pencil snapped, so he sharpened it and tried again. The eraser only made things worse, so he started a new page, and then another, and then another, finally filling the last sheet in his notebook and even the cardboard cover on the back, trying to find this one damn answer.

Paper. He needed more paper. He checked his desk drawers, dumped out his backpack. How could there not be any paper? He sprawled belly-down on the floor and scooped an armload of junk from under his bed: wrappers, used tissues, random socks, and, halle-freaking-lujah, a notebook.

But no. It wasn't a notebook. The cover was blue and faded, but the writing on the front was his own: *The Book of Luke and Jake.*

It must have been buried there since before his injury. And even worse, he'd totally forgotten about it. He opened it and read the first page:

November 4

Hey Luke,

I saw you looking through Dad's old stuff today. I know you saw me too, but it's okay that you walked away. I'm not sure I wanted to talk either.

But sometimes I do, and I don't know how to start. Sometimes I want to tell somebody how mad I am at Dad for the things he did. Sometimes I wonder what my life would have been like if things had been different. If he had been different. Sometimes I want to remember the good parts, partly because I need to know that there WERE good parts, since half of what's in me came from him.

I'm not sure if that's true, though. I think you

*have changed me and shaped me more than he
ever will. You're the kind of person I want to
be: honest, kind, good. And I'm hoping we can
shape each other. (Which reminds me, let's work
on your ball handling, especially with your left
hand, okay?)*

*So why am I writing all this in a notebook
instead of saying it to your face? Because
sometimes that's too hard. I think we both felt
that today. So anytime you have something to
say to me—whether it's heavy or funny or one of
your awesome science facts—you can write it in
here. And I will always write back.*

Deal?

Jake

Jake flipped through the notebook, lost in the good memories and jokes and things to look forward to: holidays and game days and even just letting Luke tag along for kicked-back summer days mowing the lawn and shooting hoops at Coach B's. Had there really been a time when he saw so much good in his past, present, and future? He wouldn't have believed it if the evidence wasn't staring back at him in his own handwriting.

A Jake joke

Patient: Doctor, I have a real short-term memory problem.

Doctor: *How long has this been going on?*

Patient: *How long has WHAT been going on?*

Kolt was right. Jake had changed. Of course, he already knew that, but he'd thought he'd been hiding it so well.

Luke had changed over the years too, but in all the right ways and always staying true to himself: totally obsessed with science and sports and weaving them into poems that showed the truest, deepest parts of himself. He'd turned into a good little ballplayer too.

Jake flipped to Luke's last entry.

Science Facts and Sports Stats
by Luke

Orcas stay with their families
their whole lives.
They only leave their siblings
for a few hours at a time.
Ever.
No moving out,
only moving together.

There are over sixty sets of brothers
who have played in the NBA.
Not always at the same time,
usually not on the same team.

But just to know
your brother is out there,
hustling like you,
hurting like you,
dreaming like you—
that has to feel pretty good.

I know we can't be like orcas
(I don't even like seafood),
but maybe we can be
like those brothers.
Maybe even when you leave for ASU,
we can still
somehow
be hustling,
hurting,
dreaming,
moving
together.

Jake felt sick. He didn't remember reading this at all. But he must have, because there was a sketch of two orcas next to it in his signature thick black lines. Why hadn't he written back if he'd read it? How long had Luke been waiting for an answer? He looked at the date at the top of the entry.

Since the day he had made the verbal agreement with ASU. The day he'd promised to leave Luke.

A memory came to him, of leaning on his elbows over the back of the sofa, spouting sports facts and searching for the right thing to say as his dad watched a ball game. When a scrappy, brown-haired point guard had gone for the steal, Jake had remembered something he hoped would impress his dad.

"John Stockton has the NBA steals record—3,265. Almost 600 more than the next guy. Can you believe that?"

His dad hadn't even looked away from the screen. "Stop kicking, Jake. You break the couch, and I'll break your nose."

Jake hadn't even realized he was kicking the base of the sofa. His dad wouldn't really break his nose. He wasn't like that. But Jake had stilled his feet anyway. Stared down at them, thinking how unbelievably stupid he was.

Another memory surfaced: standing in the viewing line at his father's funeral, ten years old and very aware that it was past time for new church shoes. He'd just stepped on the heel to slip out of them when a man knelt down and shook his head. "Leave them on, son. Your mother needs you to be grown up. You're the man of the house from now on." Jake had startled at the words, but as he looked over at Luke and his mom, he realized this stranger with the serious face was right. Now that his dad was gone, he had to be enough for both of them. He had to grow up, starting now, starting with these shoes. When he'd finally taken them off that night, his big toes bruised and small toes blistered, he'd wanted to show the man, to see his eyes light up with pride. But it was enough to cover the blisters with Band-Aids and know he could do this.

The man of the house. Jake had heard these words again through the years, always from well-meaning adults with serious faces. It was his cross to bear, and even though it had grown heavy over the years, there had been a certain pride in bearing it.

But now the words bore a different meaning. *The man of the house.* Destined, then, to follow in his father's footsteps. Because isn't that what he'd become? Hadn't he made Luke feel all the things he'd felt himself—stupid, unseen, unwanted, *less*—all because he was too lost in his own troubles to reach out?

Luke passed in the hallway just then, looking down at his own shoes, and Jake felt it like a shot through the gut.

"Hey," he called, trying to think of anything to ask about. Didn't Luke have club team tryouts coming up? Or was that what he was coming home from?

Luke came back, but stopped when he was only half visible through the doorway. He looked unsure about being even that close. His hair fell, matted and messy, across his forehead. His jersey hung off one shoulder because he was just so small.

"Want me to help you get ready for tryouts?" Jake asked.

"It's too late," Luke said, and the look on his face told

Jake exactly how it had gone. "Today was the last day. I didn't make it." He took a step toward Jake, and Jake was ready to pull his little brother into a hug. But Luke swept *The Book of Luke and Jake* straight off Jake's desk and into the trash can. "It's too late."

As Luke shuffled off down the hall, Jake felt a tug from the prescription bottle, heard a voice telling him that Luke was right.

It was too late. He'd become like his father.

Still, something inside him fought.

Jake had never had a drop to drink.

He had never even put anything illegal between his lips.

He worked hard at absolutely everything he did.

He had lettered in three sports; had worked all summer, laying shingles and spreading tar; had fought through summer school alone because he refused to give up.

He was not his father.

But then some monster inside him whispered that pills didn't make him like his father. They helped him be more than his father ever was. After all, he'd never gotten out of control. All the pills did was keep the edge off.

Jake googled the name of the drug on the bottle, and when it turned out to be a different generic name for the very medication he'd been taking—the one he'd been told to take by his surgeon—it felt like a sign.

But there were only thirty in the bottle, and they wouldn't last long. Not with football season ahead. He'd have to come up with a plan. He'd have to write Luke back later. Because if he could feed this monster, maybe it would leave him alone long enough that he could get back to normal. He'd be there for his brother's tryouts next time, and the time after that, and always, from that day forward. Luke would have everything he needed.

So Jake took the notebook from the trash and slid it back under his bed. He put the homework away for tomorrow.

As long as he had enough to get him through until he'd really recovered, this would all work out fine.

But the pills ran out before he was ready. After one particularly ass-kicking practice, he went looking for at least some ibuprofen in his mom's medicine cabinet and found a bottle of Norcos left over from her dental work. They weren't nearly as good as the oxys, but they did *something*. His knee still wasn't as strong as it had been, and it still hurt after any workout whatsoever. When the Norcos were gone and Jake called the doctor to see about just one more refill on the oxys, Dr. Morris didn't even make him come back in. All it took was a fax to green-light the refill to the pharmacy.

Jake knew you could get pills without a doctor. He promised himself he'd never buy from anyone, but once you're looking for it, you notice the guys coming out of bathrooms with the shady expressions and their hands in their pockets a little too casually. You start to hear hints of who's got something for sale.

It's just that it's so much safer knowing where the next one's coming from.

That's all.

No, that's *everything*.

So maybe you find ways to let them know you're interested.

After that, they find you.

Hurt Like Hell

Daphne

November, Senior Year

"**Three** hours," I tell Jake. "Those kids waited *three hours* for superstar Jake Foster, because you promised you'd be there."

I came straight from the gym, where hundreds of kids in Junior Warriors T-shirts were heartbroken when their hero never showed.

"I'm sick," he says, barely glancing away from the TV screen. "Can't you tell?"

"Okay, well, if you're sick, why didn't you text me so I could let somebody know? So I could let those kids down easy instead of promising them you were on your way?"

"Why didn't you tell them they had something much better? Superstar Daphne Sharp, who has as good a chance at a state championship but is actually passing all her classes. Who can actually afford to put gas in her car."

I'm not taking the bait. This isn't a pity party for the all-star. "It was your face on the posters, Jake. And those kids have been talking about your rim-wrecker dunk since last year."

"Well, this year has been all about the knee wreckers, but I'm glad everybody's making my injuries about them. That sounds about right. I can't even do that dunk anymore. Tell the kids that. Tell them if they come down wrong on one rebound or have one little accident, they could ruin everything."

I grab the trash can and start picking up fast-food wrappers and wadded-up tissues. "What is your problem, Jake? This isn't you."

Jake yanks an empty soda can from my hand before I can put it in the trash. "You know what, Daphne? This *is* me. I've spent my whole life trying to be the person everybody else wants me to be, and it's exhausting. I'm done. This is who I am, and clearly it's not good enough for you."

"I didn't say that."

He looks at me, his face hard. "*I'm* saying it. I think maybe we should break up."

The words take my breath away, like an elbow to the sternum. He stares at me a second longer, then turns his attention back to the TV.

I slam the trash can onto the coffee table and hit the power button on the remote. Even when the TV is off, he stares at it, his face as blank as the screen. Who the hell does he think he is, breaking up with me after I've spent the last six months nursing him through injuries and surgeries? After all the homework I've reminded him about and walked him through and, okay, even a couple of times let him copy? After all the crap I've put up with from my dad for dating him in the first place, after defending him for the last two years?

Stunned as I am, hurt as I am, my own words come back to me. *This isn't you.*

I sit on the coffee table and grab him by the jaw, turning his face so he has to look me in the eyes, willing myself to be strong so I won't fall apart. "I'm giving you one chance to take it back, Jake. Because you're wrong. I know who you are." I take a breath, drawing in memories from the feel of his skin against my fingertips.

"You're the guy who has mowed Coach B's lawn for the last six years and gets paid in raspberry lemonade. Who led the team in every category as a junior because he basically lived in the gym. Who let those kids literally stand on your shoulders so they could dunk."

"Yeah, I *was* that guy," he admits, and there's something about the way he says it that cracks my heart open.

"You were, and you will be again. I don't know what's going on with you right now, but you're still the guy I fell in love with. The guy that's going to make me cheer for

Arizona State next year, even though I grew up Arizona all the way."

His jaw tightens, and I know I'm onto something. I keep pushing, hoping to snap him out of whatever this is.

"Do you think a Division I program will put up with a player who skips out on commitments? Because I can tell you right now, they won't."

"You're right. Congratulations, Daphne. You're always right." The way he spits the words at me, I know I've missed something.

"What do you mean?" I ask.

"I mean, they called this morning. Made some assistant do the dirty work. They wish me well, but my play has 'lacked consistency' this year, so they've decided to 'go in another direction.'"

There's a sudden sick feeling inside of me. I didn't see this coming. They're not wrong; Jake's been inconsistent this year—on the court, at school, in *life*. But that just means there have been days when he's been human mixed in with the days when he's been brilliant.

I start to tell him this, but he cuts me off.

"It's over, Daphne. I'm done."

"It's their loss," I insist. "Can you imagine how many other schools will be lining up to sign you once they find out?"

"I mean, I'm done. *We're* done. I think we should break up."

The wave of sickness crests, and I sink to the couch. This can't be happening. I think of my dad, try to be as strong as he was when my mom walked away, and I cover Jake's hands with mine, knowing mine aren't nearly big enough.

"I know you're hurting," I say, trying to steady the tremor in my voice, "and I don't blame you. I know what it feels like to want to lick your wounds by yourself."

His jaw tightens. "I'm not even talking about that. I'm talking about us. The fact that I'm done with *us*."

I close my eyes for a breath. Gather myself. "If you break up with me now, I will survive. It will hurt like hell, but I'll come out stronger on the other side. Is that what you want?"

"Yes," he says, but he's lacing our fingers together the way we used to, sophomore year. He leans forward and rests his forehead on our knuckles, squeezing so tight it almost hurts. "That's exactly what I want."

A shock of pain shoots through me as he strengthens his grip. I pull my hands away. "You don't mean that. You'll feel better after you get some rest."

"I do mean it. I've never meant anything more. You should go, Sharp." He won't even look at me now. "You should get out while you can. Come out stronger on the other side."

I reach to guide his face back toward me, but he turns away.

"I love you, Jake. Look me in the eye and tell me you don't love me too."

He looks up, eyes swimming. "If I say it, will you go?"

He won't say it. He can't. As rough as things have been between us lately, he wouldn't lie to my face. Not Jake.

"Yes," I agree. "If you say it, I'll go."

"I don't love you anymore," he says, his eyes hard.

"You're lying," I say, and even knowing I'm right doesn't make the hurt any less.

"Grow up, Sharp," he says. "Did you really think this would last forever?"

I *had* wondered, and the thought makes me sick. Because now, as much as it hurts to leave, I can't imagine spending one more minute with the shell of a person in front of me. Ever since his injury, I've been trying to help him, fix him, change him. And that's my own damn fault.

I'm almost gone when I hear his voice behind me, flat and defeated.

"There's no staying on top of the pain, Daphne. You can tell your patients that someday. They're better off learning to love it."

"Goodbye, Jake," I say, wiping my cheeks. "I hope you find something to love besides your own pain."

I feel the bitterness and the bite of the words as I speak them, but I mean them, every one.

Derivative

December, Senior Year

After the breakup, it's Seth who stands beside me at Junior Warriors every Saturday for a month, getting the kids to line up and showing them the drills. It's Seth who loads the balls and takes the Rodriguez boy to the locker room to get cleaned up when he loses a tooth.

Once the kids have gone home on their last Saturday, Seth and I are sorting the tiny, sweaty jerseys into mesh bags when our hands touch, just for a second. Maybe it's all the static of the kids taking them off and the jerseys brushing past each other, but I swear there's an actual spark. I've known Seth as long as I've known Jake, but is this the first time we've actually touched?

I shake it off and we go back to sorting the jerseys, joking about who has to take them home and wash them.

"My mom buys organic detergent," he says. "They'll come out smelling like vinegar if we wash them at my house."

I narrow my eyes. "Your clothes never smell like vinegar."

I take a step closer, just to be sure, and then I'm breathing him in. Neither of us worked up much of a sweat helping the kids, but still, I'm surprised how good he smells.

"Contraband," he tells me, waggling his eyebrows to let his blue eyes bring me in on the conspiracy. I wonder if it's a move he picked up from Jake, or if I'm imagining Jake everywhere he doesn't belong. "I smuggle in the real stuff so I won't smell like salad dressing. True story. And no, I'm not using my secret stash on kid jerseys. The Chapman kid barfed on hers."

"Okay," I concede. "We'll wash them at my house, but you have to help."

Seth brings the jerseys in, turning them all red side out before tossing them in the machine. There is something sexy about a guy who not only does his own laundry but actually cares about it. Especially when you've watched him be patient and fun with kids four Saturdays in a row. Especially when you can see the curve and cut of his muscles under his worn Nike T-shirt.

While the washing machine runs, we sit at the kitchen table and catch up on our calculus, working through the problems together. The only weird thing is that it's not weird at all. When the buzzer sounds, Seth slides his hand over mine, and a little shock runs through me. "Stay put," he says. "I'll get the jerseys in the dryer if you figure out that derivative."

Forty-five minutes later, the derivatives are solved and we're on to Dickinson for AP English when the buzzer sounds again and the jerseys come out of the dryer, soft and warm. I pile them on top and start to fold.

"I'm impressed," Seth says.

I try not to roll my eyes. "That I know how to fold laundry?"

"No," he says. "That you can fold the laundry right here. Our washer and dryer are always covered with crap, so I have to fold my laundry on my bed."

I have never in my life thought about Seth Cooper's bed, but I feel my face threatening to flush. I search for something to say, but I've spent too much time with these boys, and all I can hear is Kolt's voice in my head saying, "Please don't let folding secret scented laundry be the most exciting thing that happens on Seth's bed."

Seth grabs a jersey and gives me a little side-eye and a smile. Is he blushing? As we fold, I wonder why I've never really noticed him before. If maybe it's because the spotlight was always so focused on Jake that everyone else ended up in the shadows.

And I hate that I'm thinking about Jake in this moment. I wonder how long it will take before the ghost of what we were leaves me in peace.

Maybe because I'm afraid the answer will be *too long,* I take Seth's hand and turn him to me. My eyes find his and the next breath brings us toward each other, and even as it's happening, a thought comes, unbidden, to my mind.

You kissed Jake in this laundry room once.

And then: *Seth's taller than Jake. That's a good thing.*

Before he can kiss me, I slide the jerseys to the edge of the dryer and hop up so I'm sitting on top of it. I draw Seth to me, hoping to separate this moment from that one. But it only makes the two of us closer to the same height, only makes me remember Jake's taste.

Stop, I beg the ghost. *Please.*

And somehow Seth senses it. He leans away, searching my eyes to figure out what's wrong.

"I didn't see this coming," I tell him, because I want to tell him the truth, even if I tell it slant.

He sits on the washer, and the metal pops under his weight. "Because you thought you'd be with Jake forever?"

Apparently I'm not the only one the ghost is haunting. "Through high school, maybe," I admit.

"I thought so too," he says. "Is it going to ruin the moment if I tell you I didn't see this coming, either? Because to be totally honest, I've been intimidated by you ever since honors math sophomore year."

"Wait, what?" I'm genuinely surprised. "You're the one who kept beating me on all those challenge problems!"

He shrugs, flashing the quickest hint of a smile. "You're the one who got the high score on all the tests."

"Think how unstoppable we'd be if we joined forces. We could take over the world! Or at least ace the AP calculus test." I swing my foot, tapping it against his leg. "We do make a pretty good team."

Seth hops down and pretends to think it over as he picks up the stack of jerseys. "Laundry and math and babysitting other people's children," he says. "So that's the way to impress a girl?"

I laugh, then look him up and down, taking in his shoulders and chest and arms, his messy hair and kind eyes. "Well, none of this is hurting your cause." I scoot to the front of the dryer, then wrap my bare feet around his legs to pull him to me. The jerseys are still warm when he sets the stack down beside me.

Seth gives a crooked smile, tilting the faint constellation of freckles across his nose, and I wrap my arms around his neck. When I kiss him, it's fresh and new and freeing.

Beside me, his phone rattles and vibrates on top of the dryer. I'm still leaning my head toward him as he pulls away.

He checks the screen and sighs. "I'd better go. My dad might lose it if I don't take these jerseys back and watch game film with him."

"Your dad expects a lot of you," I say, realizing we have this in common. I wonder if I should warn him now that he'll never be good enough for my dad, either.

"I guess. Walk me out?"

In the driveway, he leans against his car door and pulls me close again. "Can I take you on a real date sometime?"

I frown, pretending to consider, pretending that everything in me isn't already screaming *yes*.

"Will there be laundry?" I ask.

"No," he says.

"Will anybody puke or lose a tooth?"

"No. Not on the first date, anyway."

I reach up and tangle my fingers in his hair, and he gives a little shiver. "Will there be kissing?" I ask.

He nods.

"Okay, then," I say, leaving one kiss on his cheek like a promise.

On Monday, between school and basketball practice, Seth and I go to Ms. Li's room to borrow an AP calc practice book. He opens the door for me, resting his hand on the small of my back.

"Why, thank you," I say, reaching behind me to lace my fingers through his as I pull him into the classroom.

Ms. Li sits facing away from us. She's going over a test

with a student, and Seth and I both freeze when we realize who it is.

Jake slumps over the desk, looking totally defeated. Then suddenly he turns, enough that I know he sees how close Seth and I are standing to each other, our hands held together at my waist.

Ms. Li is the only one oblivious to it all. She flips the test back to the front page, giving us a clear view of the big red "14%" on the cover. "One way or another, Jake," she says, "we're going to get you to graduation."

Seth clears his throat, and she startles. "I'm so sorry," he says—to her, to Jake, maybe even a little to me. "We wondered if we could borrow an AP practice book."

"Of course, of course," she says, tucking Jake's test away as if we haven't all been staring at the score. She looks at us, her eyes lingering on our hands. Even though they've got their own lives outside of school, I wonder if teachers talk about this kind of stuff, and what they'll think of me if they do.

It's been a month, I want to tell her. *And* he *broke up with* me. *And neither Seth nor I expected this.*

I stare at Jake, wondering how long he's been struggling with math and why he never asked for help. And then I remember: because he's Jake, and he's not allowed to ask for help. He can't let himself be anything short of perfect, all on his own.

As Jake stands up to go, Seth steps a little closer behind me, and I give his hand a squeeze. Something in me prepares for a fight, but Jake just gives us a sad smile.

"If you need help—" I start, but Jake cuts me off with a laugh that sounds like it's been sucked dry of any happiness at all.

"I'm kind of past that point, you know? But thanks. And good luck with your stuff." He nods at the practice book, but maybe at the two of us. He looks right at me. "I really mean that."

I watch him leave. I can't help it. When you care about somebody that much for that long, it doesn't just go away. But already the feelings I had a few weeks ago have begun to change, and the voice in me whispers, *That's not your load to carry anymore.*

Except I can't seem to leave it behind so easily. Even after practice, when I'm working through more integrals at my kitchen table, my eyes search out the ones and fours, rearranging them into the red fourteen at the top of Jake's test.

I knew he was struggling, but I had no idea how much. It makes me wonder what else I missed just because it wasn't in bold red marker right in front of me.

Police Statement:
Seth Cooper

Tell us about the night Jake Foster disappeared.

I don't think I can tell you anything you don't already know. He played the game. He pretty much won the game. Nobody expected us to beat Pine Valley, but we did. *He* did.

Did you see anything out of the ordinary that night? Anything worth looking into?

[*Pause.*]

No, sir.

You hesitated before you answered that, son. And you sure seem nervous.

I *am* nervous. I've never been questioned by the police before.

There was a party at your house after the game. Did Jake come?

No. Everybody kept texting him, but he never showed up.

Why not?

I wish I knew.

Were you and Jake friends? Would you use that word?

Yeah, we were friends.

Was there ever any conflict between you?

Every day. Three sports and camps all summer—we were each other's best competition. And competition means conflict. Tackling, guarding, striking each other out.

Did it ever bother you that your dad gave so much time and attention to Jake? That Jake was a better ball-player than you?

Nope. But thank you for bringing that up. [*Sighs.*] I'm sorry. That's not me. I don't know how to act in these situations.

Apology accepted. Anything you and Jake competed over outside of sports?

[*Clears throat.*] No, sir.

What about Daphne Sharp?

She's a person, not a trophy. She'd walk away from both of us if we ever forgot that.

Okay, not "competition." But the original question was about conflict, right? You two have any conflict that involved Daphne Sharp? Maybe even the night Jake disappeared?

Like I said, he never came to the party.

But she was there before the game, wasn't she? In the training room with Jake? Even though she's your girlfriend?

Look, up until this year, nobody would have dreamed of coming between Jake and Daphne. But senior year, he's been different. Kind of checked out, kind of an ass. To be honest, he didn't deserve her anymore—and he's the one who broke up with her. We all cared about her, you know? She deserved to be with somebody who treated her the way Jake had before. I didn't even realize I wanted that person to be me until it was.

Understood. So here's the question: Did you see Jake or hear from him at any point after the game?

I saw him driving away with Kolt.

Away from where?

Away from his house.

After the game?

Yes.

But you said you didn't see anything out of the ordinary that night.

That's right. Nothing out of the ordinary. What I saw was Jake driving away from his own house with his best friend.

You sure about that?

[*Pause.*]

Wait, didn't Kolt already tell you about that?

I'll work that out with Mr. Martin, but you're sure you saw the two of them driving away together?

Yes, sir.

What time was this?

Around midnight.

Why were you at Jake's house?

Because I was worried about him.

You were worried? All on your own? Nobody put you up to it?

[*Pause.*]

Yes. It was my idea.

So you drove to Jake's house and saw him leaving with Kolt. Did you speak to either of them?

No, sir.

When was the last time you actually spoke to Jake?

Besides on-the-court stuff during the game?

Yes.

I . . . I can't remember.

Let's try that one more time, bearing in mind that we have a witness that says he overheard you talking to Jake right before warm-ups. What were the last words you said to Jake then? Before you shoved him into the wall and walked away?

[*Pause.*]

"I hate you, Foster. I freaking hate you."

Thin Red Line

Seth

Sophomore Year

Freshman ball was fun and games, but we knew things were going to change sophomore year. On the first day of tryouts, everybody worked out together so Coach could "see the big picture." After almost three hours of busting our guts, he shouted at me and Kolt and Jake to get dressed and come to his office.

I figured Kolt and Jake were more nervous than I was, but not by much. Yeah, he was my dad, but by then it felt a lot more normal to call him "Coach." (When two-thirds of the people in your household are named Seth Cooper, you've got to find a work-around.) Plus, it wasn't like we even interacted that much at home or discussed any subject other than basketball. And at the gym, he definitely treated me like any other player.

When the three of us had changed and made our way to his office, Coach got right down to business. "You boys busy tomorrow after school?"

We shook our heads.

"Well, then, you think you could stay for varsity tryouts?"

We all nodded together, like Ashland High bobbleheads.

Every once in a while, there would be one or two standout sophomores that made varsity, but I couldn't remember a time when there had been three.

Coach came around the desk, his gaze bouncing between us like he was playing pinball. Even by his standards, he was pretty wound up. "Okay, then. Get some rest, and be ready to work a hell of a lot harder tomorrow than you did today—harder than anybody else out there. I've got big plans for you guys, but I can't hand you anything. You've got to earn it. What are you going to do to earn it?"

Kolt opened his mouth, but Coach tapped his jaw shut. "Think before you speak, Martin. In fact, don't speak at all. Show me your answer on the court tomorrow."

I walked out of the office with the other guys, always careful in the gym to act like just another player, even when Coach wasn't there. The three of us were headed for the parking lot when the sound of one lone ball bouncing made us turn around.

A girl. One I didn't recognize, with a long brown pony-tail and long tan legs. She had a rack of basketballs all set up to shoot threes, even though the girls' coaches had already gone home.

"I bet she misses," said Kolt, and sure enough, she did. But she just grabbed another ball and another, like once one ball left her fingers, she was already focused on the next shot. She had great form, and a lot of them were falling.

"Who is she?" I asked.

"New this year. Her name's Daphne," Jake said, elbowing me forward. "At least, I think it is. You'd better go check."

I wanted to. I almost did. But the focus and the rhythm and the *rightness* of her alone on the court held me back. "Nah," I said. "Let's give her some space. You guys need a ride home?"

"I'm good," Jake said, still watching the girl shoot. "But take Kolt. He needs a shower."

"Your face needs a shower, Foster. Come on, Seth. I'm starving."

Kolt and I drove through at Best Burger and spent the next hour playing video games and filling our faces in his basement.

"Best of seven," Kolt said, chucking his controller onto the couch when I beat him at *Madden* for the third time.

"Or hey, how about we play something I'm actually good at. It's time to slay some demons, am I right?"

"Nah, I've got to get home. Math homework."

Kolt belched. He didn't quite have the range that Jake had, but it was still pretty impressive. "You wouldn't even have math homework tonight if you hadn't signed up for honors. You know that, right?"

"I know, I know. I'm sure I'll look back and regret not playing more *Demon Slayer* when I'm making six figures as an engineer."

"Dude, whatever. I'll try to remember to come back for you when I'm making seven figures slaying demons after the apocalypse."

At home, I'd barely had time to start my homework when Coach came through the door, dropped his keys on the counter, and went to the fridge for a beer.

"Taking it easy, huh?"

I stared at him. Could he not see my homework? And wasn't he the one who told us to get some rest?

"The Foster kid stayed after and shot around for another hour. That kid gets it."

I set down my pencil, lining it up with the thin red stripe on the side of my paper. "I'll stay after tomorrow. My shoulder was tight today, so I wanted to be smart about that."

"You can be smart *and* tough. There are ways to play through a sore shoulder. I want you in the weight room too. Three times a week. And fix your form, for hell's sake. There are mirrors in there for a reason. No wonder your shoulder's sore when you lift the way you do." He sat down, setting his beer over the corner of my homework. "We barely had a winning record last year. You know that, right? You know what that means for my job? If we don't step it up this year in a serious way, they might cut me loose. I'd be taking a real risk putting three sophomores on varsity."

I watched as a bead of condensation dripped down his bottle and onto my homework, bleeding and blurring the thin red line.

"I know," I said. "It's okay if you need to leave me on the sophomore team."

Coach slammed his fist on the table. "No, it's *not* okay. That's not how the game works. You play at the highest level you can for as long as you can. And then, if you're lucky, you do the same thing as a coach. You do not get to make your talent smaller to fit into your schedule or to keep from breaking a sweat. *You* do not decide when you're done with the game. The game will decide when it's done with you."

He picked up his beer, and when my homework stuck to the bottom of the bottle, he peeled it off like skin from a popped blister. "From now on, you never leave the gym before the Foster kid. Do we understand each other?"

"Yes, sir," I said, taking the paper from him and pressing it between the pages of my book. I shoved the book into my backpack and walked away, letting him think I was done with this thing I cared about. Knowing I'd come back to it when he turned his attention to basketball again, which never took long.

And I realized: that's how it was going to be, from there on out. Sometimes, even in a family, you keep secrets from each other.

And sometimes you keep them for each other.

Talk to Me: Part 1

After

Even in the dim light of the basement, things are beginning to come into focus. Jake remembers a fight with the man—the hand over his mouth, the taste of blood, the bite of the needle in his thigh. But somewhere in there, he's still got a gap, a gap in the footage.

Jake's not exactly in the mood for metaphors, but that night he dreams his life is literally written in a book. He grabs the spine and flips back a few pages, desperate for answers.

What is he doing here? Is it true what the man says, that this was all his idea?

Impossible.

Maybe.

But the pages are missing; there's a chunk torn out

of the middle. He finds the pages scattered along the steps leading out of this basement hellhole. He picks them up as he climbs, gathering them like the programs that litter the bleachers after a game. He stands at the top of the steps, and the door opens before him and the light pours in, illuminating the words as he strains to read them. . . .

There's one word, floating on glass, that comes back to him: *Phoenix.*

Is that where he is?

But no. He remembers now: that's the man's name. At least, he thinks it is.

Then the man—Phoenix—is back, shaking him awake, handing him the morning pills and a glass of warm water to wash them down. There are flecks of something float-ing in the glass, though, so Jake swallows the pills without the water. He'll drink from the sink later.

Unless he can get Phoenix to leave the water. No way is he drinking it, but there are plenty of things he could do with the glass to get himself out of here, one way or another.

"Good," says Phoenix after Jake swallows the pills. "Now talk to me."

"What?" Jake asks.

"Talk to me. You know, with words."

"Talk to you. Are you serious?"

Phoenix rolls his eyes. "We have to trust each other. You have to tell me stuff."

Now Jake's mad. "Talk to the person who cuffed me to a pipe? Trust the person who's kept me in this basement for who knows how long? Crack myself open and spill it all out like you're my freaking therapist or something?"

"I'd hang fancy diplomas on the wall, but I didn't earn any." Phoenix smiles, but only on the surface. Jake can tell he doesn't want to show the shame underneath the smile. Jake is an expert at smiles like these.

And in that moment, Jake judges him. He looks at the shabby surroundings, Phoenix's shabby clothes and sunken eyes. Of course a loser like this wouldn't have graduated. But then he corrects himself.

You don't have any diplomas, either. And as of last semester, you weren't exactly on track to earn any.

But that's not true. There were college scouts. There was interest. Even though Arizona State had screwed him over, there were schools willing to give him another chance in the classroom because of what he could do on the court. All he'd had to do was figure out a way to pass that damn math class so he could graduate.

Well, that was all he'd had to do before the torn-out chapter. Before he missed however many days he's missed, trapped in this hole.

"Talk to me," Phoenix says again, the patience in his

voice draining quickly as he snaps Jake from his thoughts. "You're here for me too, you know. I agreed to this so we could help each other, but first we have to trust each other. So spill. It'll be good for you."

"Talk to you . . . What, like tell you how I'm feeling?"

Phoenix shrugs. "Sure, we could start there."

Jake begins cautiously, like a creature emerging from its den. Tells Phoenix something he already knows. "I'm sick. Running over to take a crap or throw up about every five minutes."

"Still?" Phoenix asks, almost like he actually cares.

Jake considers. "Well, not now, but for a while there."

"But it's getting better?"

"Yeah, I guess."

Phoenix nods. "Good. What else?"

"I have dreams."

He laughs, the sound bitter as soap. "Don't we all."

"Not that kind," Jake says. "I mean actual dreams, with, like, metaphors and crap like that."

"You're not swearing anymore," Phoenix observes.

Jake wonders how much he swore during the missing chapter. He's always watched his language, mostly for Luke's sake. He's not sure who he is anymore, and the thought makes him angry. "Go to hell," he says.

The man's laugh is less bitter this time. "Probably will. Thanks. And how are things going when you're awake?"

"I'm worried sometimes, sick sometimes, desperate a lot of the time. But I'm bored most of all, and that makes me mad. Because it means I've given up on ever getting out of here."

"Nah," Phoenix says. "It means you've recognized that I'm your way out, and I'll let you out when I'm ready. When *you're* ready."

"I'm ready," Jake says, and this time the man's laugh is real and deep.

"You are so far from ready you're not even in the same time zone."

And there's something about the way he says it that brings something else to the edges of Jake's memory.

The championship game.

Climbing the ladder to cut down the net—and almost cutting off his finger because he was watching somebody in the stands instead of watching what he was doing.

Running to the parking lot, hoping he wasn't too late.

Too late for what?

That's when he truly recognizes Phoenix, and once he does, he can't believe he didn't see it all along.

There's a knock on the door, loud and insistent, like a crack of thunder. They both freeze, and then Phoenix pulls out the cuffs and presses the latch, swinging them open like jaws.

Jake tenses but doesn't make a move. Doesn't even

shift his gaze, but takes in the room with his peripheral vision and readies himself for a fight. The water glass is closer to him than to Phoenix.

"Trust me," Phoenix says again. "Because I'm trusting you." Then he tosses the cuffs on the cot and runs up the stairs, two at a time.

Finally Jake can turn all this agitation into motion. He pushes the cot under the window and stands on top of it. Only the back end of a car and only the first few painted letters are visible, but it's enough to know: the police are here.

Hungry

Luke

After

A Luke fact: 390,127 people in the UK listed their religion as Jedi in the 2001 census.

School days got better
and almost normal
after a while,
but Sundays were still
so hungry,
so empty.

Especially when your church has
a special fast for your brother
and you are supposed to not
eat anything,

drink anything,
all day.

I don't even realize I'm stopping,
staring
into Bishop Gregersen's office
and the jar of snack-size Kit Kats,
until I hear his voice.

"Come in," he says.
So I do.
"Have a seat," he says.
So I do because
the chair is close to the Kit Kats
and it looks like maybe he refilled the jar today.

"You haven't been in here since
before you were baptized," he says.
And I remember that he was the one
to baptize me,
to bury me under the water
but also
to bring me back out.

"I have been praying more since Jake left," I say
because I know he will like that part.

"That's good," he says.
He tips the jar toward me,
and I reach in,
hoping it's not a trap.

"I'm fasting," I say,
and he nods.

"I am too.
But I thought maybe my fast
could count for both of us.
This is a day for us to do something
for your family.
For the rest of us
to take a little part of this
off your shoulders."

"That's a good idea," I say,
even though I'm not sure
what he means about
the shoulders part.

Then he asks,
"Do you want to talk about Jake?"

"Yes," I say
as I tear the wrapper open

and snap the bar in half.
Then I take a bite,
and we both wait
wait
wait
until finally he says,
"Jake . . .
. . . is a good brother, isn't he?"

I think about that as I swallow my Kit Kat.
"You said
'is'
and you almost said
'was.'"

He nods.
"You're right, Luke. I'm sorry."

"You don't have to be sorry," I say,
and I mean it,
partly because
I'm reaching for another Kit Kat
and I want to keep things
good between us.

I'm still
just as hungry
as before.

"What do you think happened to Jake?" I ask.

Bishop Gregersen runs his hand through his hair
and lets out a long breath
as I down
one Kit Kat
after another.

"I don't know, Luke.
I've been praying about it too,
and I just don't know.
I wish I did."

Now I have a fist full of Kit Kats
and a belly that's even fuller, and
I'm starting to feel a little sick,
but I keep talking.

"The police think he ran away.
Some people think
he ran away
because he did something bad."

Bishop Gregersen nods.
"I've heard people say those things too.
What do you think?"

"I don't know," I say.
And then I tell him the other part
that I wasn't going to tell anyone.

"I've been praying to God
and Muhammad
and Buddha."
I look down and twist the orange-red wrapper
of one of the Kit Kats I haven't eaten yet
until the crunchy layers crush
when I say the next part.
"I've been praying to
the Force too.
I thought if God is real,
maybe He or She or It
wouldn't care so much
about what I call Him or Her or It,
or maybe even which way I pray."

Sometimes things make sense in my head,
but when I say them out loud,
they sound
so
stupid.

"But now I think
God isn't answering

because whichever way is right,
the rest of the ways are wrong,
and that's making God mad.
I'm making God mad."

"No, Luke.
I don't think anybody in heaven or on earth
is mad at you right now."

I squeeze with both fists
until everything is ruined.
It feels good to crush something with my
    fingers
and let the dark side win for a minute.

Bishop Gregersen looks at the mess I've made.
And he slides the jar closer to me.
He really does.
Even though I already ate some
and ruined more.

And maybe that's why I'm not afraid to ask him
what maybe I really came here to ask him.

"What if those people are right?" I ask.
"Will God be mad if Jake did something bad?
And then he ran away from it?"

Bishop Gregersen shakes his head.
"I don't think so.
I think God feels a little like we do.
Like He wants to help."

"So if God isn't mad at any of us,
why isn't anything getting better?"

"Maybe it is," he says.
"Maybe it's like *Star Wars,*
and we can't see what's going on
in that part of the story.
Maybe if we could flash to Jake's part of the story,
we'd understand."

I am glad he knows *Star Wars*
and even more glad
he might be right.
"Like Luke on the island,"
I say.
"How he wasn't who he had been
or who he thought he needed to be,
so he left.
But then,
when it was time,
he came back."

He nods. "Maybe like that."

I hold the whole candy jar in my lap
and look down
until the wrappers all blend together
and my eyes fill and splash right down,
like filling an aquarium
with Kit Kats for rocks,
and I ask
one
more
question.

"If Jake ran away because he messed up,
can I still love him?
Even if he hurt somebody?
Can I still think he's a good brother?"

Bishop Gregersen comes around the desk then.
Sets the jar back on the desk.
Takes the crushed candy bars
from each of my hands.
Puts a new Kit Kat on each of my palms.
"Whatever is wrong, God can make it right.
And Jake is one of the best brothers I've
        ever seen."

He crouches down and looks right at me.
"Next to you, anyway."

I slip those Kit Kats
into my pocket
and save them
for when I need them.

For now,
I am not so hungry
anymore.

Rumors

Kolt

After

The great thing about the weight room is that it smells like the Hulk's balls. I mean, it's not great when you first walk in, but after a while you don't notice it anymore, and then when you remember what it first smelled like and realize that not only have you gotten used to it but *you are contributing* to something as unstoppably manly and powerful as the smell of the Hulk's balls, you feel like you could lift a freaking diesel.

Technically, it's a coed weight room, but last year they finished the new weight room in the annex. I've been to that weight room—it's smaller, but the equipment's new, and it doesn't smell nearly as much.

Anyway, some unspoken rule has the girls going over there while the guys stay here, tucked underground with tunnels and storage closets that probably only creepy

Caruso knows his way around. So I don't even think twice before I go up to the mirror and pull down my waistband to check out a bump on my butt. Upper cheek, and I'm pretty discreet about it, so nobody else in the room even gives a crap.

What is this thing, though? Ingrown hair? Huge ugly butt zit? On anybody else, it would be disgusting, but when you find stuff like this on your own skin, it's a fascinating scientific specimen.

I give it a squeeze, and it bursts like a water balloon.

And that's when Jenna walks in.

I pull up my waistband and spin around. She's heading straight for me and making a face, but I hope it's from Hulk-ball smell and not because she noticed what I was doing.

"We need to talk."

"Okay," I say, walking away from the mirror and loading some plates onto a bar. "Spot me so I can finish up."

In reality, my arms are fresh and I haven't benched at all yet—it's been mostly legs and core so far. But Jenna doesn't need to know that. She lifts the weights and sets them in place like they're nothing, and I'm not sure whether I'm turned on or intimidated by how ripped she is. Probably both.

"I'll make it quick," she says. "It smells like balls in here."

"Hulk's balls," I say, swinging myself down onto the bench.

She nods. "That's about right. So, anyway, we need to talk about your boy Jake."

I wasn't expecting that, and I nearly drop the bar across my chest. Jenna catches it right before it crushes me, but I recover quickly. "Thanks," I say. "I got it now. I just wasn't ready."

But I'm still shaky. I haven't actually talked about Jake to anybody since he sent that text.

"Here's the deal," Jenna says. "I'm the admin on that 'Find Jake' page, and I gotta talk to somebody about it. Half of what comes in is totally useless, and the other half is about drugs."

This time I'm ready. And, okay, it's not as much of a surprise.

"What kind of comments? What kind of drugs?"

Jenna shrugs. "All kinds."

Referring to both the drugs and the comments, I guess. "So what are you saying?"

"I'm saying it sure seems like he had a problem, and since we're filtering those comments out, I don't think the police know. Did you tell them?"

My arms and chest burn as I do another rep, and another, and another.

"I'll take that as a no. And I'm guessing by the way you're sweating that you knew. Or you suspected, anyway."

I let the bar fall back onto the stand with a loud clang,

then sit up to face her. "What difference does it make? The police went through his whole house. If there was anything to find, they found it, and they know what they're working with. I'm not going to snitch on my best friend when they already know. If there's anything to know."

Jenna nods. "So you won't mind if I pass this stuff along to them."

"Do what you gotta do," I say. I don't mean it, but I also know it doesn't matter what I say. Jenna's going to do what she wants anyway. Not sure why she's even asking.

"You messed up in this with him?" she asks, looking a little like she actually cares.

"Nah," I say. "I never touch the stuff."

She straddles the other end of the bench, and we're facing each other, like it's another damned police interview, except this officer is way hotter. And closer.

"What do you think happened to him?"

That's all anybody's been asking for weeks. The people who really care aren't throwing the question out there in the halls, but everybody else talks about Jake disappearing like it's a plot twist in a movie or something.

I decide to be straight with her. Mostly.

"I think he lived and breathed basketball for so long that when it was over, he snapped. I don't know if he's hiding away in the woods or trying out for the Harlem Globetrotters or what. But bottom line: nobody has found a body. Because he's out there. I have to believe he's out there, and he'll find the way back when he's ready."

"Okay. Let's say you're right and he's out there. You don't think he was abducted?"

I grab the bottom of my T-shirt and wipe the sweat from my face, just in case she wants to check out the washboard. "Nope. Hard to see Jake being held anywhere against his will."

"And you don't think drugs have anything to do with it?"

I think drugs have everything to do with it. But I can talk myself out of it every time. And I know that even if Jake did get himself messed up in that, there wouldn't be a damn thing anybody else could do for him unless he wanted to quit.

"Why are you so interested in whether Jake was on something? You asking all this for a friend?"

She bites her lip. "Maybe."

I've heard the rumors about Jenna. How her dad came up a few pills short in the pharmacy once and she hasn't been behind the counter since. How she passed out in the woods behind Seth's house at a party last summer.

So I look her in the eye, try my best to tell my truth. "He promised he'd never touch the stuff. We both knew the only way drugs don't ruin you is if you never let them in."

Jenna looks away, and— *Oh, shit*. I rethink my words and realize how judgmental they sound. I know my choice not to start has to be an easier one than quitting. I'm about to try to tell her that when her face changes. Now she's looking in the mirror, smirking.

"Thanks for the morality lesson, Kolt. By the way, your ass is bleeding."

I stand up and twist to see a small red circle where I pinched earlier. Great.

"You were looking, huh?" I say, and she reaches around to give me an attaboy slap.

"Take care of that thing. It's not so bad."

Then she stands up and walks away.

I grab a towel and dry off before running to catch her in the hall.

"So what are you going to do about Jake?" I ask. "About all the stuff coming in on the 'Find Jake' page?"

Jenna shrugs, like we got too close to something real. Like she'll never let it happen again. "I'm going to do exactly what you said." She steps forward and tucks one fingertip inside the waistband of my shorts. "I'm going to do what I gotta do." She locks eyes with me and we step toward each other, and I have no idea what's about to happen, but I can't wait to find out.

"Hey, guys!"

And then there's Daphne.

Jenna and I snap out of it and spin to face her.

"What's going on?" she asks. The girl's smarter than Socrates, but she is not reading this room. Hallway. Whatever.

"Nothing," we both say.

"Have either of you seen Seth?" she asks. "We were supposed to hang posters."

"Nope," Jenna says. "And I've got to go to work. Good talk, Kolt. Now go take a shower." She slaps me on the butt again, then walks away, and damn if I don't watch her do it.

"What was that about?" Daphne asks.

"Nothing." I try to ask my question all casual. "So, what's the deal with her?"

Daphne gives me the side-eye, and then her face clears. "You like her. Kolt! You like Jenna, don't you?"

"Your face likes Jenna." Definitely not my best work. "Seriously," I beg. "Forget it." Knowing Daphne, she's about to do anything but that, so I cut her off. "Want to go shoot around?"

She looks at me like I am . . . not Socrates. "Um, Kolt, the season's over."

"Exactly! No pressure. No points. Let's just play. You can study for the ACT later."

"Kolt. Please tell me you're joking. We're seniors. You should have taken the ACT junior year, or at least last fall."

Of course I'm joking. I got my acceptance letter from New Mexico two weeks ago. But she doesn't need to know that. "Come on. My arms are Jell-O right now, so you might even be able to keep up."

The gym is dark and echoes as the doors close behind us. "I'll grab a ball, you get the lights."

I'm in and out of the locker room with two worn leather basketballs, but the gym's still dark.

"Sharp?" I call into the darkness. She's across the room, over by the one safety bulb that's always on. But she's not really moving.

"I still can't be here without thinking of him," she says. "Just seeing you standing there was enough."

I toss her a ball. "Can you be anywhere without thinking about him?"

She shakes her head, like she's saying no, but also like she's trying to clear something out.

"Sometimes I even think I see him. At the pharmacy, running down the street, coming out of Ms. Li's room. I see him because I expect to and I don't expect to. If that even makes sense. I wish it would stop, but I'm afraid of that too. Like it would mean he's really gone for good."

This makes two serious conversations with girls in the same day, bringing my all-time total to . . . two. I love

Daphne like she's my hella-smart sister, and I wish I could help her for real.

But there's nothing I can do to bring Jake back. The best I can do is distract her.

"You'd better be afraid of *me*," I say. "Because I have a serious medical condition. It's called asskick-itis, and I'm about to show it to you on the court."

Daphne can't help herself. She smiles. "You know that '-itis' means inflammation or swelling, right? So you have swelling in your butt from having your ass kicked? Is that what you're telling me?"

She doesn't know about the butt zit, does she?

Before I can ask, she knocks the ball from under my arm, and the game's on, even though it's still pretty dark.

The thing about me versus Daphne is that it's really only interesting when she's got the ball. She's crap on defense and I'm no good at offense, especially one on one. But when she's cutting and I'm anticipating or she's head-faking and I almost fall for it—that's when we're both at our best.

She pulls up, but I block her shot and clear the ball past the three-point line. I may suck at offense, but I outweigh her enough that I can post up against her pretty well. My butt's against her hip when I remember my secret weapon.

"Bad news, Sharp," I say. "You're right up against my butt zit."

She backs off so fast I almost fall to the floor. "Gross, Kolt! Are you serious?"

I spin around and make an easy five-footer off the glass. "Yup. And it just gave me the lead." I slap five on the tiny red circle on my shorts.

"I'm out," she says, throwing up her hands. "Game over." But she's laughing so hard I can't let her leave.

"Sharp, no! We're sorry! That wasn't fair. Two on one. How could you ever win? Stay. I'll spot you five points in the next one." I wrap my arms around her from behind, and she tries to pull my hands apart, but we're both just playing. "If you've got one, you can invite her! It'll be even teams again."

Then the doors open, and there's blinding light and a dark silhouette.

"Wow, sorry. Am I interrupting?"

Daphne and I break apart.

"Seth," she says. "I tried to find you to help hang posters. We were supposed to meet at the weight room."

"I was in the weight room in the annex. But I guess you found Kolt first."

"It's not like that—" I start, but he cuts me off.

"Heads up, Kolt," he says, and I swear I've never heard him sound so bitter. "Daphne comes here sometimes to get guys to fall for her. Right? I mean, first Jake, sophomore year, and then me, with Junior Warriors, and now . . ."

"Now nothing," Daphne snaps. "Stop giving me a guilt trip for letting myself lighten up for five freaking minutes." She's fired up, and part of me wants to grab some popcorn and watch this thing from the bleachers.

But then she turns the murder eyes on me. "And while we're all here, you two need to bury the hatchet on whatever crap you've got going on and stop lying to each other and to me and especially to the police. None of that solves anything."

"I never lied to the police!" I say. "I didn't tell the police I left with Jake that night because . . . wait for it . . . I *didn't* leave with Jake that night. Seth is the one who has information worth hiding."

Daphne turns to Seth. "What information?"

He looks at me and shakes his head, but she deserves to know.

"Seth told Jake he hated him. Right before the game. Right outside the training room."

Daphne's face goes so white that I wonder what I'm missing. Did something happen in the training room before I got there?

"I've never lied to you, Daphne, and I never will. I saw what I saw." Seth can barely look at her now, and I *know* I'm missing something. But then he clears his throat and keeps going. "Kolt and Jake left after midnight. It's not my fault if he was too impaired to remember it."

I step up in his pretty-ass face. "Impaired? Are you serious? Are you calling me a liar and a drunk in the same sentence? Because I'm a lot of things, but those aren't on the list."

Seth throws his hands up. "I'm just telling you what happened. Spin it however you want, but I'm going to trust what I see with my own eyes."

"You see what you want to see, Seth. But are you noticing the pattern here? 'Jake's missing? Blame it on Kolt!' 'Trouble with my girlfriend? Blame it on Kolt!' Take responsibility for once in your freaking life."

I've gone all Hulk and I don't even realize it until we've switched places and it's Daphne's arms reaching around me from behind.

"We're done here, Kolt," she says softly right in my ear. "Take it easy. Let's go. He'll let us know when he's ready to apologize."

I stop struggling. She's right. And he's not worth it.

But also he's lying. He has to be. And I can't let him get away with it.

"The police are about to get some new information," I say. "It's not coming from me, but I can promise you this: they're going to figure out what happened, and then they're going to know who's been telling the truth."

Seth's face goes blank. He steps away from us, back into the shadows. "I'm done here," he says.

Daphne's watching, wary. "Aren't we going to go hang posters?"

"Go ahead," he says. "It sounds like Kolt has enough info to break this thing wide open, whether I help or not."

Daphne and I stand there in the half dark as he walks away. She takes the ball, dribbles it a couple of times. Picks at a corner of leather that's coming up.

"Were you being serious about the police getting new information?" she asks.

I nod. I picture Jenna's face, and there's no doubt she's got the guts to tell them what I haven't.

"Is something finally going to happen?"

"I don't know," I admit. "But it wouldn't surprise me if Jake turns up by the end of the week. One way or another."

One Small Thing in Return

After

He's been sneaking to the parking lot to watch the construction crew all week. They're remodeling the offices and bathrooms on the second floor of the pharmacy, and some loudmouth on the crew happened to mention which day they'd be painting. Sure enough, they left one small, high window open that night to let things air out. Must have figured nobody would even think to look for an open window when it's this cold.

He climbs the fire escape and eases himself onto the ledge that runs below the windows. He still exercises constantly, so he's got the strength and the trust in his body he needs to climb all the way to the open window without worrying too much about the brick courtyard below. It feels right that the game he's given everything to is giving him this one small thing in return.

His muscles are tight against his T-shirt as he grips the top of the window frame and lifts himself through the opening. He has sixty seconds to disable the alarm, but he installed this very alarm system last summer to make some extra cash. Of course, they've changed the code, but he still remembers the manufacturer's override.

The alarm is already flashing its final ten seconds by the time he gets down the stairs and to the box, but it's enough time to punch in the code, and he exhales, long and deep, when the light turns from red to blue. With any luck, it's the only time he'll see anything flash red and blue tonight.

The hardest part is over. His plan is probably going to work.

He hesitates then. This isn't who he was raised to be. He sees his father's face, the one who taught him to hold his head high, even in defeat.

The thing is, he shouldn't be defeated. His team redeemed him. Everything was supposed to be better on this side of a championship. But it's all gone to hell. If he could see any other way forward, he would take it. He would hold his head high, and he would take it.

But there is no other way, so he straightens his shoulders, snaps the gloves tight, slides off his backpack as he crosses to the controlled-substance cabinet. Maybe this isn't who he was raised to be, but there's no denying it's who he is now.

One by one, he takes bottles from the shelf and dumps each into a gallon-size ziplock bag, returning the empty bottles to the exact right places. It'll buy him a little extra time, anyway. Nothing will look off when they open the store in the morning. But enough people in this town are addicted to these pills that no doubt it'll all be discovered tomorrow.

He could probably sell some of the pills to those very same people. God knows he could use the money; that's why he was installing alarms last summer in the first place. But he's not so desperate that he's selling them. Yet.

When he has everything on his list, he does it all in reverse:

Puts the bag in the backpack.

Resets the alarm.

Eases out the open window.

Slides along the ledge.

Climbs down the fire escape.

It's not until he's safe in his car that he really stops to think of them: the people who would have taken these pills. Some of them are recovering from surgeries or injuries, sure. But he knows most of them are like him, trying to dull a pain that will last the rest of their lives. Trying to quiet the voices inside as their bodies grow tolerant and it takes more, more, more to do the same job.

He knows these people, knows their pain. But he also

knows that he isn't taking anything from them. When the missing pills are discovered, the pharmacy will have to file some paperwork, but the insurance company will cover the cost. And before the day's even out, a new batch will be on its way from the wholesaler. No one will go hungry for long.

That's the thing about painkillers. There are always plenty more, if you're willing to do what it takes to get them.

The system has made sure of that.

Talk to Me: Part 2

After

Voices murmur above, but they're no match for the screaming in Jake's head.

The police are here. If he yells, if he finds a way to remove the bars and break the window, he can get out of here. It will all be over.

And then he realizes: if he gets out of here, it *will* all be over.

Everybody he loves, the whole town that looked up to him—they must know who he has become. By now they must have figured out all the terrible things he has done, and not one of them will look at him the same.

He can't go back there.

He can't.

The cuffs lie on the bed, hungry jaws still open. And Jake realizes something else: the police will have cuffs of their own, and until he knows what happened in that missing chapter, he can't be sure those cuffs won't be for him.

He sinks to the bed, knowing Phoenix is right. He isn't ready to face his past or his future; he isn't strong enough. It's better to stay down here. And Phoenix was right about another thing: down here it's getting better. There's a growing feeling inside that maybe Phoenix is here to protect him. To save him.

Stockholm syndrome. He hears the words in Daphne's voice. They were watching *Beauty and the Beast,* and she was trying to talk herself out of liking it. "Imagine being so stressed and desperate that you get attached to your captor like that. It's not healthy."

Jake wrestles against the idea. This isn't Stockholm syndrome. Phoenix is trying to help.

Which is exactly what you'd think if you had Stockholm syndrome.

There are footsteps on the front porch. The police are getting ready to leave.

Jake folds his lips between his teeth and bites down, blood seeping between his lips, eyes closed against the tears.

A few minutes later, Phoenix comes back. He stops

when he sees Jake there, broken and bleeding from wounds he inflicted on himself.

"Talk to me," he says again.

Jake struggles against it, but he's been so lonely for so long that in the end, Phoenix wins. He always does.

Jake talks.

Judge and Prosecutor

Daphne

After

Dad and I stuck it out in the city for years after my mom left, but eventually his caseload wore him down enough that he took a smaller job in this small town to escape from the heavy and hard.

But it turns out those things are in small towns too.

Over the years, I've watched the light in him grow dim as he confronts the shadowed side of society: armed robbery, domestic violence, every sort of assault. Every day, he sits at the front of that courtroom and tries to hold his head up as he bears witness to all the ways people can hurt each other.

I used to think I could change things for him. Whenever I brought home a perfect report card or showed how fierce I could be on the basketball court, he'd smile and escape from it all, even if just for a little while. Every night, he tries to shed that sadness with his robe before he comes home to me. But it still shows through. And he's been getting lost in his thoughts more lately. Getting more protective of me all the time.

But tonight, he turns on an *SNL* clip show from back in the day. He kicks his feet up on the coffee table and laughs, real and deep, right from his belly, as the Spartan cheerleaders chant on the screen.

I watch him for a minute: his body relaxed, his mind released.

"How was your day?" I ask. It's a normal question, one that millions of people are probably asking each other tonight. I realize too late that it's the wrong one. In only four words, I've taken him from *SNL* slapstick to the real-life troubles of this town and the weight of the role he plays in them.

"Custody hearings," he says. "It got ugly."

I know these are his least favorite days: deciding the fate of kids caught in a storm they didn't cause and can't control. Worrying he'll get it wrong. We don't talk about the gratitude he feels that he never had to go through it, and the guilt he feels over that. But it's not his fault my mom walked away.

"I'm sorry," I tell him. "I'm sure you did what was best."

"I wish I were sure," he says. The scene's getting

funnier, but Dad only stares, glassy-eyed, looking like real laughter is something that belongs only on the screen.

Maybe a different question will bring him back to the present. I search the room for anything to talk about and notice his shoes by the back door, the bottoms caked in mud.

"Did you go to the cabin?" Our cabin is old and junky and barely up the mountain, but it's his favorite place in the world.

"Yup," he says, without looking away from the TV. "Water's on already, and I took some lumber to replace the boards in the deck."

"Did it help?" I ask.

"Not really."

I try another question, even though it's one I ask almost every day.

"What are they saying about Jake? Anything new?"

Even though he was never a big fan, Dad's been worried about Jake, asking around and telling the cops to fill him in the second they have a new lead. And I love him for it. He's my only source of information now that the "Find Jake" feed has dried up, and even the local newspaper seems to have lost interest.

He sighs and turns off the TV. "There's only one development, and it may or may not be related—I want to say that right out of the gate. I'm not accusing Jake of anything." But he looks away when he says the next part.

"Somebody robbed Ashland Drug last night."

I stare. "And what? There were fingerprints? Someone was seen wearing a number thirty-two basketball jersey? Why would this have anything to do with Jake?" I'm desperate to know Jake's alive but, apparently, not so desperate that I want to believe he could do this.

He rubs a finger along the rim of his glass. "It appears that the suspect was . . . in top physical condition."

"Dad," I say. "That's not even enough for probable cause, let alone to convict."

"I'm not convicting," he protests. "Just thinking about this with you." He gets up and paces the room, then settles himself on a barstool. "Daphne, how much do you know about Jake's medical history?"

"He had two accidents and two knee surgeries. Other than that, he was in better shape than anybody I've ever met. No asthma, no allergies, no other injuries. We were together two years and he never even caught a cold. What else is there to know?"

But even as I say it, I know what I edited out: family medical history. His dad's alcoholism, so bad it led to his death when Jake was in elementary school.

I shake the thought from my head. That has nothing to do with Jake. "He's never had a drop to drink," I say, with as much confidence as I can gather.

Dad nods. "But didn't you tell me he's been different this year? Isn't that why you two broke up?"

I think of Jake then: how he'd resisted the pills right after his surgery and how, later, he hadn't.

But there's something about the way Dad's sitting, the way he's looking at me, that makes me feel like I've got something to confess. And then I look up at him on that damn barstool and figure out what it is.

"Nope. No, no, no." I stand and try to pull myself taller. "Don't you sit above me like we're in your courtroom. You don't get to play judge *and* prosecutor. I've always respected you. Always. But I won't be put on trial in this house—and neither will Jake."

"I don't ever set out to convict anybody," he replies. "Not ever, and you know that. I make the best judgment I can, as fairly as I can, with the information I'm given. I'm not asking you to do anything different from that." There's fire in his eyes as he defends his judicial honor. More fire than he'd ever use to defend Jake.

"Bullshit." His jaw tightens, but I keep going before he can give me some stern reminder about language. "You never liked Jake. And now you think he robbed a pharmacy, based on what? The fact that he was in shape?"

Dad hesitates. "Jake fills his prescriptions with Jenna's dad at Ashland Drug."

"So do we!"

He holds up his hand, so I let him finish. "He also filled them at Walgreens and at CVS. He got prescriptions from three different doctors. He was getting painkillers in all three places at the same time, paying cash for most of them. And not just a few pills."

The news cuts sharp inside me. I thought I wanted any information at all about Jake, by any means necessary. But everything about this feels wrong, wrong, wrong.

"Says who?" I demand. "Some Pine Valley fan who's bitter about the state title? Some gossiping clerk who wanted to feel important?"

"Jenna's dad."

The answer makes me sick.

But something doesn't make sense. "Jenna's dad is a health-care professional who's not allowed to discuss what his patients are taking. Even if you're friends. Especially if you're friends."

Dad looks away, out the window. "I'm not really allowed to have friends. You know that. Too many conflicts of interest. And he didn't tell me as a friend."

"How did he tell you?"

"He told the police. It was in the warrant I signed to search Jake's house. They tried to do it the easy way, but Jake's mom wasn't cooperating."

I'm stunned into silence for a moment, but then I force myself to swallow down the sick and stand my ground. "How could you do that to them? They're grieving, Dad. They don't need police searching their house."

He's so calm I could scream. "The police have already searched their house. You know that."

"With permission, when Jake was a missing person! Not with a warrant, when he's being accused of breaking and entering and burglary and whatever else. Can you imagine how that's going to freak Luke out? And what, you think Mrs. Foster has something to hide? If there was anything there, you wouldn't have needed a warrant. She already let them search, and she knew there wasn't anything left to find. So she stood up for Luke's emotional health, and you plowed right through her wishes."

Dad's eyes soften. "Those boys need more than their mom is able to give them." Then he clears his throat and swirls the ice in his glass, trying to dodge the daggers I'm staring at him.

"What's that even supposed to mean? You think because your job pays better that you'd be able to parent them better? You don't know the first thing about the Fosters, Dad, but you sure as hell made things worse for them. Trust me on that."

I take the glass from his hand, forcing him to look at me. "What else?" I ask. "What haven't you told me?"

Dad chooses his words carefully. "There has been some information coming in through your 'Find Jake' page. I thought you'd seen it, but I can tell that's not the case."

I'm not following. "There hasn't been anything on the page for days."

He nods, and I hate that he knows something I don't. "It sounds like Jenna deleted the entries before they were posted. She didn't feel it was good to put the information out in public, but she shared it with the police. There are a number of individuals who say they've witnessed Jake taking prescription painkillers when he thinks nobody is watching. And one who says he walked in on Jake buying them in the bathroom at school."

I'm actually struck dumb: by the fact that idiot online trolls have any part in this conversation, by the fact that the page I started to help Jake has so completely turned against him. I'm stung too by the fact that Jenna hid this from me, even if she thought she was protecting me.

"Jake didn't rob the pharmacy," I say, willing truth into the words. "And the sooner you and your colleagues figure that out, the sooner we'll find him." I turn away, disgusted. "I can't believe I thought you'd help. You've wanted Jake out of the picture from the second you met him. Go back to watching your show. We'll find him on our own."

Even as I say it, I'm not sure who I mean by "we" anymore, only that I can't do it alone.

My dad is wrong about Jake robbing the pharmacy. I have no doubt about that. But looking back over the last year—the mood swings, the terrible grades, the inconsistency on the court, and especially the things Jake said to me before the championship game—I'm sick as I realize he might be right about the painkillers. And maybe that's why I got so mad.

Because what kind of pharmacist will I be if I don't even notice when somebody I care about is suffering from something this serious? If I'm the one who practically forced him to take the pills in the first place?

Then I hate myself for making this about me, about this dream I have that Jake always supported.

Was I like this when we were together? Was it always all about me? Where was I for his dreams? Did I ever even ask what he wanted to do beyond basketball, or just go on and on about what *I* was going to do? Am I part of the reason he couldn't see past senior year and college ball?

I open the text on my phone—the last four words Jake sent.

It's not your fault.

He's wrong. In my case, anyway. Kolt and Luke loved Jake longer and better than I ever did. They didn't abandon him. And even though I know I shouldn't feel guilty for walking away from a relationship that wasn't working, I'm sick knowing how completely I shut out a person I loved who needed me.

And what am I doing to help? So far, all I've done is mess everything up. Sure, I've read every article online and pried every piece of inside information out of my dad. But hardly any of that has translated to actual action. And what have I been doing instead? Filling out scholarship applications and graduation paperwork, pretending I'm trying to distract myself from tragedy but really just doing what I do best: focusing on me.

No more.

Even though I fundamentally disagree with pretty much everything my dad said, a memory surfaces that makes me wonder how many conversations I read wrong—and if money might have something to do with this after all.

When we were watching so much *Grey's* last summer, Jake actually walked away from the TV during one episode. I found him out front, lying on his back in the grass.

"Must be nice," he said.

"What?" I asked.

"To have enough money to go to rehab whenever you need it. To check in and come out changed after thirty days, as many times as it takes. Like a freaking magic trick."

It took me a minute to make the connection between what we just watched and what he was saying. "Did your dad ever go?"

"Once," he said. "We hadn't even finished paying it off before he fell off the wagon again. My mom tried to get him to go back, but he never would. Too expensive. Too hard." He closed his eyes, let out a long, slow breath. "They had started fighting about it again when he died."

I couldn't think of the right thing to say, so I filled the silence with the only words I could think of. "I'm sorry. I wish it had turned out differently. I wish he could have gone back."

Jake's smile was forced and bitter. "It wouldn't have worked anyway. They're happy to take your money, but they can't make you change."

"It's not about the money," I started.

"No," he said, with a look that let me know just how thoroughly I didn't get it. "When you've got it, it never is."

I picture him now, needing help but thinking it's out of his reach.

Maybe I still don't understand. Maybe he's too stubborn to accept help, even if I offer it. But I can at least try.

I spend the next two hours researching rehab facilities and programs and payment options. I print anything that's promising, just in case. And when I'm done, I send a text to Jake, praying that maybe he'll see it somehow.

It *IS* my fault, and I'm sorry. Whatever you're going through, I am here.

Search Warrant

Luke

After

Dictionary.com says
search means "to look carefully to find something
    missing or lost"
and *warrant* means "authorization, sanction, or
    justification."
And *search warrant* means the cops can
    dump out your brother's drawers,
    where the clothes still smell like him,
    scatter the mail from thirty-nine colleges
    you stacked on his desk,
    grab the mattress so hard it rips
    in exactly the spot he'd let you sleep
    when you were lonely and sad
    after your dad died.

I don't think they would need the warrant
if they'd done a better job with the "search" part.
Because Jake has been gone for twenty-seven days,
and Mom says they haven't even been looking,
not really.

She never shouts, but she shouts at them tonight.
"Don't you think I've searched this room
for any clue about
where he went?
What are you even looking for?"

"Drugs," says the short one,
and the tall one looks at him with an angry face,
like maybe
he wasn't supposed to tell us.

"Drugs," my mom repeats.
"Are you trying to *find* my son
or convict him of something?"

"We'll need you to wait in another room, please,"
says the short one, and my mom says,
"Yes, I'll do that.
I'll be in another room
calling my lawyer."

She shakes her head at me
when they're not watching
so I won't tell them
that we don't have a lawyer,
because lawyers cost money
and we don't have money, either.

I hold so still,
am so silent,
that they let me stay.
Jake would want somebody
keeping an eye on his stuff.

But when they're done searching,
the short one turns his laser eyes on me.
"When my partner said 'drugs,'
you didn't look surprised."

"Sometimes people's facial expressions
don't match social norms,"
I say,
which I know is true
because the school counselor said so,
but is also not
the whole truth.

"Okay," he says.
"Were you surprised?"

I try to blend into the wall again.
It doesn't work.

"You can tell us," says the tall one.
"We really are trying to find him,
and it might help."

I look at the clothes folded wrong,
the books stacked wrong,
the rip across the mattress.

If they really wanted to help us,
    I could tell them how to
    fold the clothes and
    stack the books
    the way Jake likes them.

If I really wanted to help them,
    I could tell them there won't be anything
    hiding in the mattress,
    because he always kept the pills
    in the little metal tin
    that says
    FIRST AID
    in his nightstand drawer,
    and that tin
    disappeared
    with Jake.

If we both helped each other,
could we help Jake?

Maybe I could have kept all this from happening
if I hadn't kept my secret.

"You have a story to tell us,"
says the tall one.
"I promise, we're only trying to find him.
And help him, if he has a problem."

"Will I be in trouble?" I ask.
"If I should have told somebody before
but I was
too afraid?"

"No, honey," she says,
and even though
I don't like being called food words,
I like her better.

"Can I write it down?"
I ask.

"Of course,"
she says.

So I get a pencil
and a piece of paper
and sit at Jake's desk.

Mom comes in and tells me
I don't have to tell them anything,
but it's too late.
I've already stepped off the edge.

The story falls from me.

Anytime, Anywhere

September, Senior Year

Jake stands on the roof, watching lights blink on across town. It hadn't even seemed dark to him, but that's how night comes on. You don't realize how dark it's gotten until there's light again in contrast.

Today was their third day laying this roof. Hours of black underlayment and heavy shingles that would have been unbearable in the summer just felt like a solid workout now that the air had turned cooler. Plus, it's impossible to look at the straight rows of shingles and not feel a sense of pride. He did that. His work would keep a family safe and dry for years to come.

Jake has come to like these quiet moments when the rest of the guys have gone. He offers to stay and clean up almost every day now. The extra work is worth the moment when he can sit down with a cold Gatorade and look out over the rooftops and unwind. Especially at this house—a two-story on a hillside where you can see all of Ashland, from the community college to the elementary school, from the Dollar Depot to the car dealership. Especially tonight, his last night on the job, since he's got to get ready for basketball season.

Then a new set of lights comes on, brighter even than the dealership's. Any other year and Jake would be down there on the football field. He's never been all that great at football—good enough to make the team but not good enough to make any kind of a difference on the field. After struggling through summer conditioning, though, he talked with the football coach and told him he couldn't play anymore. He needed to focus on basketball this year, because that's where his scholarship was coming from. Needed to avoid another injury, especially after he'd already messed up his knee playing summer ball.

The football coach tried to talk him out of it. "I hate to see you miss your senior season because of a hypothetical. And you know, Jake," he said, "an injury could happen anytime, anywhere."

But when Jake insisted his mind was made up, they let him go without a fight, and that stung a little. He was helpful on the field, but not essential. Not really enough.

Jake tried to tell himself it was because even the football coach knew this was the basketball team's year, that everything was on the line.

Now, watching the headlights streaming into the high school parking lot, Jake knows his reasoning was stupid. He hasn't spent any extra time in the gym these last few weeks; he just kept the roofing job. And even though the money has been nice, he wishes he were down there with his friends tonight.

But it's too late to turn back now. On a lot of things, really.

Jake heads to the boss's trailer and pulls a Glacier Cherry out of the cooler. He's not sure whether he always picks it because he likes it or because Daphne does. Either way, he's looking forward to drinking it.

Back up on the roof, he checks his phone, thinks about texting Kolt and Seth to tell them good luck. Or Luke, to see if he wants to go to the game. Or maybe Daphne, to see if she wants to join him here.

But there's a distance between them now. He wishes they could go back to the way things were, to the way they fit together at the beginning of the summer. Those weeks after his injury were some of the best times they'd spent together.

Now she's writing college essays and elbow-deep in AP classes and he's . . . spreading tar and laying shingles, barely keeping up in his classes. He's still hoping for college, and the verbal agreement with Arizona State makes it seem possible, because the only way he can afford it is with that scholarship.

But the football coach's words echo inside him. *An injury could happen anytime, anywhere.* What happens to scholarship players if they get injured? No way colleges would spend all that money for a damaged product, right? Do you have to pay the scholarship money back? Do they kick you out right when it happens?

Jake paces the roof. He has to relax. He forces himself to sit, breaks the seal on the Gatorade, and leans back on his elbows. But damn, that doesn't feel right. His left elbow screams when he puts any weight on it at all, probably from lifting shingles all day.

No worries. Jake has planned for this. He rolls onto his side and reaches into his pocket for one little round circle of relief, better than any coin or currency.

But it isn't there.

He hasn't even put his hand in that pocket all day. How could it have fallen out? He stands up and reaches deeper, his fingers hoping for anything but soft, worn fabric. He turns the pocket inside out.

No.

No.

No.

The pill is small, but it would stand out on this black roof, wouldn't it? Jake crawls over the whole thing, darting around like an animal. He scrambles to the edge and looks at the dirt below. Could it have fallen there?

The ground is a muddy mess of boot prints and tire tracks. But maybe he can find it and clean it off. Hell, he'll take it dirty. All he needs is enough white to see it. He jumps to his feet, and the ground seems to sway beneath him.

The desperation leads his mind to even more desperate questions:

Even if he does find this pill, what then?

Where will the next one come from?

How many does he have at home?

How many refills will the doctors give him before they want more testing or at least some answers?

It's one more reason Jake should have played football: four months when he was expected to hurt, when there wouldn't be so many questions.

He needs a plan. A way to get more. Because with or without football or basketball or roofing or school or any of it, he knows there is hurt ahead, because he can feel it and see it stretched behind him for all his life: the hurt that comes from never being enough.

Something inside whispers, *Your mom can't afford this anymore.* But they've met their deductible, and really, he doesn't have to quit roofing to focus on basketball after all. They tell you sports shape character, but won't this job build muscle and character and his ability to work with a team in ways that shooting around in the gym or reps in the weight room never could?

He sends a text to his boss: **Hey Tim. Never mind about today being my last day. I can stay until November.**

But none of this answers the real question: Where will the painkillers come from? How can he fix this problem of the empty pocket—and his empty wallet—and thereby fix all his other problems?

And then there they are. Those words again.

An injury could happen anytime, anywhere.

The thought is so surprising and so perfect it makes him laugh: a short, clipped sound with no happiness in it at all. He steps to the edge of the roof as a plan begins to form in his mind.

Careful with the arms and hands. You can rehabilitate an injury in time, but you can't rebuild a shot.

It was your left knee that was injured last time, so better to protect that one.

Even from here, he can hear the roar from the football stadium as the Warriors score without him.

He flexes and stretches the muscles in his back that he's counting on to soften his landing. He realizes how lucky it is that he knows his body so well, knows exactly what it's capable of. Knows how to hurt himself just enough that he can get what he needs to heal.

But what if he can't drive to the hospital afterward? Better to have a backup plan than to lie here for who knows how long. Kolt brought girls to this hillside—probably this very cul-de-sac—for postgame make-out sessions last year. "Cul-de-sex," he called it, even though Jake knows for a fact Kolt's never gone all the way.

No, Jake doesn't want Kolt or his girl-of-the-week or anybody else to find him. But he still needs a backup, so he texts his boss again.

Finishing up now. Leaving your slate cutter at the site in case you need it this weekend.

Tim is a good guy, but he's obsessed with his new slate cutter. He'll be here in ten minutes, and if Jake's not already gone, it'll be for good reason.

He leans over and gauges the distance to the ground below. Maybe fifteen feet. A hoop and a half. Not so far, really. But far enough.

It's startling how quickly the plan formed and the details fell into place. Almost as though it were meant to be, as if this were the only way forward.

Because honestly, if there were another way, Jake would take it. But the emptiness in his pocket and the hurt in his heart are too much. He'll do what must be done.

Then three things happen at exactly the same time:

Jake closes his eyes and steps off the roof.

Luke steps out from behind the construction dumpster.

From the stadium below, the crowd roars.

Freefall

Luke

After

Here's what I write for the police:

You maybe know about the accident.

The night of the first home football game
I rode my bike up to where Jake was working.
Thought I would surprise him with some
    Laffy Taffy,
since it seemed like he'd run out of Jake jokes.
See if I could jump out and scare him
and then do my porg eyes
and my porg squawk
that always make him laugh.

I hid behind the construction dumpster
that looked like a drone barge,

that smelled like sawdust and cigarette butts,
and waited
waited
waited.

The plan was this:
    I hide until
    Jake gets in his truck, and then
    I jump out and scare the crap out of him.
    We both laugh like Jabba's little monkey lizard
            (that's what Jake calls him).
    We load my bike into the truck.
    We go to the football game together.
And also this:
    Jake sees me.
    Jake laughs.
    We're together.
    Jake sees me.

Instead, he stayed up there on the roof
f o r e v e r
and right when I was about to give up:
He closed his eyes.
He stepped to the edge.
He stepped off the edge.

I ran to him,
saw the bones of his leg

bent all the wrong ways
like the rabbit we hit with his truck last Halloween.

    At first, Jake was mad
    when I made him stop the truck,
    because he was already late to pick up Daphne,
    but I could hear the sorry in his voice
    when he said to the rabbit,
    "I didn't see you there,"
    and to me,
    "It's too late for her."
    I saw his eyes, sad and shining, when
    we drove the truck
    thump thump
    over her small body
    so she wouldn't have to hurt anymore.

And I thought about that rabbit
at the construction site
as I knelt by my brother's body,
both of us breathing hard,
and whether he was speaking the words
or I was just remembering them,
I heard his voice again.
    "It's too late"
and
    "I didn't see you there."

But then
   "I thought I'd land it better."

I was crying, screaming
over Jake,
my heart all *thump thump,*
which made me cry harder,
and I knew it wasn't helping.
I KNEW,
but it was all I could do.

Then there was a man
with the kind of face that could be
Jake's age
or twenty years older,
and he was
   making sure Jake could breathe,
   calling 911,
   telling him help was on the way.
All the things I should have been doing
when all I could do was cry.

When the ambulance arrived,
the man touched my arm,
whispered,
"They'll let you go with him
if you can settle down."

And because he looked at me
like he knew I could do it,
I could do it.

I buried my crying
and climbed in next to my brother,
and by the time I looked back,
the man was already gone.

When I came up the hill, I had a plan.
The scare part was meant for Jake,
but it was only supposed to last half a second.

Instead, I was the one who was scared
when I saw his body
falling from the roof,
crumpling, crumbling to the ground,
crying out like no animal I ever heard before.

I think I have been scared about my brother ever
        since.
Because the accident
wasn't an accident
at all.

When I think about those words
   I thought I'd land it better
I see
it wasn't like the rabbit.

He wasn't trying to make the hurting end.
He was trying to make it start again.

The Mess
That Wasn't Mine

After they read it,

everyone is quiet for a minute,

and then the tall one asks,

"Are you sure, Luke?

Are you sure it wasn't an accident?"

"I'm sure," I say.

"And you said

you know why he did it.

Can you tell us?"

She asks this in a way

I think she might already know the answer,

but I tell her my answer
to see if they match.

"Because the tin was empty,"
I say.
"And after, it was full again.
He needed it to be full again."

"Was the tin gone when he disappeared?"
the tall one asks.

I nod.

Then we all look to the corner
where Mom is
listening,
crying.

"I didn't know," she says
so quietly I almost miss it.

"People get really good at hiding these things,"
says the tall one,
and I wonder if maybe
somebody hid something
from her once.

"You think he robbed the pharmacy?" Mom asks.

The short one folds his arms.
"We think it's worth looking into."

Mom nods. "If he did it, he's alive.
Or he was then, anyway.
If he did it, there's still hope."
Then her eyes go bright
and wild.
"Is there security-camera footage?
Can I see it?
Can I see him?"

They shake their heads.
"Cameras were down all week.
Probably because of the remodeling."

The short one gets up to leave,
but the tall one leans toward me.
"Is there anything else you want to tell us?
About that day?
Or before?
Or after?"

"Only that," I say,
already breathing easier,

like the story was something
hard
and small
that had been blocking my throat.

The officers leave,
and Mom takes me to the kitchen
for a glass of milk,
and I think about how
it's easier to tell the hard things
on paper,
not in person.

And then I think about
all that blank paper
that covered this table
the morning Jake went missing.
The mess that really
wasn't mine.
And I wonder,
Is it important?

But the cops are gone,
and my mom has stopped crying,
and anyway
how could blank pages be trying to tell us
anything at all?

The thing
hard and small
in my throat
is back,
so maybe it wasn't the secret
after all.

But
I have learned to breathe
and swallow
and live
with it inside me.

Metal on Metal

Part of me has wanted
to stay home from school
every day since Jake disappeared
and especially
after they searched
and I told my story.

But Mom won't let me.
Not until I'm
      hot as Venus,
        cold as Neptune,
          aching everywhere,
            coughing up chunks,
              too sick to enjoy a sick day, even a little.

Then she lets me stay home and promises to check
    on me at lunch.

I try watching TV, but
all that light plus
all that sound
makes my head hurt.

So I'm lying there,
lights off,
blankets on
(current temperature: Venus),
wondering again
if I should have told the cops
anything after all,
when I hear it:
        metal on metal,
        key in lock,
        soft footsteps crossing the kitchen.
I close my eyes and slow my breathing,
pretend to be asleep so Mom won't bug me.

But the footsteps pass my door,
keep going down the hall,
and then they stop,
and another door opens.
A creaky one
that we never open anymore.

Jake's room.

And there's only one person in the world
besides me and my mom
who would know where the spare key is,
who would walk straight to that bedroom
where Jake belongs.

I'm not sure if it's a dream
or the fever
or something,
so I tell myself to
wake up,
look for the droid or the Wookiee
that means
this isn't real.

But it's still just me,
sick and sweating under all these covers,
which means
the other footsteps, breaths, heartbeats
belong to him.

I slide the covers back and tiptoe to the door,
not wanting to scare him,
just in case.
Turn the knob so slowly there isn't even a click
and sneak down the hall to Jake's doorway.

And there he is,
digging through a desk drawer.
He dyed his hair black,
lost some weight,
has different clothes
that look
frayed and worn
like the rest of him.

But it's Jake.

It has to be.
It has to be.

"Jake," I whisper, and he snaps up, spins to face me.

We stare at each other, me and this man who is
not
NOT
NOT Jake.

At first I want to scream,
            run,
                      call the police,
and then I notice what's in his hands:
Jake's Wildcats sweatshirt.

The one I gave him last Christmas
that has the ketchup stain
right in the middle.

The one that's not worth anything
to anybody but us.

And then I see a list in his other hand,
and I know who wrote that list,
because only Jake makes the lines so dark and thick.

I think of how this person
passed by the TV downstairs,
and the laptop and the iPad,
and I know that he's not stealing from us.

He's stealing for Jake.

And then I recognize him.
I even remember his name.
"Hey," I say, "you're—"

But he cuts me off.
"Not anymore. Are you going to call
    the police?"

I think of the tall police officer's face,
hear her words.
Let me know if you hear anything.
Anything at all.

BUT

she is not here,
and he is, and
I'm sure he is the one
who helped me once
the time I was most afraid,
when nobody else was there.

What if he's trying to do what is right,
and the cops are too?

What if we all are?

"Would it help Jake if I called the police?"

He shakes his head. "I promise, it wouldn't."

I am afraid,
but the same amount of afraid
as when the police were here.
The same amount of trust too.

So

finally

"Okay," I say.
"I will not tell the police
if you tell me something:
Is he okay?"

The man stops.
Thinks.
"He will be."

And even though he broke into our house
to take Jake's things,
I know he is telling the truth.
I can tell he is trying to help.

I remember a speech Coach B gave
when they dedicated the gym to him.
If you want somebody to do what's right,
let them see you believing that they can.
I remember Bishop Gregersen telling us a story
of an escaped prisoner
and a priest
and candlesticks.

And then I know what I need to do.

The man is already at the door,
reminding me I never saw him,
but
I say,
"WAIT."

He turns,
eyes narrowed like a cat,
but he waits while I run to my room
and back again
with something in each hand.

I look him straight in the face
so he'll know this isn't some kid game,
but also
so he'll see I believe he can do what's right,
and I hold out
The Book of Luke and Jake
with that same dark, thick handwriting
and
my duct-tape wallet
with all my money
($239)
still inside.

"You forgot these," I say.
"The most important part."

He looks at me real close,
then slides the notebook into the black garbage bag
with the rest of Jake's stuff
and the wallet
into his own pocket.

I'm glad he doesn't ask me if I'm sure,
because it's hard for me to be sure
of anything
anymore.

I keep my promise to the man.
I will not tell the police.
But there's someone else I have to tell
because brothers deserve to know.

The Divide

Sabrina

After

It's my third trip to the grocery store since he disappeared. Everything is split neatly now into "before" and "after," like a great chasm in the earth, a divide we can never cross but only gape at.

It was Luke who spurred me to come to Price Saver today, not just because the kitchen is bare and he's finally feeling well enough to eat again. We're also here because of the square on the calendar I should have noticed weeks ago.

"I want pad thai and chocolate cake for my birthday," he told me. "And we need other food. I made a list. Your wallet is in your bathroom. Your outfit is fine, and your hair is fine." I'm about to tell him I'm not sure where my shoes or my keys are when he hands me both.

There's no excuse, then. So we go to the store, and I pray we won't see anyone we know. It will be hard enough to smile at all the well-meaning people who somehow know us.

Not *somehow*. We all know exactly how.

We nearly make it through without a single sad smile or forced conversation. But as we wind through the produce, Mrs. Braithwaite rounds the corner, pushing a cart of fresh vegetables and nutritional supplements.

I can't talk about Jake right now. I just can't. So I search my mind—and my shopping cart—for any other topic.

My answer comes in the cake-mix box, lying right on top like my own Betty Crocker cue card.

"I'm so sorry," I tell her. "I still have your platter. The cake was delicious, and I washed it and was ready to return it the very next day, but . . ."

She brushes the words away. "Keep it as long as you like. I'm not worried about the platter, honey. I'm worried about you."

My mouth goes dry even as my eyes well up. I try to bring the conversation back to safe territory, to subjects that won't make me break down in Price Saver.

"Why coconut cake?"

She smiles and lays a soft hand on my sleeve. "Because he told me it was your favorite, but that you always make chocolate instead for your kids."

The tears come, swift and sudden, as I stare down at the chocolate cake mix and frosting in my cart. "Jake told you that?"

She nods. "That boy loves his mother," she says, and I'm grateful for the present tense. She thinks a moment. "I've changed my mind. Bring that platter back, and I'll make you another. How does that sound?"

"I'd like that," I say, desperate for this small thing that will connect me to my son.

She gives me a smile and ambles away. Soon Luke comes back to the cart with limes and red peppers, which I asked for, and caramel apple dip, which I definitely did not.

"I saw Daphne," he says. "I invited her to my party."

I stop, stunned. Luke has grown so much quieter since Jake disappeared. Now he's invited someone to our house tonight? To what I'm afraid will feel nothing like a party, in spite of our best efforts?

But one look at his face and I can't say no. His connection with Daphne was always particularly meaningful, and I can tell he's missed her.

"Okay," I say, gripping the cart handle as I try to adjust to this curveball. "What kind of party is this? Are you inviting your friends?"

He shakes his head. "Everything is weird with my friends."

I should have known, should have noticed. But I was

too caught up in my own grief. I try to slip into a playful tone. "Well, if you'd rather invite Jake's friends, do you think we should invite Kolt and Seth too?"

Luke thinks this over. "Kolt, but not Seth. Seth is Daphne's boyfriend now. And he underperformed in the state tournament." As he talks, his thumbs dart across the screen of his phone. He looks up a second later.

"Kolt's coming. We need more food."

"You have his number?" I ask. "Have you always had his number, or just since the text?"

There's no need to tell him which text.

"I already had it," Luke says. "I've been texting Kolt ever since I got my phone." I marvel at the way Jake is still helping his brother connect to the world, even in his absence. He's always been so good at that: drawing Luke in with sports statistics, drawing him out with pickup games, passing that notebook back and forth.

And now Luke is one of the people Jake trusted with his four-word text, and I am not. As good as my son is in connecting others, the omission cuts me fresh every time I think of it. *It's not your fault.* He must have known that the person he didn't send that text to would get as clear a message as the ones he did.

It's my fault.

Except that sometimes I wonder if I can see my son more clearly in his absence. Jake is not cruel. Is there another meaning? Something to decipher not only in the words themselves but in the people he sent them to? Luke, Daphne, Kolt, and the fourth number. No doubt the police know who it is, so why don't I ever remember to ask?

I send Luke off to get a little more of everything. It helps and hurts, knowing exactly how much more we'll need for Kolt because it's exactly the amount we would have needed for Jake. And like a hundred other things today alone, this sets off a chain reaction that finds its way to the same set of questions, like water running a constant course until it's carved a canyon.

Is he safe?

Is he eating?

Is he sleeping?

Is he scared?

Is he hurt?

Is he ever coming home?

Across the crates of colorful produce, Daphne comes into view, and I fix a smile on my face, hoping it looks genuine enough.

But she's not smiling. She doesn't even pretend, doesn't try. She just comes and wraps her arms around my waist and lays her head against my shoulder and cries. This motherless girl, so small but so strong. I smooth the hair from her face and hold her close, and we stand there, weeping softly, surrounded by what should nourish us—but emptied, gutted all the same.

Until, once again, Jake bridges the divide by giving me the right words.

"It's not your fault," I say, dropping a kiss on top of her head like I did with my own boys until they grew up and laughed and blushed and pushed me away.

She only holds me closer, and my mind reels in reverse, all the way back to when Jake was a toddler. I had to follow him around all the time then, just to keep him from hurting himself.

What would I have seen if I'd followed him the night he disappeared?

Could I have kept him safe?

Could any of us?

The Moment
That Defines You

Six Hours Before the Game

The knock on the door isn't a surprise. Coach B has been expecting it. Hoping for it, even. He's been dizzy today, which isn't unusual, so he's had plenty of time to think of what to say while lying in his bedroom, the curtains tightly drawn to guard against the spinning world outside.

He'll admit it's selfish—wanting to feel he played some part if Ashland takes home the trophy tonight. But when he sees the figure before him on the front steps, he wonders how many others have looked at Jake Foster and hoped to take a little of his light and make it their own. How many people see him as the boy he still is: unsure, anxious, too much riding on him? So Coach B will do what he intended all along—sit and listen and give only the advice the boy's actually asking for. And he will remind himself that every bit of it's for Jake.

"Come in," he says. "It's cold out there." And then, with surprise, "It's snowing. And you've shoveled. Oh, my boy, I wish you'd saved your energy for the game tonight."

Already he is saying the wrong things. Jake's face falls; he starts back down the steps.

"What do I know?" Coach B says, opening the door wider. "It's probably the perfect way to warm up. And you've got plenty of time to recover."

The tournament is being played in the university arena three towns over, a couple of hours' drive away. Still, the neutral site is closer to Ashland than to their opponents, so most of the crowd will wear the same red and white as Jake and his team. The boys have been able to sleep in their own beds and eat at their own tables throughout the tournament. They're all hoping it will feel like a home game; the Warriors are undefeated at home this season.

But all that is hours away. Now Jake comes in and sits at Coach B's table, eating the chicken and rice Mrs. B started in the slow cooker this morning for just such an occasion.

"She'll be so glad you came by," Coach B tells Jake. "In fact, I hope you'll see her before you leave. She just ran to the pharmacy for me."

"I hope so too," Jake says, and there's still a bit of

that sixth grader in him, so hungry to be seen. This year has been rough on him, but things are getting back on track.

Still, Coach B notices the way the boy winces as he shifts in the chair. He shouldn't have shoveled the snow.

They talk strategy for a while. How the Warriors aren't as big as their opponents, but they're quicker. Smarter. How they can come out with the win if they control the pace of the game. It's nearly time for Jake to leave for the school and get on the bus when Mrs. B comes through the door.

"Well, there he is," she says, like she's been looking for Jake all morning. "Can I fix you some cocoa?" She frowns. "And which one of you shoveled the walk? Somebody at this table is in trouble for wearing himself out on game day or disobeying doctor's orders." She looks back and forth between them as she takes a bag of cinnamon bears—Jake's favorite—and sets them in front of him. "Good luck tonight. And you don't have to share those. Not with the team, and certainly not with anyone watching their sugar intake." She gives Coach B a stern look and leaves them to talk, but they hear her voice once more from down the hall. "Wallace, I'm putting your pills in the bathroom. Don't come to me asking where they are, and don't forget to take them this time."

They talk a little longer. Coach B tries to get back into

the strategy for finding the gaps in the opponent's defense, but the focus has shifted. The boy is nervous. He's spinning the package of cinnamon bears on the table, a quarter turn at a time.

"I should probably go," Jake says at last. "Mind if I use your bathroom first?"

"Of course, of course," Coach B says, waving him away. "I'll make you a sandwich while you're in there so I don't get in trouble later for not feeding you enough."

But he can't help but look back and worry at the hitch in the boy's step as he walks away.

Quietly as he can, Jake picks up the orange bottle. Pushes the lid and twists it open.

Sixty pills, perfect and round, but pale green instead of white like his.

Jake checks the bottle. Same stuff, different strength.

Eighty milligrams.

Holy shit.

Even after his accident, the most they'd give him was twenty. Not that you can't make eighty out of four twenties. Even Jake can do that math.

If it weren't for all that white outside, he'd be fine. But shoveling really did tweak something in his knee. He pictures the scars from last summer's surgery. Nothing will ever be the same. He'll never be as strong as he should be, never be whole again.

And he definitely can't play his best ball if he's distracted by his knee. One pill will take the pain away, but two would help him relax. Two pills and he'd really see the court clearly.

He shakes two pills into his palm and holds them there. Two out of sixty. Hardly any at all. And didn't Coach B say he'd help any way he could? Isn't two pills a pretty reasonable price to pay for six years of lawn mowing, snow shoveling, dirt hauling—just generally being Coach's manual laborer?

Jake is sweating now. The pills are beginning to stick to his palm.

He knows it's wrong, knows *he's* wrong. Coach B needs these pills for his own pain—decades of pain left as a legacy of war and not some stupid game. Jake knows too that Coach B has given him a thousand times more than he's ever received in return. Not just in sandwiches and cinnamon bears but in basketball advice and encouragement and a clear picture of the kind of person Jake hopes to be.

He tries to imagine himself as an old man, somebody who means something in the world. Somebody people have pointed to for decades as the one who made a difference in their lives. He imagines spending all those years with somebody by your side who still looks at you like Mrs. B looks at Coach. And when he imagines it, the figure beside him, gray-haired and weary, definitely has echoes of Daphne.

That's the life he wants. Even if they don't grow old together, maybe he could still fix things with Daphne if he goes back to being the guy she fell in love with. The person he was before . . .

The pills make a small sound as he drops them back in the bottle and secures the lid. He closes his eyes and turns on the water, splashing it on his face, rubbing it along the back of his neck.

There's a gentle knock at the door. "Your sandwich is ready, son."

Son.

And because Coach B is the closest thing Jake's had to a father for a long time, Jake chokes on the words.

"Thank you."

He'll take the sandwich and go. He'll see the floor and control the pace and bring home the title and make Coach B as proud as any father ever, anywhere. And it will all start with this moment—the one that defines him, the one when he is strong enough to say, once and for all, *no*.

The small orange bottle calls to him as he washes his hands.

No.

As he dries them on a hand towel with the Warriors logo on it, embroidered by Mrs. B.

No.

But when he reaches for the doorknob, the bottle, perched so dangerously on the edge of the counter, falls to the floor.

And when he bends to pick it up, a shock of pain stabs into his knee.

And then, somehow, the whole bottle is in his pocket as he opens the door, takes the sandwich, turns to go.

Coach B stops him, a firm hand on Jake's arm. "You okay?"

"I'm fine," Jake says, his fingers curled around the bottle so Coach won't recognize the shape in his pocket.

Coach B nods once, winces at the pain as he lowers himself back into the chair. "I'll be there, Jake. At the game, and after. I'll always be there if you need me."

Jake nods back. Closes his fingers tighter around the bottle. Hates himself.

And then he is gone.

If

Seth

Two Hours Before the Game

I'm almost through the arena doors when I realize I left Daphne's good-luck Gatorade bottle on the bus. The tournament hasn't been going well for me—a dozen points and barely more rebounds across three games—so I'm not actually sure how much luck it's given me. But she'll notice if I don't have it on the bench, and she means more to me than the outcome of any game. I turn and trudge back to the bus.

But as I stand at the door, out of sight, I hear Coach's voice from inside.

"How are those knees? I saw you limping a little when you got out of your truck."

"Nah, they're good," Jake says. "I'm ready to play."

"You still got prescriptions for those things?"

"No. Not for a long time."

There's a pause. A shuffle of equipment. "You sure about that? I thought I saw you swallow something before you got out of your truck."

"Just some aspirin."

"Would you be willing to open your bag for me?"

I'm sure they'll hear my heart beating in the silence that stretches between them.

Jake clears his throat. "I'd rather not, Coach."

This is none of my business. I sneak along the side of the bus, then head straight to the locker room. Maybe I can come back for the Gatorade bottle later. I don't say a thing as I dress for the game, but everybody's pretty quiet. Focused. Or freaking out.

Jake dresses in silence too, then walks out without a word. I can't stop myself from staring at the bag he left behind. Were there pills in there? Did Coach take them away?

It's none of your business, I remind myself. It's a little early, but I head to the training room to get my ankle taped so I won't be tempted to look.

But it really is too early; none of the athletic trainers are here yet. A voice drifts from behind the divider, desperate and pleading.

"I've messed everything up."

I've known Jake nearly all my life, and I've never heard

him sound like this, talk like this. I'm not sure whether he's on the phone or there's somebody back there with him. "Not just with you," he says, "but with everybody. I've tried so hard to fix it, but I can't. It's not like some surgery, where you take out the tumor. It's in me everywhere. It *is* me." He's sobbing now, gasping. "I'm not even sure I can go out there."

But before I can even wonder what he means, there's another voice behind the divider.

"You can. I know you can. I believe in you, Jake. I always have."

Daphne.

I hear the truth in her words, and I can't blame her. I believe in Jake too. The only person I've ever believed in more than Jake is Daphne herself: the way she walks through the world with grace and grit, the way she beats me to the answers in calculus and somehow still makes me feel good about myself. The fact that there's nobody I'd rather have talking my friend down from this ledge before the biggest game of our lives.

I've never said the words out loud, but I know in this moment that I love her.

And in the very next moment, I realize what it might mean that they're here together, and I wonder: *Do I even matter to her at all?* The question cuts me across the chest, and I can't move, can't breathe.

"You should go," Jake says, emotion still thick in his voice. "You should get out while you can."

"I can't," she says, softer now. "I can't walk away, Jake. I'm afraid I'm going to love you for the rest of my life."

It's quiet then, and I know I do not want to see what's happening on the other side of the divider. But then I'm moving and breathing again, all at once, and I can't stop myself from crossing the room silently, slowly, until I see their mouths pressed together and her fingers snaking through his hair. The slash of pain widens, leaving me sliced open, raw, gutted as I stumble back through the door.

Neither of them notices me at all.

The locker room is nearly deserted. Only one figure, hunched over Jake Foster's bag.

"Find anything?" I ask, my voice dry and flat.

Coach startles, straightens. "Nope, he's clean." There's a hint of disappointment in his voice.

But no. What kind of coach would want to catch his star player violating the rules right before the championship?

And what kind of captain would want that? *Don't be stupid,* I tell myself. *If Jake screws up right now, that hurts you too.*

Too late.

"We get a little time on the floor," Coach says. "Head on out there. You seen Jake?"

"Try the training room," I say. Then I jog out to the arena, knowing Jake won't be far behind.

The team and assistant coaches are scattered around center court, stretching and chatting and probably just waiting for the rest of us. I sit down next to Kolt, determined to act like a captain even if I want to punch the other captain in the face.

And in spite of how pissed and broken I am, I see the scene in front of me for exactly what it is: a bunch of teenagers who have sacrificed family and school and sleep, who have put their bodies through hell—all to get better at dropping a ball through a metal hoop ten feet in the air. Which would be ridiculous if we weren't all doing it for each other.

"You know what I see on this court today?" I ask Kolt, loud enough that the rest of the chatter stops.

"What?" Kolt asks, playing along.

"A team that's worked their asses off all season."

The guys murmur their agreement.

"You know what I see?" asks Kolt. "A team that's ready to dissect the Panthers like frogs in bio lab."

Louder cheers.

"You know what I see?" Jake asks, coming up from behind us. "A team I'm proud to play on." The guys whoop their agreement, and I try to hold in my hate as he keeps going, his back to me as he claims this moment that Kolt and I built. "A team that knows the three keys to winning a game: head, hands, heart."

They shout it back at him. "Head, hands, heart!"

"You know what I see here, gentlemen?" Jake shouts, and the guys are all on their feet, ready to follow him anywhere. "A team that's going to take state tonight!"

Coach takes his turn trying to pump us up as we stretch, but I don't hear a word of it. I see Jake in my peripheral vision, trying to get my attention. I ignore him until I can't anymore, until the speech is over and everybody starts for the locker room and he's pulling me by the elbow back to center court.

"Seth, I have to tell you something."

Six years I've been listening to Jake call the plays as we come down the court, and I've run exactly what he's called, every single time. I'll do it again tonight—for the team, for Coach, for the dream they keep telling me we all share—but I won't do it right now. It's all I can do not to deck him.

"Let's focus on the game, okay?" I try to turn away, but he grabs my elbow again and spins me back.

"Please. Let me explain."

When he puts his hand on me a third time in the hallway—right next to that damn training room—I lose it.

"Explain what? I see you so clearly, Foster. I know every single thing about you that I need to know. You're a crap friend. You're a crap boyfriend. I mean, if Daphne picks you, I'm going to step aside. But know this: she deserves better than me, but she deserves a hell of a lot better than you." I steady my fists at my side, even though he looks like I've already decked him.

Good. He's scared. He's sweating, shaking. And then I see all the shaking and sweating for what it is.

"Oh, and you're a crap captain. Because we're about to play the most important game of our lives and you're hopped up on painkillers. Aren't you? Are you high right now?"

Jake looks away, and there's my answer.

I shove him, hard as I can, right into the wall.

"I hate you, Foster. I freaking hate you."

Good thing he doesn't try to stop me this time, because I would lay him out. I walk outside to the parking lot and lean against the cold, rough brick. The snow soaks into my expensive new basketball shoes, but I don't give one single shit what Coach will say about it.

I swear, I almost walk away right then, Jordans and all.

But a junky old Jeep pulls up, rattling and sputtering like it must have done all the way from Ashland. The door swings open, and Coach B eases himself out, then circles around to open the door for Mrs. B. Arm in arm, they move through the slush with tiny steps, pausing here and there to share some little bit of information that makes them both smile.

Then Coach B slips and Mrs. B struggles, pulling me out of my own mind and back to the moment. I hurry over and offer an arm to each of them.

"Why, thank you, Seth," Coach B says.

I know Coach B follows the team, that he and Mrs. B are not the kind of fans who just show up for the championship. Still, it surprises me that he knows me. There is something warm in the way he speaks my name.

Inside the gym, Mrs. B settles herself into the bleachers. "You'd better get in there with your team," she says to me. "And find yourself some dry socks. It'll be hard to get many rebounds with your feet soggy, now, won't it?"

I nod. "Yes, ma'am."

She laughs and pulls needles and yarn from her bag. "Wallace, will you buy me some of those Dots from the concession stand before the game starts?"

"Yes, ma'am," he echoes.

I walk with him across the gym, and somehow, instinctively, we both pause before parting ways. "It's quite a game, isn't it?" Coach B asks. When I look over, he's watching the court with pure joy carved across his face.

The Panthers have taken the floor and begun their warm-ups, dribbling down, laying it up, passing the ball to the next player in an endless figure eight. It's hard to judge how we'll match up with them by layups and warm-ups, but all at once, it doesn't matter. In that moment, I see the game through Coach B's eyes and even think of it in his words: the fluid beauty of it all, the effortlessness that comes at the culmination of all those years of effort.

"It's quite a game," I agree. "Like poetry."

Then he starts reciting in his gravelly voice.

> If you can keep your head when all about you
>> Are losing theirs and blaming it on you,
> If you can trust yourself when all men doubt you,
>> But make allowance for their doubting too . . .

He trails off, like he only just realized he was speaking the words aloud. I know the poem—we studied it in AP English a few weeks ago, and Daphne said something about the poet's sexism and imperialism and rewrote the ending with her own feminist twist. But now I remember the ending the way Kipling wrote it, like I need it to face this game.

> If you can fill the unforgiving minute
>> With sixty seconds' worth of distance run,
> Yours is the Earth and everything that's in it,
>> And—which is more—you'll be a Man, my son!

Coach B still faces the court, but his gaze flashes to me as he smiles. "That's right. There's a lot hanging on that one word, isn't there? That 'If.'" He clears his throat. "Almost every lesson you need in life can be learned out there on the hardwood. Grit, determination, teamwork, loyalty, both winning and losing graciously. How to pick yourself up after you fall. But for me, one of the greatest gifts is that, even during the war, the game was the game. Whatever burden you're carrying, you can set it down for a time and just play. And yes, it'll be there waiting for you when you're done, but it might not seem so heavy."

I let the words settle on my wounds as our team streams from the locker room, Jake leading the charge, and then they begin the same fluid layup drill. But now, as my teammates circle past, one by one, I see the faces and know the stories of each player, and it strikes me how much I want to win this. For each of them, maybe even Jake. But also how much we'll have gained, even if we don't win.

"I suppose I've always seen him as Sirius," Coach B says as Jake lays the ball up and in, gently as the last snowflakes falling outside. "The brightest star in the sky."

Something inside me wants to close off, but then he continues. "I've been watching all season, you know. Teams are good when they have a bright star to build on. Even better when they have a comet, like Kolt, who's everywhere at once. And they're champions when they have a Polaris, a true north to follow." He turns and looks me right in the face, lays a hand on my shoulder. "This is a team of champions, regardless of the outcome tonight. And let me add, young man, that it has been a pleasure to watch you play all these years." He gives me a crooked smile. "Now go get some dry socks on and join your teammates. They need their Polaris, and I've got to find myself some Dots."

So I go to the locker room, and I leave my burden there along with my wet socks. Back on the court, I slide into warm-ups as the team welcomes me into the flow of it all, as natural as stepping into a river on a starry night.

Savior: Part 1

Before the Game

Jake stands in the stall and looks at the pile of pills in his hand. Two now and one at halftime will still leave enough to do the job after the game is over, if he swallows them all. It might give away his secret, but the way Seth spat those words at him just now—*You're hopped up on pain-killers. Aren't you?*—he's afraid they all know anyway.

He counts out three, putting the rest of the pills back in the small ziplock and shoving it inside the lining of his bag. His fingers find the few stitches that have come loose on his warm-up jersey, just the right size to slide the oxy inside. The last two still lie in his palm, staring up at him like blank, barren eyes. He wonders how he ever thought they were his savior from anything: pain or sorrow or the monster of Not Enough.

You won, he tells them. *You'll always win.*

It's a new feeling to Jake, but he's seen something like it in opponents' faces often enough he thinks he recognizes it: the moment you know with absolute clarity that you'll never win, and you make peace with it because you're too weary to try anymore.

And he is so, so tired. The sounds of the arena are dulled by walls and distance and the fog forming in his head, but the pull of the game is as strong as ever. He has to go out there. *Do this one more thing,* he tells himself, *and then you can be done.*

Jake opens his mouth and slaps his palm to it, letting the twin circles sit there a moment, bitter spots that will turn sweet inside his belly, inside his blood. Out in the arena, a new song blares over the loudspeakers, deep and thrumming.

It's time. Jake crunches the pills once between his jaws. He closes his eyes and swallows, then stuffs the bag in his locker. The bass seems to follow his footfalls as he runs through the tunnel and onto the court.

Maybe it's the pills, or the relief at finally having made the decision, but as the team warms up, Jake's worries fall away like a shed skin. The game becomes as pure and perfect as it was all those years ago, when they'd rush outside for every recess or gather in Kolt's driveway on summer nights until it got too dark to see the hoop.

It's right to spend his last hours here. Whether drive-way or playground or ten-thousand-seat arena, the bas-ketball court has always been the most sacred place in the world to Jake, even though he's been to church nearly every Sunday all his life.

At church, he has learned that he should be perfect, even as his Savior was perfect, and it seemed like a worthy goal. Be perfect, and the aching emptiness inside you will go away. Be perfect, and be loved, unconditionally and forever, by a Father who is perfect too.

But all his life, every time he fell short—barked at his brother, ignored his mother, felt so angry at his father he threw something, broke something—Jake knew he be-came less worthy of God's love. Of anybody's love, really. Because to really be worthy, you're supposed to be perfect.

He sometimes looks up at the picture of Jesus in the church foyer, eyes kind and hands stretched out, and he knows, just knows, that he doesn't deserve that love.

"Ask of God," the scriptures have told him, and Jake wishes he could. It's fine for the others to bow their heads and clasp their hands and pour out their hearts, asking for anything and everything they need. They're not as flawed as he is.

How can he ask for help from the very Being he has disappointed most? The One who asked him to be perfect in the first place?

He's had moments of perfection, he knows. Moments of goodness and clarity. In the beginning, the pills helped those moments last longer. They dulled the teeth of the monster of Not Enough.

But now, even with more pills, it never lasts. "There is no peace, saith the Lord, unto the wicked." And here in this arena, before the starting lineups are even announced in the biggest game of his life, the monster has returned, teeth bared.

Coach B will know he stole the pills.

Coach C will find the others in his bag, if he hasn't already.

They'll know, like his dad knew all along, that Jake isn't worthy or worth it.

There's no such thing as a Father who loves you unconditionally.

It doesn't matter anyway. Jake is ready—head, hands, heart—to lay it all on the court one last time. And then he will walk straight into the monster's mouth.

Any Night but Tonight

Daphne

After the Game

They did it. They won. And Jake had the game of his life. As I pull up to the after-game party, it still feels surreal.

Seth's house pulses with music, the laughter inside louder because the season's over and Seth's dad will turn a blind eye to the fact that it's not always Coke in our plastic cups. I watch eleven cars arrive but quickly lose count of how many people have piled out and gone inside. They make it look so easy: flirt and laugh and walk through the door. It used to be like that for me.

But I don't want crowds or music tonight. And I definitely don't want to see Jake. All I want is to talk to Seth, to tell him what happened in the training room—how Jake was so broken that I wanted to fix it any way I could, how I regretted it before it even really started.

Who would believe it, though? Who would believe that even before my lips met Jake's, I knew I'd always care about him but I didn't love him like that anymore?

It's a lot to ask, even of Seth.

Still, I gather my courage and go to the door. As much as Seth's dad likes to be in the middle of everything his players do (which is probably why he offered to host in the first place), Seth's family lives on the edge of town. Their property backs up to a scraggly forest with a creek running through it. For me, it was love at first sight. Even better than our cabin, not because it's nicer (although it is) but because they get to wake up to it every morning. *How would it be,* I wonder, *to walk a hundred yards out your back door and see only what's natural and wild?*

Seth and I came out to the forest after a snowfall one night, and we sat silently for so long, just watching the flakes fall, that a doe led her fawn right in front of us, the spots on its back barely bigger than the flakes.

I never told Seth that I came here with Jake too, one night when Seth had invited us both to a party. I never told Seth that Jake was the first boy I kissed in these woods. Not because it was something to hide, but because I've tried so hard to leave everything about being with Jake in the past. In this moment, I wish I could erase it all. Wish these woods could only be the place where Seth and I watched the fawn in the snowfall, pure and simple.

It's Coach himself who answers the door, smiling and waving me in. "You don't even have to knock, you know. You're welcome here anytime."

Coach has always liked me. All parents seem to like me. Maybe it's because my dad raised me to be polite and respectful, or maybe my name is in enough news articles for sports and academics that parents sort of pay attention. And okay, it probably doesn't hurt that my dad is the judge.

Whatever it is, I've learned to work the advantage. To like it, even. Bad news is, high schoolers aren't so easy to impress. I'm about to brave the crowd when I hear Coach's voice calling me back. "Hey, Daphne," he says, the scent of beer on his breath. "I meant to tell you, congratulations on your win tonight."

My team won too—but in the consolation bracket. I was coming to the training room to get some ice for my ankle after my own game when the whole mess with Jake happened.

"Thanks," I say. "And you too. Pine Valley got outplayed tonight, but they got outcoached too. You deserve to celebrate."

Coach looks down into the red-and-white plastic cup in his hand. Warrior colors, even tonight. Especially tonight. "Oh, I'm having a great time," he says, but it doesn't sound like he believes it. "Seth's out back." I look past him and out the sliding glass door to see Seth with a plastic cup of his own and an arm slung over Kolt's shoulders.

"Thanks," I say. "And I meant what I said. They couldn't have done this without you."

Seth smiles when I come through the sliding door, but there's something sad in it. I think of his smile as he stood between Jake and Kolt and hoisted the trophy above his head. It's been only a couple of hours since the game. It seems so unfair that our worst moments stain for so long but our best fade so quickly.

"Hey," I say, slipping my hand in his and giving it a squeeze. "Can we go down to the basement? To talk?" I give the last two words extra emphasis for Kolt's sake.

"Maybe not tonight," Seth says, his gaze flickering back toward the house. He doesn't return the squeeze, but he doesn't pull his hand away. "I just . . . Maybe not tonight."

"Okay," I say, steeling myself against the sting.

"*Annnndddd* Daphne gets shut down," says Kolt. "Hey, don't feel bad. It's your night too! Congratulations on winning the loser bracket."

"Thanks," I say. "Congratulations on your two points tonight."

"And twelve rebounds!" he insists, but by then we're both laughing. "Hey, have you seen Jake?"

Seth's hand tightens around mine, and when I look up, I wonder if he knows somehow.

I've got to explain. Got to fix it.

"No," I tell Kolt. "Probably still got kids lined up for autographs or something." I say it as a burn on Kolt, but I feel the way Seth tenses beside me. He's never been jealous of Jake's success on the court, but even Seth must have his limits.

Kolt laughs and goes to look for Jake, and Seth lets me pull him back into the house.

I keep hold of his hand and hope he won't hate me when I've said what I need to say.

"I made a mistake."

He unfolds his arms, starts to walk away. "Come on," he says, not even really looking at me. "It's too loud in here."

If those words had come out of Kolt's mouth, they would sound like a line. But even if nothing had happened in the locker room, even if nothing needed to be fixed between us, Seth wouldn't have stayed long at his own party. Deep down, he's an introvert. He loves that people are at his house, having a great time. He loves that he played a role in the victory that brought them all here. But he'd rather watch it all from a distance.

Seth grabs two quilts from the hall closet, and I follow him out the back door and straight onto a path that leads to the woods. (Of course, Kolt gives us crap on our way out.)

Once we're alone in the cold clarity of the forest, Seth hands me one quilt and wraps the other around himself. We're not wrapping up together, then. He sits, and I sit beside him, unsure how much space he wants between us.

"I made a mistake," I say again.

"Okay," he says.

Even through the blanket, I can see that his knees are bouncing, and it can't be from the cold. I'm not sure there's a right time to say it, so I start again. "Something happened before the game, and I—"

"Could we not?" he asks. He starts to stand up, changes his mind. "I mean, whatever it is, can we talk about it another time? I really want tonight to be about the win."

"Okay," I say, and I swallow it back down with one part relief and nine parts remorse.

After that, we just sit on the rough log bench at the edge of the tree line, watching the golden glow of the party from the cocoon of our separate blankets.

Eventually we talk, and even now it's not as hard as it probably should be. But the topics are safe; we're both guarded. He asks about my game, and we talk about what's next. Track for me, baseball for him, AP prep for both of us. We don't talk about what's beyond that. We've applied to some of the same colleges, but neither of us has decided on our top choices. Even though graduation is months away, it feels like high school is winding down.

Seth watches as a new song begins and everybody dances, the music and laughter muted by the distance and the windowpane. "It's like a metaphor or something. Like we're already looking back on the party, but not ready to step into the forest. You know what I mean?"

I laugh. "That is exactly what I was thinking, but not quite in those AP English–essay terms." I lean my head on his shoulder, hoping he won't pull away.

After a few seconds, I feel his temple against the top of my head. I draw the blanket closer around me. "Thank you for letting me share this metaphorical purgatory bench with you, Seth Cooper."

It's a more perfect moment than I deserve right now.

And yet Jake lingers like a ghost on the edges of this happiness. I can't stop thinking of the way he looked in the training room, the desperation in his eyes. Even during the game—the greatest performance of his breathtaking high school career—there was something off. Something I'd been seeing glimpses of all season. For the first time, I think of the fact that he's not here tonight and feel worry instead of relief. I hate to break the moment, hate that it might hurt him or us, but I look straight up at Seth, and I ask, because I have no choice.

"Will you check on him?"

Seth's face tightens. "Check on who?" Of course he knows who, but it's fair that he's going to make me say it.

"Jake. I promise I'm over him. I know that more than ever. But something's wrong, Seth. Really wrong. And he won't answer my calls or texts."

"You called him," Seth says, pulling away. "You texted him. Tonight?"

I nod. "Before I came over."

He closes his eyes and lets out a breath. "Yeah, I'll check on him. How long do you think this will last?"

"I don't know." I'm not sure if he's asking how long Jake will need us or how long I'll feel like I have to help or whether he and I will stay together long enough to go off into those metaphorical woods side by side someday.

Tonight, I have no answers at all.

Later, as I lie in bed, trying to make sense of the day, I realize the list of people I trust is shorter than ever.

I don't trust Jake like I used to.

I don't trust myself around him.

And no matter how many times I chase the thought away, I wonder for the first time if Seth might be hiding something too.

Taillights

Seth

After the Game

I watch as Daphne's taillights recede in the distance, headed toward home. Why the hell would I promise to check on Jake?

Because you didn't want her to do it herself. Because who knows where that would have led.

I text Kolt, just so I can say I've done something.

Did you talk to Jake?

    I tried but he didn't answer

You think he's OK?

    I think he's the MVP of the state tournament

    So yeah he's OK

Will you go check on him? Daphne said he was acting weird. I'd go but this place is a disaster and I still have to clean up.

U serious?? It's almost midnight and my cars out of gas

My mom whisper-shouts at me from her bedroom doorway. "Is everybody gone?"

"Yeah, the last people just left. Can I talk to Dad for a second?"

Mom gestures at a mound under the covers. "Good luck. I barely got him horizontal before he passed out."

I watch the rise and fall of the comforter as Dad lies there, his face slack and blank. What does she mean by "passed out"? That he was so exhausted from tonight's game—and this season, and the six years of late nights leading up to it—that he fell asleep, hard and fast, the second his head hit the pillow? Or does it have more to do with the empty beer bottles lined up along the windowsill that he snuck in over the course of the party?

I learned discipline from my parents, by their instruction and their example. Mom has put up with so much from both of us for so long, and she never even breaks a sweat. But lately Dad has been so focused and disciplined when it comes to the game and the season that things have started slipping in other areas. He's still as fit as most of the guys on the team, but instead of running three miles every day, it's ten or nothing. (Usually nothing.) Instead of lean protein, it's greasy burgers. And now the line of beer bottles, when he'd always limited himself to two.

When my phone shakes my pocket, I hope it will be Kolt. Normally I'd rather have a text from Daphne, but tonight all I can think of is what I saw in the locker room—and the fact that she's still thinking about Jake.

It's her. And yup, she's still thinking about him.

> **Jake will be fine. Don't check on him—I didn't mean to dump that on you. He and Kolt are probably passed out in front of Demon Slayer or something. I'm going to sleep. You should too. xoxo**

It's impossible not to picture her in her soft shorts and the Stanford T-shirt she sleeps in. She always could fall asleep so quickly, so peacefully, even on bus trips or curled up on a couch during movie nights.

Jake must know that about her too. The thought burns me up. And even though I'm exhausted, I'm too mad—at Daphne, at Jake, at myself—to fall asleep. I lie there listening to Coach's passed-out snores keeping no time whatsoever with the tick of the clock on my wall.

Everything is out of sync, and there's no chance of my brain shutting off until I clear this up.

There's still a light on in my parents' room, so I knock softly. Mom's awake, reading. "I need to check on something real quick," I tell her. "Jake was acting weird tonight, so I'm going to make sure he's okay. I'll be back in half an hour."

Mom rests a hand on my arm. "You are a good kid, Seth. Wake me up when you get back."

I don't pass a single car on the long drive into town, but when I get to Jake's, there's one parked at the curb. A beat-up truck, actually, with Kolt hunched over the wheel in an old basketball hoodie, looking pretty ticked off. He must have borrowed one of his dad's semifunctional trucks since his truck is out of gas. And Jake's truck is in the driveway.

I pull over—across the street and far enough back that they won't notice me—and cut the engine and the lights. If Jake's home and Kolt's on it after all, maybe I don't have to get involved.

Jake comes out of the house then, hood up and hands stuffed in his pockets.

As he walks to the truck, though, there's something off. The way he keeps looking around, maybe, or the little bit of stagger in his step.

Jake shrugs out of his backpack and tosses it in the bed

of the truck, then climbs in the passenger seat. I swear, Kolt gasses it before Jake's door is even closed, and they tear down the street.

Straight toward me. Shit. I pull up my own hood and duck down, but still, I want to get a good look at Jake's face.

Even in that split second, though, I can tell he isn't okay. His face shines too pale in the dim glow of the streetlamp. His eyes seem sunken somehow. If I had to pick one word for it, I might pick *haunted*.

In the very last instant before they pass, those sunken eyes lock with mine, and I shiver deeper into my hoodie and crank the engine to start the heat back up. For half a second, I think about following them, but I talk myself out of it, using the same excuses I've been hiding behind all night.

He'll talk if it's just him and Kolt. He doesn't want you there.

He doesn't deserve your help after what happened in the training room.

And most of all: *Jake Foster is a lot of things to a lot of people, but he is not your problem. You deserve to go home and check out for tonight.*

So that's exactly what I do. I send Kolt a quick text: **Let me know if you need backup.** And Daphne too: **He's with Kolt. He's fine.** Then I drive straight home.

As I'm driving, it's hard not to hope karma kicks him in the ass. Because I still can't guarantee I won't do it myself.

———

When my alarm blares Monday morning, it still takes everything I have to haul my butt out of bed.

I slide into the desk next to Daphne's in calculus. She doesn't straight-up ask me about Jake, but I can tell she's wondering, especially as the day drags by and we still haven't seen him. After the last bell, she comes to my locker, and I can see the question in her eyes.

"I drove by Jake's house Saturday night," I say. "He and Kolt were headed somewhere. They probably decided to take today off. It's pretty rough on those two how they have to go to class every single day during the season."

Daphne doesn't laugh. "Kolt's here today."

That's a surprise. I haven't seen him all day, so I assumed he and Jake were still out together, maybe getting themselves stuck in that truck in the hills somewhere or heading south to find someplace warm enough to camp.

I check my phone. No texts from either of them.

"Kolt's here?" I ask. "Are you sure?"

We walk out to the parking lot, and I can see Kolt's ugly orange Ford, plain as day. He must have gotten gas in the last thirty-six hours.

"We could go over to his house together," I say, realizing I didn't really mean it when the look on her face tells me that's exactly where we're headed.

Except we don't make it that far. As we start down the sidewalk, a police officer walks up to us.

"Daphne Sharp and Seth Cooper?" he says.

"Yes, sir," we say together. It might be funny if I wasn't starting to freak out.

"Nice job at state," he says. "Both of you."

"Thanks," we say, but out of sync this time. We're ready to walk straight past when the officer puts out his hand, stopping us without even making contact.

"I wonder if you'd be willing to talk with me for a minute."

"Is something wrong?" I ask, even though that sick, sinking feeling inside me knows there is.

"Come inside," he says. "I just want to ask you a few questions."

I think I might puke. I was pulled over once and wanted to puke then, but this is a thousand times worse.

Daphne goes first, and I sit and stare at the closed door of the counseling office the whole time, trying to think about anything other than being interviewed by the police. We came here together two weeks ago to talk about summer internships. I've missed some of the deadlines already, I realize. That's got to be first priority when I go home.

But when I see the look on Daphne's face as the door opens, my priorities are shot to hell. "Are you okay?" I ask.

She buries her head in my chest.

"Daphne, what happened?" I ask, wanting to hear it straight from her.

She looks up at me, eyes brimming.

"He's gone."

No Going Back

After

Phoenix comes in and drops a paper bag on the long, low table in the center of the room. The smell makes Jake sick. He notices the translucent spots on the bag where grease has seeped from the food.

"I can't eat that," he says.

"You have to eat that," Phoenix says. "Tonight's the night we plan our next move, so I need you fueled up and ready to think."

Our next move. That's what he said. Jake feels something in him loosen. He's been hearing the unmistakable rip of packing tape and the dull thud of things being dragged around. He's been so afraid that Phoenix was planning to leave without him, and then what? There was no going back, but he had no idea what forward might look like.

Because everything has changed since he's been down here. He still thinks of home, misses his mom and Luke, but he sees now that Phoenix has saved him. That this really was the only way.

"Make a list," Phoenix says, sliding a burger and a pile of fries across the table. "The shorter the better. Once we grab what we need, we can get out of here."

"Am I going back with you to get the stuff?" Jake asks, hopeful in spite of himself.

Phoenix gives a short bark of a laugh. "Hell no, you can't go back. You're barely ready for forward."

Jake picks at his food. "When are you making the grab?"

"Maybe tomorrow. Probably the day after that."

"What day *is* tomorrow?"

Phoenix looks surprised—maybe that Jake doesn't know, or maybe that he cares. "Friday. The fifth. You've been here awhile."

If tomorrow is the fifth, then the next day is Luke's birthday. Jake's not sure exactly what that means to him tonight, but it means *something*.

"Don't go on the sixth," he says.

"Why? You got other plans that day?"

Jake nods. "You know me. Calendar's always full."

Phoenix laughs. This time it sounds like a release.

"Tomorrow it is. We can take off the next day."

"And then you'll give me my phone back." Jake expects Phoenix to ignore it or shut him down like before, but he stops and thinks as he eats fries, two at a time, from the bag.

"Maybe," he says. "If you're ready."

Jake doesn't believe him.

Phoenix finishes his can of off-brand soda, pulls off the tab, and slips it in his pocket. He notices Jake watching this. "Just something stupid I do for good luck. You superstitious, Foster?"

Jake pulls the tab off his own soda and puts it in his pocket. Phoenix laughs again; Jake likes making him laugh. "Maybe. Comes with being an athlete, I think." But is he still an athlete? Even in this broken, bruised body? He lowers his gaze, unsure—and catches a flash of metallic red in a split seam of the cushion of Phoenix's chair.

Jake needs Phoenix to lean forward again, to see if he really saw what he thinks he saw. So he asks another question, trying not to let his words betray the new thought in his mind. "Can I have your ketchup if you're not going to eat it?"

"Holy shit, Foster. When did you become such a diva?" Phoenix throws a pair of half-eaten fries at Jake, who catches them. As he leans forward, reaching for the ketchup, the seam splits further, and Jake can see it clearly.

This is where Phoenix is hiding his phone.

———

When they've finished eating, Jake writes the list of things he needs Phoenix to take for him, noting the location of each and keeping the list as short as he can. He's got to be in and out as quickly as possible. As Jake writes, the knot inside him loosens just a little more. Tomorrow, when Phoenix leaves to make the grab, he'll be able to take the phone back, at least long enough to send a message.

But the next day, when the moment comes, the cushion is empty. Jake swears, realizing Phoenix has taken the phone with him.

In the end, all he gets is a few stolen seconds with it around dinnertime the following day, while Phoenix is in the bathroom. Jake taps the group message at the top of the list and types as quickly as he can. There's no time to check what he's written, but he hopes it's enough. Hopes it's worth something, even if it isn't worth nearly what a kid deserves on his birthday.

He sends the text and shoves the phone back into the seam just as the light spills in from the open door.

Do. Or Do Not.

Kolt

After

This is the second time in two days I've been sure Luke's shitting me.

The first time was yesterday, when he texted to tell me he saw my brother. I might not be in AP psych, but even I know that's called "projecting." "Remember your brother who disappeared? Great news: he's back! Everything's fine!" You can't blame the kid for wanting to believe that so bad he says it to somebody else.

And now he's inviting me over for his birthday party. I haven't been to a twelve-year-old's birthday party since I was—you guessed it—twelve. What do you even do at a party like that, when there's a Jake-size elephant in the room? What do you say?

But when it's time for the party, I go over there. Mostly for Luke's sake, but also because there's something nice about being around people who are as worried as I am. And maybe they're even mad at Jake too, like I am some days, even if that's not totally fair. People who know him and, okay, love him like I do.

Daphne pulls up right after me, and Luke comes out the front door wearing the *Space Jam* T-shirt Jake gave him for his last birthday. I wonder if Daphne's even seen the movie. I wonder what memories the two of them have that I'm missing. If each of us were a circle on one of those Venn diagrams, is there anything but Jake in the section where we all overlap? Anything else in the world that would bring the three of us together?

Mrs. Foster comes out, looking like she partied a little too hard last night, even though I know she doesn't drink and she sure as hell hasn't been partying. She wraps Luke in her arms.

"Thanks for inviting us," Daphne says. "I've missed you guys." She joins in the hug, and then I'm the sucker just standing there by myself. *This is it,* I think. *The point of overlap for all four of us. They literally have their arms around each other. I should get in there.*

But by the time I've talked myself into it, they're pulling apart. "Come in," Mrs. Foster says. "Dinner is almost ready."

Mrs. Foster's pad thai is probably about as authentic as an eBay Da Vinci, but it's pure Jake. I look around and wonder how many times each of us has eaten chicken and red peppers and noodles and peanuts, with little wedges of lime to squeeze on top, here at this table. It would feel exactly right if it weren't so disturbingly wrong.

While we eat, the four of us talk about the schools Daphne has applied to, the way the baseball team is shaping up for this season, the fact that even if Luke believed in astrology (which he doesn't), today's signs are based on the position of the constellations two thousand years ago, so they're extra wrong. You know: normal dinner conversation.

When my plate is pretty much empty, I scrape together the last little pieces of peanut and scoop them up with my fork. "Mrs. Foster, that was amazing. It would be a special kind of hell to be allergic to this stuff." Then I remember Seth's peanut allergy, and when I see a way to tease Daphne, I have to take it. "No making out for you tonight, huh?"

It's the wrong joke. I don't even need Jake here to tell me. Wrong because Daphne used to be with Jake and it's pretty obvious the Fosters still miss her, and because Seth's so allergic something like that could actually kill him, and, most of all, because we're all sitting here pretending to party when we don't even know if Jake's alive.

Daphne's speechless, which isn't Daphne.

"I'm sorry," I say, crushing the peanuts with the tines of my fork.

"It's okay," she says, even though nothing is.

"I made my own cake," Luke says, and we all smile

because it's kind of a perfect bittersweet, not-so-smooth reminder of why we're here.

Luke's cake is covered in chocolate frosting and leans a little, but it's better than I could do. He puts twelve candles in a constellation across the top, and we sing (badly).

Right as we finish, there's a buzz and a chime and the rustle of three people reaching for their phones when they get a text all at once.

Three, but not four.

Mrs. Foster makes the connection first, maybe because she's the one on the outside. Or maybe a mother knows stuff like this. "It's Jake, isn't it?" she whispers. "What does it say?" Her face looks so pale in the flickering light of the candles. "Is he okay?"

It's Luke who reads the text out loud.

> **I'm so sorry I wish I would have done everything differently maybe when this is all over you will find a way to forgive me**

Then we all put our phones down and sit there, sick, while cheap candles weep wax onto Luke's cake.

Maybe it's just the candles, but there's a fire in Mrs. Foster's eyes now as she reaches for Luke's phone. "He's alive, and he's asking for help. That's what this is. I'm calling the police. No, I'm *taking* this to the police. They have to be able to figure something out."

"I can stay with Luke," Daphne says. "If you want."

Mrs. Foster nods. She pulls Luke close and kisses the top of his head. "I can't sit here waiting or wishing. Not anymore. I have to find my son."

She throws Luke's phone into her purse and strides out the door. Part of me wants to follow her, to say *Screw it* to the world like she did. But at least she had somewhere to go. Where would I even start?

I read the text again. What does "when this is all over" mean, anyway? That he's thinking about suicide? That he's about to overdose? That he was so desperate for drugs that he crossed the wrong kind of people and really is locked away somewhere, taken prisoner or brainwashed or something worse? Daphne catches my eye, and I can tell her mind's going to the same dark places.

When her phone rings, we all jump. She relaxes a little when she sees the screen.

"It's Seth," she says, silencing the call and forcing a smile for Luke. "I'll talk to him later. Luke, it's your birthday. What do you want to do?"

"I want to find my brother. I want to go look for him and find him. Tonight."

I rake my hands through my hair. "We're trying. . . ."

Luke looks up at me, serious as a heart attack.

"Do. Or do not. There is no try."

Rebel Alliance

Daphne

After

I've never seen Luke look so determined—or so much like Jake. And he's right. Something fundamental needs to change if we're going to go from *try* to *do,* like Mrs. Foster did tonight. I could kick myself for all the time I've spent scrolling through the garbage on the "Find Jake" page and waiting for the police to take me up on my offer to help. For all the hours I've wasted hanging posters and following the rules instead of following my gut and actually finding him myself.

Kolt tips back in his chair. "Well, sure. I should have realized all we were missing was a Yoda quote."

"Not helping," I snap at him. Then I turn to Luke. "You're right," I say. "But maybe we have to start with the *try*. We know he's not in this house, so let's look somewhere else."

I turn back to Kolt. "You coming?"

He looks down. "He's my best friend. Of course I'm coming."

"Good," I say, stacking the dishes and scribbling a note for Mrs. Foster. "Let's go."

Luke leans forward and blows out the candles, and nobody needs to ask what he wished for.

Outside, Kolt strides to his truck, then falters. "Wait, I'm almost out of gas."

"Are you ever *not* almost out of gas?" I ask.

"Nope," he says, and changes direction. "But I could drive Jake's truck. Maybe there's some kind of clue there anyway." He lifts the handle, but the door's locked again.

"I know how to open it," I say. "I'm going to pull up on the handle, and you grab it from the bottom. . . ."

Right as we're reaching for the door, Luke pulls the key from his pocket and slides it in the lock.

"Did you have that all along?" I ask, feeling like an idiot.

"Yes," he says. "So if he ever came back, he couldn't leave again without saying goodbye."

He climbs in first and slides all the way across to unlock the driver-side door, and then all three of us are on the bench seat.

"Okay," Kolt says, taking the key from Luke and

turning it in the ignition. The truck coughs and sputters but eventually starts.

"Where are we going?" he asks.

"Whenever I lose something," Luke says, "I'm supposed to retrace my steps. So maybe we can retrace Jake's steps."

"Okay," Kolt says. "We know he drove the truck home, and we're in the truck. So now we go . . ."

"Back to the school?" I say. "I mean, we know he's not there, but maybe there's a clue, or it could trigger a memory for one of us."

"Sure," Kolt says, gunning the truck backward down the driveway.

Luke reads the text again. "'Maybe when this is all over . . .' What does that mean?"

Kolt and I look at each other. "We don't know for sure," I say, although it's hard to interpret it as meaning anything good.

My phone rings, and I glance down.

Seth. Again.

Kolt sees it too and rolls his eyes. "Might as well answer it, or he'll just keep calling. Dude doesn't know when to give it a rest." He grabs my phone and answers the call on speaker.

"Hey," I say, hoping Seth will hear in my voice that I'm not looking to talk.

"Hey," he answers, his voice tinny over the rumble of the truck. There's a silence long enough that I wonder if he thinks I called him first.

Kolt sees his opening. "I gotta be honest, bro. We don't have time for whatever this is."

"Kolt?" Seth sounds confused. "What are you doing there? Daphne, who else are you with?"

"Well, technically, she's with you," Luke says. "Because you stole her from my brother. That's you, right? Seth Cooper, center, six four, two hundred ten pounds," he recites. "Team leader in rebounds and foul-shot percentage and not much else."

"Is that Luke?" Seth asks. "What's going on, Daphne?"

"We're trying to find Jake." I don't say it to hurt him, but I don't care that it might.

Seth clears his throat. "Okay. Look, I was just calling to tell you not to come over tonight."

"I wasn't planning on it." Seth knows me, knows I'd never put up with a boyfriend who tries to control me. But there's something off in his tone. Something different from the ridiculous jealousy in the gym the other day. "Why shouldn't I come over? What are you doing tonight?"

"Staying home," he answers, quick and suspicious. "I'm not feeling great, to be honest, and I thought maybe you would want to go home in case it hits you too."

What's he hiding? It can't have anything to do with Jake or the text, can it?

"Good talk, bro. We gotta go." Kolt picks up my phone and thumb-stabs the screen to end the call.

Two seconds later, it rings again, and I grab it away before Kolt can turn this into another group conversation. "I'm not coming home," I say. "I'm going to find Jake."

There's a few seconds of silence before Dad answers, his tone tight and tense. "Absolutely not."

"That's not your call to make," I say.

"Absolutely not," he says again, as if repeating the words will make me obey. I'm used to him trying to protect me, but he's never sounded this afraid.

"I'll be safe," I promise. "But I'm not coming home, and if you call again, I'm not answering." Then I hang up and turn my phone on silent. I've had enough of men trying to tell me what to do or not do tonight.

I'm looking for a place to stash my phone when a small white triangle catches my eye. Something's stuck in the space above the ashtray.

I tug at the corner of the paper and unfold it to find some indecipherable scrawl on the back of a McDonald's receipt. Jake *hates* McDonald's. Plus, the handwriting isn't his, and it's pretty much impossible to read.

"Do you know what this is?"

Luke shakes his head, and Kolt says, "Looks like a

305

receipt, genius," but I pocket it, anyway. Maybe if I tell the police I have new evidence, they'll actually talk to me.

When we pull into the gym parking lot, Kolt swings his door open before he's even in park. "Okay, so, retracing his steps. We all went in the locker room for a minute to deliver the trophy. I can get us in."

Luke and I watch as he shimmies through a high window, and thirty seconds later, the door groans open.

"How long have you been doing that?" I ask.

"Since sophomore year. Caruso showed us."

"The creepy custodian showed you how to break into the school?"

I shiver, but Kolt only shrugs. "He's not creepy. Just socially awkward or something. And be nice. He might still be here."

Luke and I follow Kolt through the maze of stalls and showers and lockers. From the tile to the smell to the buzz of the lights, it's both different from and the same as our locker room across the gym. Familiar, yet somewhere I've never been.

We search Jake's basketball locker for any hint or sign or anything significant, then make our way to his regular locker and do the same thing. Between Kolt and me, we can patch together Jake's full schedule, and even though the classrooms are locked, it feels significant to walk the halls as he would have walked them.

But, of course, that doesn't mean actual evidence, and pretty soon we've walked the whole school.

"Now what?" Kolt asks. "We go back to the arena where we played the championship game? I mean, we know he made it back to Ashland, but I guess that makes sense. . . ."

"Not yet," Luke says. "I felt closer to him in the gym. Let's go back there."

The gym is eerie in the glow of the one emergency light in the corner. Without another word, we sit in a circle at center court: Kolt splayed out and leaning back on his hands, me with my knees tucked to my chest, and Luke chewing on his bottom lip so quickly I know he's working through something in his mind. Is he discouraged that his idea didn't work? Wondering what was behind all the locked doors we passed? When he finally speaks, his words are soft but clear.

"'In a dark place we find ourselves, and a little more knowledge lights our way.'"

"What?" Kolt asks. "Wait, are you quoting Yoda again? You know this isn't *Star Wars*, right? We're not your princess and your Wookiee or something."

"Of course," Luke says. "But I'm still a Luke trying to save somebody I care about. And Yoda helps me think."

"It helps me too," I say. "And we *are* a little bit of a Rebel Alliance. But we still need a plan."

"Not a plan," Luke corrects. "A little more knowledge."

"To light our way." Kolt doesn't sound totally convinced, but he shrugs and decides to go with it. "It actually is easier to think in here. Maybe because we don't have Seth distracting us with his drama."

Kolt's right, but his words catch inside me. My boyfriend—if that's still what he is—is not drama. Something is up, and the timing of his call so soon after Jake's text makes me wonder if they're related. Does Seth know where Jake is? Has something happened and he doesn't want me to see? Doesn't want me to worry?

Everything is upside down; somehow Seth has become the ghost I can't stop thinking of when all I want to do is focus on Jake.

"Seth is trying to do what's right, same as you," I say.

"You really believe that, don't you?" Kolt asks. "Even after that crap he pulled with the police."

I feel my eyes narrow. "I'm still not sure who to believe on that one."

"Me! You should believe me. Seth told them I picked up Jake at midnight that night. I don't know if he grabbed the wrong cup at the party or made up a story or what, but that's straight-up not true. I never saw Jake after the locker room."

I hadn't thought about it before, but Kolt's right. I've trusted Seth so completely that I had assumed Kolt was the one bending the truth to keep himself out of trouble. But what if Seth felt so bad about not checking in on Jake like he'd promised me he would that he made it all up? And then he couldn't back down and had to repeat the lie to the police?

Still, I bristle. "Seth wouldn't lie to the police."

"Lots of people lie to the police," Luke says. "I did. I mean, I tried to tell them the truth, but the last part turned into a lie."

"The truth about what?" I ask, trying to approach it gently. "Can you tell it to us?"

And then he tells us the real story of Jake's accident on the roof, a story I lived too but saw through a lens I refused to remove. By the time he finishes, I'm crying and pulling my knees closer, fat tears falling to my arms as guilt slices me open again.

I didn't see.

I didn't listen.

I told him to push through the pain to get himself back on the court.

"I lied to the police too," Kolt admits, tipping his head back like he might be trying to keep the tears in. "I knew he might have a problem with pills, and I didn't tell them. They asked me straight-up, and I didn't tell them."

"I didn't lie," I say, my voice soft but full of false strength. "But I'm the worst of all. I'm the one who made him take them. When he first got injured, he didn't want to. I told him he had to if he wanted to recover."

Jake's words circle the room. *So sorry . . . all over . . . forgive me.*

"They think he robbed the pharmacy." Luke whispers the words. "Do you think that's true?"

Kolt stares at the ceiling. "If he did, he's probably getting ready to run. That's what my brother would do."

"What do you do when you are getting ready to run?" Luke asks.

Kolt thinks a second. "Try to get some cash. Anything else you can't live without."

Luke sits up straight, like a bolt of energy just came through the floorboards. "Cash and your favorite sweatshirt? Is that what you would need?"

"Luke," I ask gently, "what are you talking about?"

"When Kolt's brother came to my house yesterday, that's what he took. That plus I'm not sure what else."

My pulse quickens; I feel it throbbing at my temple. "Kolt's *brother* came to your house?"

"Yes," Luke says. "Yesterday."

I spin to Kolt. "Why didn't anybody tell me?"

Kolt sighs. "Because it's not true. I didn't know about the rest of it, but apparently Luke gave stuff to some rando who claimed to know Jake—which is its own problem. But I promise you it wasn't Kmart. Luke just thought it was him because he's projecting. That's when—"

I cut him off. "I know what projecting is. Luke, did he say anything else?"

Luke hesitates, and there's a little fear in his eyes.

"You can trust us. Did he tell you not to tell anybody?"

Luke nods. Thinks. "Well, maybe he just said not to tell the police. . . ."

"Yes!" I say. "I'm sure that's what he said. So you can tell us."

Luke presses his lips together for a few long seconds, but then he lets the words out in a whisper. "He said Jake would be okay but I couldn't tell them." He looks up at me, eyes big and pleading. "Did I ruin it?"

"No," I insist. "You didn't ruin anything. Kolt, tell him."

"She's right," Kolt says. "You did the right thing telling somebody. And I wish it was my brother, but it wasn't. You want to see who my brother is?" He pulls out his phone, and two seconds later, he's showing Luke a mug shot. "This is him. Kade Martin, a.k.a. Kmart."

Luke takes the phone. Studies it. "Yes. That's him." He swallows. "But we still can't tell the police."

Kolt and I stare.

Finally he speaks. "You saw my brother."

Luke nods. "The scar above his eyebrow is smaller now. Is this an old picture?"

Kolt answers with questions of his own. "And all he took was cash and some sweatshirt? What did he say?"

311

"He said not to call him Kmart and not to call the police. He said Jake will be okay."

"Are you sure it's him?" I ask.

"Yes," he says, and I have to believe him.

We're finally getting somewhere, and I realize it's happening because we're finally sharing everything we have—and finally taking each other seriously. So I pull out the receipt from Jake's truck. "Look closer," I say, pointing to the indecipherable words on the back. "Could this be his handwriting?"

Kolt grabs the receipt and flips it over. "No way," he whispers. "No way no way no way."

He gapes, then takes his phone back from Luke and taps the screen. My phone dings, and I look down, hoping it's Seth or, even better, Jake.

But it's that same mug shot staring up at me. I'm struck by how much it does look like Kolt.

"Send it to Seth," Kolt says, and he's up on his knees, bouncing. "He might not answer if it comes from me. Ask him if that's who picked Jake up at midnight that night. If he's with my brother, that's seriously bad news."

So I forward the photo and ask the question. We all stare at my screen, but the answer never comes, which is not like Seth. The call wasn't like him, either. What's he doing that he wants me to go home so badly? I'd be worried about him if I had any room at all left for more worries.

But I don't, and I can't wait any longer for an answer. If it really was Kmart who came for Jake's stuff, then it's looking more than ever like one or both of them might have been responsible for the pharmacy break-in. And the text makes it sound like things have gone downhill from there.

Still, this new information seems to mean Jake is finally found—and with his life on the line, that's all we need. It feels like a wall has cracked open right in front of us, and we have to keep moving even before the dust settles enough for us to see what's waiting on the other side.

"Do you know where he lives?" I ask Kolt.

"No," he says, and my heart falls.

He gets up and paces along the half-court line. Then his head snaps up. "But I think I could figure it out."

"A little more knowledge lights our way," Luke says, and nobody can argue with that.

Savior: Part 2

Championship Game Warm-ups

Jake makes every layup during warm-ups.

Big deal. So does everybody else.

He sinks shot after shot from midrange. Never misses. Somebody notices.

"J-Money," says Kolt. "You came to play."

Jake smiles, grateful that this game has fixed what was broken between them, like it has so many times before. He wouldn't want Kolt to think anything that happens after is his fault.

They pair up for shooting warm-ups, and Jake dribbles back behind the arc. Pulls up for three and drains it. Kolt grabs the ball and fires it to Jake, who drains this one too.

One after another, Jake sinks the threes, each one confirming and clarifying the plan in his mind. Tonight is the night. He has no doubt they'll win, and after they win, he'll be done. It'll be better for everybody, really. Everywhere but the court he messes up. He takes and he takes and he takes. So he'll give back this one last time, and then it'll all be over. And what a way to end it.

He must have hit a dozen threes in a row, but he just keeps going. Maybe it's the chemicals thrumming through his veins. Maybe not.

Most of the other guys—on both teams—have stopped to watch now. Jake's aware of it, but that's not to say he cares. He's past pride or shame. He knows where the ball needs to go and how to get it there. Simple as that. The world has been stripped down to his body and the ball and the hardwood and the hoop. When that's all there is, how can he miss?

He continues around the arc, hitting every single shot, Kolt still feeding him. The crowd is watching, cheering. He's almost to the baseline now and facing his own bench, and even though he's focused on the court, not the crowd, he knows they're all there.

His mom and Luke.

Daphne.

Coach B.

And near the back of the arena, someone else he almost recognizes.

The ball hits Jake in the chest, but he still catches it.

"Sorry," Kolt says. "I thought you were ready."

Jake looks at Kolt, then back up to the hooded, bearded face that caught his gaze. Has he seen this man before?

"You okay?" Kolt asks. "You gonna shoot it? Or are you posing for the statue they're gonna make after you win this game for us?"

It's because he looks like Kolt, Jake realizes. That's why the man looks so familiar.

And then it all fits into place, as perfectly as the planks of hardwood beneath him.

The man looks just like Kolt.

And Jake has seen him once before.

He almost laughs now, because the man has aged more than he should have. He looks not unlike the picture of Jesus that has stared down at Jake every Sunday of his life.

But this is no perfect savior. This is the only person Jake knows who is like him—who has hurt everyone he loves and sold his very soul to the same monster.

And yet, here he is. Dirty and drawn, yeah, but almost smiling. And very much alive.

The rumor is true, then. It has to be.

He got clean.

Suddenly Jake feels something. Just a hint of a wonder whether there may be another way. Not to die, but to be reborn. Maybe it's his imagination or maybe it's the drugs, but he thinks he sees a glimpse of his salvation, his redemption, his path forward, in the man's haunted eyes.

"Who you looking at?" Kolt asks, following Jake's gaze to the back of the arena. The moment Kolt turns, the man pulls down his hood and bows his head.

"Nobody," Jake says. All his life, he would have believed that too. That someone who struggled with addiction was basically nobody.

He certainly believes that about himself.

But when he looks back up at the man, time slows. The crowd disappears. Suddenly Jake sees that this person he has never really met has been shaping his life for years.

Seven years ago, Kmart was the team leader who showed up at the championship game too high to play.

It was benching Kmart—the team's top scorer—and losing that game that cost Coach B his job.

It was Coach B's losing his job and Kmart's showing up in the parking lot that turned Jake and Kolt into best friends the day they met.

It was going to a hearing when Kolt couldn't bear to—even though Kmart himself never showed up—that made Daphne notice Jake in the courtroom that first day.

And now Jake remembers one more time when Kmart was there at a crossroads, and he's as sure of this one as the others.

It was Kmart who picked him up from the dirt at the

construction site on that worst, most desperate day of all, when the pain was so searing, so blinding that he could barely recognize the face of the man who saved him, who spoke so soft and steady to him and Luke both.

The noise of the crowd is still dull in Jake's ears. All he can do is stare at Kmart. All he can see is salvation. Jake knows he's not worthy to cry out to a perfect God for help, but the savior he is looking for is sitting here in the stands. He has felt this frightening clarity, this need to hurt himself only once before. And the same person saved him then.

The immediate plan has not changed, he realizes. Play the game. Win the game, for Seth and Kolt and Coach B and Daphne and Luke and his mom and all the people he's hurt. Do this one small thing for them, and then . . .

When the announcer calls Jake's name, Kmart looks straight back into his eyes, gives him one slight nod that means more than the roar of the crowd. Something sparks in Jake's belly, and the spark gives way to something like a summer rain.

Jake remembers this feeling.

He thinks it might be hope.

Perspective

Championship Game

Kade Martin knows he shouldn't have come. He *knows* this. He's always heard that it's smells that bring back memories, and maybe there's some truth in that. Popcorn and sweat and rubber soles.

But it's the sight that really gets Martin tonight. The red-and-white uniforms rush out onto the floor, and he's gone back in time to when he was part of it all: the whole human condition—comedy and drama and especially *history*—played out in thirty-two minutes on forty-two hundred square feet of hardwood.

It's not the same, of course. Back then, he was looking at the game from down on the court. Back then, he was the guy with the ball. Had he looked this young, though? This innocent?

They start with layups, fluid and graceful, and he knows for certain it's not the game that's changed, only his perspective.

He's been following the team—*his* team, his brother— all season. It's the only way he's found to stay connected to his family without crossing the boundaries he's drawn for himself. It started with the football games he watched from the hillside, but the pull of the basketball court was even stronger. So just this once, just for tonight, he wants to be inside the arena. To see if this team can make some history of its own, or if their season will end in heartbreak the way his did. To be in the same room as his family, even one as cavernous as this.

Across the arena, his parents huddle together a few rows behind the bench. They have new Warriors gear—of course they do—but the same expectant energy as they did for his games, all those years ago. He can almost feel the crackle of their nerves from here. Hoping for the best for their son, like the other parents, but also knowing how terribly it can all turn out. Because of him.

He watches Kolt leave the team just long enough to bound up into the stands and say something to them. His mom throws her head back with laughter; his dad shakes his head but with a smile on his face. They are knit together for one perfect second before Kolt rejoins the warm-ups, and in that second Martin knows: walking over there would tear open every wound he ever caused them. They've healed now, with him on the outside. And just because that's exactly what he wanted for them doesn't mean it can't hurt like hell.

So Martin tears his attention from his family and lets it settle, like the rest of the crowd's, on Jake Foster. Not only because the kid's so damn good, but because he sees himself in Jake. Even in warm-ups, there's a tension between the power of his play and the hunger and desperation beneath the surface.

They've never formally met, but that doesn't matter. You'd only notice it if you'd felt it yourself, and he has definitely felt it too. He knows Foster's family has even less than his own, but the uniform is the great equalizer. You walk out on that floor with the same slick synthetic jersey as everybody else, and it doesn't matter whether your family lives in a mansion on Evergreen Vista or a run-down apartment in Subsidy Square.

The game is about to start, and a thrill of adrenaline rushes through him. That's the same too. It's not only about the outcome of the game, though. It's the danger of being here in the first place. What if it's all too much, and he can't walk away again after the final buzzer? What if somebody sees him?

And like lightning, like karma or kismet or just plain fate, Foster looks up at him, and their eyes lock. Just for a moment. Just long enough for Foster to mouth one word at him.

Help.

Foster looks back at him at every timeout, between every quarter, even when he's standing at the foul line. No way should the kid be able to play this well when he's this distracted. When he's this high. But he's unstoppable. Unbelievable, honestly. Pure poetry. Like MJ in the 1997 NBA finals—if Jordan had been playing through a handful of oxys instead of the flu.

Help.

Foster's lips don't form the word again, but it's written on his face every time he looks up.

Martin knows he should go. He can't be pulled back into anything from his past. He won't survive it. He knows his own weaknesses too well.

But he can't walk away, because when the ball's in motion, all he sees in the Foster kid is himself. He has to stay to see the ending, because maybe if they win, things will be different for Foster. And if things are different for Foster, maybe they really can be different for him too.

After the ceremony, Martin goes out to his truck. Blows on his hands and prays the engine will start. He doesn't even jump when the fist pounds the glass, because he's been expecting it. Maybe even waiting for it: the chance to pay off his greatest debt, but to pay it forward.

"I need your help," Foster says, the window making his words sound like he's underwater. It's even worse now that Martin can hear his voice, can see so clearly in his eyes that the kid is battling the same demons he did. He knows he won't be able to drive away.

"Get in the truck," he barks.

Foster climbs in, shaking from the cold and the chemicals inside him.

"I have to . . ."

"I know," Martin growls.

"I can't . . ."

"I know," Martin says, a little softer this time.

But no. Soft will sink them both.

"If we're doing this, we're doing it my way, and we have to start tonight."

Foster nods. "Whatever you say, Kmart."

"If I'm going to help you, you can't call me that." Martin grips the steering wheel, the muscles in his hands as taut as those in his jaw. "Use that name again and I'll kick your ass so hard you'll have loose teeth."

"Then what am I supposed to call you?"

"I don't care," he says. "Just not Kmart."

"What about . . . Phoenix?"

At first he thinks Jake's trying to be poetic or symbolic about rising from the ashes or some shit like that. But then he follows the kid's gaze to the PHOENIX LUBE AND

TIRE sticker on the windshield, reminding him to change his oil two thousand miles ago.

"Okay," he says, because it's sure as hell better than Kmart. He lets his own gaze drift to the stream of people still coming from the gym doors in the distance: high school sweethearts and old-timers and young kids with stars in their eyes and dreams of state championships.

"You'll have to cut ties with everybody you know," he says.

Foster swallows. Tries to make a joke. "Good thing I never knew you."

"By the time this is over," Martin says, "you'll wish that was still true." He fishes a scrap of paper from the floor of the truck and scrawls a list on it. "Pack everything on here, nothing extra. Be watching for me at midnight. If you're not there, I'll drive away, and you can keep heading down this path you're on. But if you come out, that's like signing a contract. Next time you get in this truck, there's no going back."

Foster nods. Climbs out and runs away before Martin can change his mind.

This could be the end for either of them.

Or it could be the beginning.

Unmarked

Postgame

Jake took more pills after the game.

Too many too many too many.

But not all of them. He empties the first-aid tin into the toilet. Flushes. Ditches the tin in the trash can outside.

The pills have brought the whole world into focus. He has a little more time before the crash, and he's got to use every minute of it.

So he grabs his backpack. Kmart said not to bring much, and this is his first chance to prove that he's willing to do whatever it takes, whatever Kmart asks. (Including not calling him or probably even thinking of him as Kmart. *Phoenix,* he reminds himself.) So he only packs a few clothes and a toothbrush before searching his mom's medicine cabinet for the things on the list.

Gauze and bandages.

Antiseptic.

Imodium.

Sleeping pills.

Blood-pressure pills. (Jake feels an undeserved flush of pride as he drops these into his backpack. Phoenix will probably be surprised he could get them.)

There are other ways to get clean. He knows this—but he also knows his mom can't afford any of them. *He* can't afford any of them, and he's not sure they work anyway. So he takes a permanent marker, thick and black, and explains all of this to her, page after page, in the note that he writes: how he's got to go off the grid for a while, but he'll be in touch when he can. How she shouldn't worry, but he knows she will. How she's got to trust him and not get the police involved. How he promises he'll write to her when he's clean, but not before then. How he's sorry for this, just like he's sorry for everything else.

He cries when he writes this part. He is sorry for absolutely everything. But maybe that's a good thing. Maybe that will be one of Phoenix's twelve steps or something. He almost laughs, then he almost doubts this whole idea.

But no. Jake Foster is a man of faith, and his faith was never stronger than in that arena tonight.

He looks at the marker in his hand. He will get through this, and it's that word that will carry him through. So he writes it in thick black letters down the length of his arm.

FAITH.

There's a little space left in the backpack, so he grabs a few granola bars and Gatorades. It almost makes it feel like just another bus trip instead of a step into the unknown.

Later, he will look inside the backpack and wonder what happened to the granola bars and the Gatorades. He will look at the unmarked skin of his arm and realize that he must have imagined it.

He will not realize that the marker was real but he never uncapped it, that there was no note left for his mother at all.

Too Many Questions

Luke

After

I know sometimes
I ask too many questions
and it's annoying,
distracting,
exhausting.

So I follow Daphne and Kolt as they sprint to the truck
and I don't ask
    Is Kmart bad after all?
    Is Jake in trouble?
    Is Jake in danger?
    Is he getting ready to run?
    Is he getting ready to die?
I keep my questions inside

while Kolt runs into his house
and comes back out with no lightsaber, no blaster,
only an envelope.

"He still gets mail,
and sometimes my parents forward it.
They think I don't know."

I'm not sure what any of this means
until
he points to an address crossed out
and a new one next to it
written in blue pen.

"Same town as the receipt.
Go there," he says.
"We should be there in less than an hour."

Even if that's true,
it will feel like forever.

We go back to my house
to switch to Daphne's car
because Jake's truck
is sketchy on fast roads
(and sometimes on slow roads).

I make them wait
while I put Jake's key in the ashtray—
and because the mail reminded me:
Jake has mail too.

Daphne's car can go fast
but not fast enough.

Before we're even out of town,
lights flash behind us,
red blue red blue red blue.

Daphne and Kolt just look at each other
and we go faster.

"They're not coming for us,"
Kolt says,
but even I can tell
he's not sure about that.

This is not good.
When the cops come, you pull over.

The sirens chirp, just once.
Daphne drives faster.
This is really, really, really not good.

"Maybe we should . . . ," I start to say,
until
at the edge of town
the cop cars turn down some side road
and we are alone again.

We all breathe out together.

But then I have to wonder:
    If we're going this way
    and they're going that way
    and Jake is in trouble,
    getting ready to run,
    and my mom might have given them
    a clue how to find him,
    are we going light speed
    in the wrong direction?
    Or are they?
    Or are they looking for someone else
    and still not looking for Jake?
    And will anybody find him
    before he runs away?
    Before something worse?

One Small Stroke

After

My finger hovers over the phone. All it will take is one small stroke to do what's right. I've known it in my head all along, but it took my heart a while to catch up. Now that it's up to my hands, somehow I can't finish the job.

I grew up on the basketball court in the shadow of so many heroes, but none of them turned out to be who I needed them to be. And sure, we won the championship, but at what cost?

True integrity takes tremendous courage. Isn't that what Coach B says? And in the end, isn't Coach B the only person who has never let me down?

I don't realize I've completed the call until I hear the soft ring in my palm. I put the phone to my ear before my fingers have a chance to hang up.

"Ashland Police Department. How may I direct your call?"

I take a breath. Close my eyes.

"I know who robbed the pharmacy. I know exactly where he is and exactly where you can find the pills." I stop. Swallow. "I'm sorry. I should have called a long time ago. I'll tell you everything you need to know."

Alive Isn't Enough

After

"Let's go," Phoenix calls down the dark stairwell.

"I'm still packing" comes the reply.

"Packing what? All you brought was a backpack."

He can hear the hesitation in Jake's silence. Jake isn't ready to leave, too afraid of what's next.

Finally a reply. "I should probably shower. If we're going to be in the truck for a while, you definitely want me to shower."

"Fifteen minutes. This truck is leaving in fifteen minutes, and you're going to be in it. Don't make me bust out the handcuffs again."

He wonders if it's too soon to joke about it, but then he hears Jake's laugh. "I'll be there as soon as possible. Thirteen minutes, max."

Phoenix hopes it's soon enough. He's seen the headlines. He knows the cops are narrowing down suspects in the burglary, knows there are too many trails that lead to him, whether he's guilty or not.

It's time to leave town anyway, and no better time to go than when they're well supplied. The roll of cash in his pocket might be enough to make a fresh start, even farther from Ashland.

He takes one last look down the stairs, then walks through the small main floor: kitchen, bathroom, bedroom. More space than one person should need, but it still felt like a prison so much of the time.

But no. He stops himself. It wasn't prison; he shouldn't compare the two. He actually hates it when people do that, because a small house where you can come and go and eat what you want and close the door to take a crap is nothing, *nothing* like prison. The furniture is full of holes and smells, but it's been his these last few months, here in the only furnished place he could afford.

Phoenix leaves a prayer behind for the next person who will call this place home, because anyone who would live here is already someplace dark and may be on their way down from there.

He's wondered a hundred times whether this was all a mistake, but seeing Jake tonight—so hopeful, so clean— helps ease the guilt and doubt a little. When he steps onto the front porch and shuts the door behind him, he is determined not to look back, literally or otherwise.

But a car turns down the rutted drive, and as the front passenger comes into view, his past rushes toward him in a way he is not prepared for.

"Kolt." The name falls from him, heavy but soft, like the breath has been knocked out of him.

In an instant, he is Kmart again. In an instant, he sees his little brother in all stages of his life: the baby who hid carrots in his diaper; the preschooler who tried to scam the tooth fairy by putting white pebbles under his pillow; the teenager who stood before him the day he returned from prison and shoved him, hands on chest, saying the same words with every push: *I hate you. I hate you. I hate you.* And his only response: *I hate me too.*

Kmart left town that very same day, and they haven't stood face to face since. Of course, he has seen Kolt: as a red dot against the field when he watched football games from the hillside, and from the stands at the championship game, when he was feeling particularly reckless. He'd wanted to come closer so many times, to try to make things right in the place it had all gone wrong.

But if he came back, so would all the questions and stares and whispers. No denying the burden it would be on his family, and he has already been burden enough.

He knows too that he could never stay clean in that

town. *Environmental cues are one of the most common triggers for relapse.* He's recited it to himself—and now to Jake—so many times it feels like a mantra. Any place or person or smell or feeling that reminds you of when you were using can send you straight back, and that makes Ashland a minefield for them both.

Even now the sight of his brother so close reminds Kmart of where it all started: sneaking a Norco at the lake one day when Kolt was too little to notice, the sun warm on their skin and summer stretched out before them. That happy, floating feeling, even though they weren't on the water yet. The drugs are tricky that way, calling up the one good memory in an ocean of bad.

Kolt jumps out as the car rolls to a stop, and he's more than twice the size of the boy at the lake. Kmart is so stunned by it all—his brother, here, tonight—that he doesn't have time to react or even brace himself as Kolt winds up and punches him in the face.

Kmart staggers back, cheek throbbing, nose bleeding. He deserves whatever Kolt throws at him. Even now he wants to pull his brother into his arms and apologize for a thousand things. But the anger in Kolt's eyes makes him keep his distance as he tries to stanch the blood with the back of his wrist.

"Where is he?" Kolt demands, shaking out his fist and cradling it in his other hand. "Where's Jake?"

He's only here for Jake, then. Kmart is suddenly grateful Jake stalled and stayed inside. Jake isn't ready for this. Kolt could easily be the trigger that takes him right back where he started.

"Not out here. And you shouldn't be, either. Trust me, it's better for everybody if you drive away."

Kolt steps up into his brother's face. "I'd be happy to leave and never see you again. It would make my freaking day. But we're not leaving without Jake."

Daphne steps between them. "Please. We just want to talk to him. We want him to know that this doesn't have to be the end."

"I'll be sure to pass along the message," Kmart says. "If I see him."

Then the back door of the car opens, and the kid climbs out too.

No, no, no. This isn't good. The kid can't be here. Jake could be coming up any minute now, and Kmart knows too well how it tears your heart in half to walk away from family.

Kmart studies the kid. He's not afraid. Not now, not in his house yesterday.

The kid studies him back. "Did you give him the notebook?"

Truth be told, Kmart keeps forgetting to give Jake the notebook—he thinks he may have put it in Jake's backpack. He was too busy counting the cash that came with it. He searches for a line that will satisfy the kid enough to leave. "It's with him right now," he says. True enough—Jake and the notebook are probably both in the basement. He might have found it while he was packing up. He might be reading it this very minute.

Then the slam of the screen door. Four heads snap toward the noise as the beam of the porch light cuts through the dusk.

Kmart swears. How can he be done already?

Even in the failing light, they all see the moment when Jake sees them. He steps to the edge but not down off the porch, so his face is sharp lines of light and shadow under the single bulb. At first he's frozen, but then he steps back and kicks the metal frame of the screen door, just once—hard enough that they can hear it, even from down the drive.

Then the tears come, and Jake's body shakes with sobs.

Not one of them dares step forward. The yard falls silent—hell, the whole world falls silent—until the old wooden steps creak and crunch on the gravel drive under Jake's sneakers, their soles worn smooth on hardwood.

"You're alive," Kolt says.

But it doesn't take long before being alive isn't enough.

Kolt barrels toward Jake, and it's Kmart who catches him and holds him back.

"What the hell is wrong with you?" Kolt spits the words

at Jake. "Texting us to say it's all over and please forgive you. Who does that?"

Kmart tightens his grip as Kolt strains forward. "You sent that, Foster? When? Holy crap, no wonder they tracked us down."

Jake protests. "They didn't have to track us down. I left a note. I told my family exactly what I was doing and why."

Kolt shrugs his brother off. "Luke," he barks at the kid, who's still standing behind the open car door like it's a shield. "Did Jake leave a note?"

Luke shakes his head, hard. "The paper was blank. He didn't leave us anything."

Jake steps toward him, and he flinches.

"We thought," the kid says, choking on a sob, "we thought it was almost over. Like you were maybe dying."

"I'm not," Jake says. "Luke, I'm not. I'm okay. I just . . ." He sputters, stalls. "I'm sorry. I'm so sorry about all of this."

It's a start, but Kmart knows better than anybody that it will take a lot more than that to make things right.

Jake will be apologizing for the rest of his life.

Right Is Right

Daphne

All this time, Jake has been a ghost to me, and now that he's standing in front of me, I'm still not sure that's changed. The smile, the swagger—everything that made him Jake—have been stripped away, replaced by this pale, hollowed-out shell of the Jake I loved.

"I'm so sorry I didn't see it," I say. "I'm sorry I wasn't there when you needed me." My words are soft; they need to be after the way Kolt went after him. "But I'm here now. We all are. We want to help."

I approach gently, still unsure how to interpret Jake's text.

Maybe when this is all over . . .

"What did you mean in your text?" I ask, aware that Luke is listening to every word. "Maybe when *what* is all over? Are you . . . leaving?"

Jake nods, slow and solemn. "We have to go away for a while. Hopefully not forever."

"Go where?" Kolt demands, but when I raise a hand, he backs off.

They're going away.

He's not going to hurt himself, then.

Relief rushes through me, but reality's right behind. Jake still needs help, and running away won't lead to any lasting solution. I wish I could tell him it's all okay, that whatever he's done, it's already forgiven.

But it's not. It can't be. I stare at him, knowing I can't turn him in for the burglary, but I have to.

I can't.

But I have to.

Right is right. The words are Dad's, but they're mine now too, even if the edges are still a little softer for me.

I reach for my phone. "If you make a deal, they'll go easy on you. Especially since it's your first offense."

I don't look at Kmart when I say this. We both know he's already used all his chances.

Jake shakes his head. "Daph, we're getting out of here. We have to."

"You can't run from this," I plead. "Please let me make the call."

He comes to me, takes the phone. Just when I'm about to protest, he slides it into my coat pocket.

"I'm not running away. I promise. But I can't be here anymore."

It takes everything in me not to pull my phone back out. To trust Jake again.

Kolt steps up beside me. "So this has nothing to do with trying to ditch the cops?"

Jake lets out a short bark of a laugh. "What? No."

"And you're not on painkillers anymore?"

Jake shakes his head, serious this time.

I want to trust him, and I almost do—but I have to be sure. "You haven't stolen any pills since I saw you last?"

"Just my mom's blood-pressure meds." He looks at Kmart, like he's realized something. "Is that what you were shoving down my throat in the beginning?"

Kmart nods. "It helps with the withdrawal," he says, and the knot in my chest loosens a little.

Neither one of them robbed the pharmacy.

They have been out here getting Jake clean.

The same feelings rush through me again: relief, then reality.

I turn to Kmart. "What the hell?"

He looks almost amused, which makes me want to punch him.

"I mean, I know you were trying to help, but seriously. What. The. Hell? Sketchy detox in the middle of nowhere with somebody else's blood-pressure meds? You could have killed him."

He takes a step back, hands up. Smile gone. "If I didn't do something, he was going to kill himself. So I helped him the only way I knew how. The way somebody helped me once. And it worked, okay? It worked."

"It worked?" Kolt looks like he wants to strangle his brother, and I'm not sure I want to stop him. "There was a freaking missing-person report. A search warrant. Everybody who cares about him has been scared shitless for weeks. You're calling that a success?"

"He's alive, isn't he?"

I'll leave Kolt to argue with Kmart. I'm done with him, anyway. This is about Jake. About moving forward.

"Come back," I say to Jake. "There are people at home who still care about you, no matter what. You don't have to hide out for the rest of your life just because you made some mistakes."

"I wish I could go back," he says, his voice thick. "But it's better for both of us if you climb in your car right now, Daph. Without me." He reaches a hand toward me, then lets it fall to his side.

Tension crackles between us. I know exactly how it would feel to take one step forward and rest my head against his chest. And he must know exactly how it would feel to thread his fingers through mine and kiss the top of my head. Impossible as it may be to quantify, we both know exactly how much comfort we could find in each other's embrace if we just gave in to the gravity pulling us together.

But in all of this, we never actually touch each other.

"There are other options." I hold out the stack of papers I've been driving around with for weeks. "I've been reading about addiction," I tell him, knowing how ridiculous I sound. How different reading about it is from living it.

But the words are all I've got, and I promised myself I'd say them if I ever had the chance. "I know coming back would be hard. But I also know you're more likely to get better if you're surrounded by people who love you. And, Jake, we love you. That's why we're here."

Instead, he steps back. Looks toward the truck. "We have to go."

"You don't," I say, holding the papers out toward him. "You said you wished you'd done everything differently. If that's true, do it differently. Starting now."

He looks down, ashamed. "We can't afford any of that. We're still paying off my surgeries. How can I ask my mom to pay for this too?"

Tears sting my eyes. "You have to trust her enough to let her make that choice. Please, Jake. Come back."

"I can't," he says. "Think about it, Daphne. You're smart enough to understand why."

So I try to see the world the way Jake sees it right now. The fact that the cops really might be after him, even at this very minute, ready to drag him back to Ashland and put him through the trauma of arrest and questioning and who knows what else for a crime he didn't commit. The people he loves but feels he has let down in unforgivable ways. The incredibly intimidating prospect of surrendering himself to an inpatient program in spite of his lifelong fear of doctors and hospitals and anything like them. The memory of his father and how rehab wasn't enough. The impossible cost of it all.

Or he can go with the person who has pulled him out this far, in search of a truly fresh start.

But just because I can see why he believes this is the answer doesn't mean I believe it. It's too easy to imagine all the ways this could end in tragedy.

"I'm terrified," I tell him.

"So am I," he says, and he raises his hand to reach for mine.

I'm about to take it, hold it, keep it close to my heart, when I realize he's reaching for the brochures. I riffle through the stack, wishing I'd written myself a script for this part.

"I can show you statistics," I say. "We can compare programs. Figure out costs. There's a way to make this work—"

Jake cuts me off. "I'm not saying I'll do it," he says.

"But I'll think about it. We'll talk about it—after you guys are gone."

No. This isn't how it's supposed to go. "I'll think about it" is not good enough.

"You'll talk about it? With *him*?" I don't even try to keep the venom out of my voice.

"Yes," Jake says. "After you leave." He closes his eyes, swallows hard. "Just go, Daphne. Please."

I scrape and scramble for the right words to make him change his mind, but even as I do, I see the decision set in his jaw.

"I'll think about it" is all I'm going to get, because all my hours of worry and preparation weren't enough.

Jake extends his hand one last time.

I nod and hand him the stack.

Our fingers do not touch.

Then I walk away so he won't see me cry—and so he can have a moment with the person who missed him most.

Force Field

Luke

While Kolt tries violence
and Daphne tries diplomacy,
all I can do is hide
behind the car door
    like it's a force field,
    keeping me from this shapeshifter.

I mean, I know it's Jake,
    but I want it to not be Jake
    because he is smaller, sunken,
    and this place is dim, dirty,
    and if this is Jake,
        then my hero
        left me,

hurt me,
made mistakes,
and all of it was
    his choice.

Jake looks at me.
Tries again.
"Happy birthday," he says.

"It isn't," I say, because
I
am
angry.

"Where have you been this whole time?"
    "Here."
"Why didn't you tell me?"
    "I thought I did."
"I felt like you were frozen in carbonite."
    "I felt like that too."
"You said it's not my fault."
    "I meant it."

I swallow my sob,
step out from behind the door.
I don't know if I want to hug Jake
    or hurt him back.

He steps toward me.

I let him.

"You said 'when this is all over.'"
    "That was stupid.
    I didn't think.
    I didn't realize."
"What do I tell Mom?"
    "Tell her I'm okay.
    Or that I'm getting there."
    He can't look at me for the next part.
    "Tell her I'm sorry."
"What about me? Are you sorry to me?"

My force field must be down because
Jake pulls me in,
holds me tight.

I am surprised how much he feels
like my big brother.
    "I'm sorry to you most of all," he says.

It takes a long time
before either of us lets go.

Rearview Mirror

Kolt

As Daphne and Luke say their goodbyes, I'm watching Jake and Kmart. Their steady movements, the way they stand their ground. Finally I believe it.

"You're clean," I say, and it's not a question. "Both of you."

Jake looks away, like he's still so superstitious he thinks saying it out loud will make it all disappear.

Kmart, on the other hand, looks me straight in the eye. After all these years, the anger inside me isn't going to burn out anytime soon, but I'm not going to let it keep me from getting answers. "Is that why you came out here? Because it's easier to stay clean outside of Ashland?"

He half shrugs. "It'll never be easy. But yeah."

"So now what?" I ask. "You drive away and never come

back?" I try to keep my voice level. Try not to sound like I care.

"Nah," Kmart answers, sliding his hands into his pockets. "It'll take two years for his dopamine receptors to start working naturally, but it'll get better after that."

I can barely believe this is my brother. "Thanks, Professor." It's supposed to be a joke, but even I can hear the sharp edge on it.

Good.

Then I play the odds. "It's been longer than two years for you, though, hasn't it? You could come home. Mom and Dad would want that. We could, you know, be a family again. Don't you think you owe them that?"

Kmart kicks at the gravel. "I owe all of you a lot more than that. But I need to see this through for him," he says. "Somebody did the same for me a while back."

"Who?" I ask. My brother is even more of a mystery than I thought.

"That's a story for another day," Kmart says, fishing for his keys.

Another day. He said it like this won't be the last time we see each other. But I don't want to care whether that happens, so I remind myself he came back for Jake, not for me. And he's choosing Jake again right now.

"Where will you go?" I ask.

Kmart leans against the truck. "I'll let you know when we know. It wasn't supposed to happen like this. I mean, it was always going to be rough on Jake and me, but it wasn't supposed to be so bad on your end. I didn't know about the search until it was too late to smooth it over with the authorities, so we had to dig ourselves in deeper and wait it out."

I look to the house, which is pretty sketchy, even by my standards. "So you've been here the whole time? Running some kind of vigilante rehab?"

Kmart laughs. "You could call it that, I guess. The only kind guys like me and Jake can afford."

"And you didn't break the law?"

Kmart hedges. "Well, I'm not sure the cops would see it that way. There were . . . struggles, let's say. Times when Jake didn't want to be here."

Jake shudders, and I can see it's still raw. I try to come up with the perfect joke—something about the creepy setting and the horror-movie house—but nothing quite clicks. Then I realize I don't want to make a joke right now, anyway.

But he still owes me answers. I nod at the soda-can tab on his key chain. "You still collecting those?"

"You remember that?" he asks. "It was just for fun at first. But now I keep one for every day I've been clean. Almost a thousand now."

"I found one on the sidewalk outside Jake's house the day after he disappeared. I almost showed it to the police, but even I couldn't believe it was anything but trash."

"Might have been," Kmart says. "Or maybe I dropped it. Maybe they would have believed you, maybe they wouldn't."

We stand there, probably both of us thinking about the millions of ways this might have gone down differently. And even if I'm still pissed, I can't stop myself from picturing how much worse this could have turned out. I feel something building inside me, and then, dammit, I'm crying, even though everybody knows Wookiees don't cry.

"We gotta go," I say, swiping at my eyes with the back of my arm.

I'm halfway to the car when Kmart's arms wrap around me from behind.

"I'm sorry, Kolt."

His words are dulled against my shirt. His hold tightens, and panic sears inside me. In a flash, a thousand painful thoughts surface: Kmart picking me up from practice high, Kmart missing his own hearing, me holding Mom one night while she cried until Dad came home to take my place. Because of my brother, I had to grow up way too quickly. I've had the suspicions of every teacher in Ashland on me like a freaking magnet. I've felt police officers' eyes following me all my life. And I didn't deserve any of it.

Maybe when you've been hurt like that for so long, you can't forgive somebody in less time than it takes to play a basketball game. Even if they saved your best friend.

"I know," I say, turning and pulling back until he and I have our hands on each other's shoulders.

"I wish Jake could go back with you, for Luke's sake," he says. "A kid deserves to have a big brother he can believe in."

"Yeah," I agree, but there's not as much bitterness in it as before. "That makes a difference."

I look back at Jake one last time. Decide maybe he's ready for a joke now.

"I miss you, asshole," I say.

It's only there for a second, but I catch a twitch of a smile at the corner of his mouth. "Thanks," he says.

"You shouldn't swear," Luke says. He hands Kmart the envelope that led us here. "We brought your mail."

Then he hands a stack to Jake. Even from here, and even though I didn't get nearly as many, I can tell they're letters and mailers from colleges. "I made you a new highlight video with the state tournament on it. Arizona State is too focused on their big men, anyway. You might want to look at New Mexico State or Southern Utah. Let me know if you want me to look up stats on any of the others."

"Thanks," Jake says, pulling Luke in for one more hug. "I will. I promise I will."

Then we tear ourselves away, divided between Daphne's car and the junky old truck. It all feels wrong, but what can I do about it?

Back in Daphne's car, we follow the truck to the end

of the long gravel drive, and then they turn right and we turn left. In the mirror, I watch the taillights of the truck— one steady, one flickering—until they disappear around a turn. When I look over, Luke is watching too. And he's crying.

The kid needs a big brother, or at least something like it. Maybe Mrs. Foster will let me take him to Best Burger, or to play catch. Or maybe we could even go out spotlighting—if he can stop talking about the stars long enough that the animals don't all run away.

"Hey," I say, tossing him a bag of chips I find next to my seat. "If those two are going to take care of each other, you and me might as well do the same thing."

Luke turns the bag over in his hand and studies the nutrition information. "One hundred sixty milligrams of sodium."

I look at Daphne, but she just nods like I should know what to do about this. "Is that okay?" I ask him.

Luke shrugs. "Could be worse. Did you know that there are significant amounts of sodium on Mars? And in the stars? But not in cars."

"Luke," I say. "You're a poet."

Luke crunches his chips. "Of course I am."

"The Rebel Alliance makes a pretty good team," I say.

Daphne laughs. Luke doesn't.

"Of course we do," he says.

Reckoning

Seth

I'm in my room, pretending to do homework, when a car turns down the gravel drive, lights flashing blue and red off its slick black body. I stare at my calculus book, knowing they're here because of me, wondering whether I should run while I still have the chance. But it all piles on—the drugs, the lies, the perfect public persona—and I'm so sick of it all, so ready for it to be over, that deep down, I know I wouldn't run, even if it weren't too late.

It's my mom who answers the door. Her voice is faint, but only because I'm not man enough to actually go downstairs and face what I've done. Not because she has anything to be afraid of. Yet.

"Come in, Matthew," she says. Then her tone tightens. "Is this about Jake Foster?"

"No, ma'am." It's Officer Vega—Matthew, I guess—sounding like he's trying too hard to be tough and professional. "We've got a warrant to search the house," he says.

"I—I'm sorry?" she stammers.

"Me too," Officer Vega says. His boots beat a rhythm across the wood floor and up the stairs, purpose and direction in every step, his partner following close behind. I spin the state championship ring on my finger, watching to see if my doorknob will turn.

But no, they pass by, headed down the hall to the little room over the garage where Coach keeps his tools and a small steel box I used to think he'd forgotten about.

Speaking of Coach, I hear another set of footsteps coming up the stairs. Quicker. Catching up. Then his voice, almost cracking. "Now hang on a second. What did you say you're looking for?"

I open my door, just a sliver. Hear them looking around for something, know exactly what the something is.

Then another thought hits me: it was probably Judge Sharp who signed the warrant. He probably knows they're here right now and knows exactly what they're looking for. Daphne's dad has never liked me much. What will he think of me now?

I hear the heavy *thunk* of the box as they pull it from its hiding place.

"You can't take that," Coach protests.

"I hope we won't need to," Officer Vega says, and he tells the combination to his partner. "Zero-nine-one-nine."

Nine nineteen: 9/19. My parents' wedding anniversary. It took me only three tries to guess it. The box was sleek and silver with a dusting of white across the bottom—the perfect place to hide something small and valuable.

"Now hang on," Coach says again, his voice rising. "My family doesn't deserve this. We're good people. We've given a lot to this town. You know that as well as anybody. Didn't I take a chance on your boy playing JV this year?"

Through the crack in the door, I see him step forward, like he's ready to yank the box right out of their hands. For all his faults, he'd do anything to protect me. Her. Us.

"You're going to need to back off," Officer Vega says.

"Not until you tell me what it is you're looking for."

It's time to face what I've done. I push the door open, sick and scared, and they all turn toward me.

"Drugs, Dad." I hope they can't hear the panic in my voice as I walk toward them. "They're looking for drugs. Painkillers. The ones that were stolen from the pharmacy."

Coach is so stunned that he forgets to fight as the other officer raises the lid. Even from the hallway, I can see the stash and hear the sharp intake of breath of everyone in the room.

Then my mom looks at me and Coach with so much pain in her face that I know she's put it all together.

But Coach. Dad. Whoever he is, I'm pierced by the hate in his eyes.

"How could you?" he asks. "How could you do this to me? To us?"

I don't answer. I can't. I have no words for this.

Officer Vega takes the cuffs from his belt. "Seth Cooper, you are under arrest," he begins, and there's a part of me that's floating above the whole scene, surprised that it really is the same words you hear on TV. "You have the right to remain silent. . . ."

What would have happened if I'd remained silent? I wonder, that same floating feeling taking over. *How long could I have kept this secret?*

But it's too late now. The cuffs click into place, and no one speaks as Officer Vega follows us down the stairs.

We stop for a moment by the door. "Seth," my mom whispers, and I think she's speaking to my dad. The man I'm named after. The man I've spent my whole life trying to live up to.

But no. She's looking at me.

"It will be okay," she says. There are tears in her eyes, but she won't let them fall. She will be stronger than any of us. Always is.

Officer Vega agrees. His face softens for a moment, and I remember that he and my dad played ball together, that they won a championship of their own for Coach B.

"This isn't the end," he says to my dad. "Just the part where we turn it around."

Then he takes Coach by the shoulder and walks him out to the waiting squad car.

I sink to the steps as they drive away. My shoulders shake; I can't breathe.

My mom pulls me against her shoulder, and I hate myself for letting her, because it's all wrong. She should hate me right now. Or at the very least, I should be holding her, comforting her. I'm the one who found his stash, who made this happen. Our family has been splintered and broken for a long time, but I'm the one who tossed a match on top of it all when I called the cops from the sketchy pay phone down by the gas station, because I was too afraid to use my own phone or my own name.

"I'm sorry," I tell her between gasps. "I'm the one who called the cops. I'm so sorry."

"This is not your fault," she tells me again and again as her tears fall like rain on my hair, my neck. "I should have seen it. He struggled off and on for years, but he told me it was okay." She smooths my hair, and I feel her strength as she hugs me close. "You did the right thing, Seth. And it will be okay."

I shift on the cold concrete steps, and my mom rests her head against my shoulder. We stay there like that, not saying a word, until headlights cut through the night and

Daphne's car pulls up. I should have known telling her not to come over would make her do exactly that.

"You should tell her," Mom says, standing up and waving Daphne over. "She'll find out soon whether you tell her or not, and it's better if she hears it from you. I've got a couple of phone calls I need to make anyway."

Then Mom goes inside, and it's just the two of us out here.

"Hey," I say to Daphne. "I'm still not feeling so good."

But when she steps into the porch light, her eyes are red. "Me neither," she says. "I think we need to talk."

Not tonight, I beg. *I can't lose you tonight too.*

But then she rises up on her toes and pulls me down with one hand behind my neck and she kisses me. "Can we go out back?" she asks.

So I get the same quilts and we go out to the clearing and we look at the stars, surrounded by a dark halo of trees. Then we lie on our backs and, after a false start or two, we tell each other everything. Jake, my dad, Kmart and Kolt. All that's happened between us, including what I witnessed in the training room—what it meant, and what it didn't mean. Maybe it takes an hour, or maybe four, but finally there's something like peace in the clearing.

"I never lied," I say. "I really thought it was Kolt in the truck. Does this mean I have to apologize to him?"

"Yup," Daphne says. "Even though I think he's forgiven

you already." She pulls the blanket closer; I feel the heat of her side against mine under the stars.

"Sodium," she says with a little laugh. "After all that, somehow my mind goes back to potato chips and Luke and sodium and space." She props herself on her elbow and looks right into my eyes. "Everything is going to be okay," she says.

Once two of the people you believe in most have told you something, you kind of have to believe it.

So I do.

The Other Side

As soon as the other car disappears around a bend, Jake's reading the papers: Daphne gave him printed pages underlined and scrawled on in her handwriting. He mutters to himself. Taps his fingers against the handle of the door.

Kmart knew everything had changed before they even climbed into the truck. "Talk to me," he says, not for the first time.

So Jake talks.

Kmart listens.

After twenty miles, Jake finally calls a new play.

"Turn around. I need to go back."

Kmart sighs, but he pulls over.

"You sure about this?" he asks as the truck idles.

Jake nods. "I'll find you on the other side," he says.

Kmart shrugs. "If you want to."

Jake turns to him. "Of course. You're my sponsor, man."

They both laugh at the absurdity of this, at how true and untrue it is all at once. They laugh because sometimes the only way to do something this difficult is to laugh. Whether they realize it or not, they have both learned this from Kolt.

"Here," Kmart says. "It was time to give this back, anyway." He tosses Jake's phone onto the seat between them, then peels out of the gravel and onto the road—heading for Ashland this time.

Jake's almost afraid to pick the phone up. Was it really just a few hours ago he snuck it out to send that text? How has so much changed so quickly?

When he finally turns it over, there's a message from Luke. The highlight video, as promised.

Jake watches himself on the court and aches to get back there again. When the screen fades to black, he picks up the stack of mail from Luke and opens one college envelope after another. Some are just generic mailers, but most seem personalized, and a few are even signed by the whole coaching staff. For the first time, it seems possible that somebody could still want him, that this could still be his future.

Eventually the truck pulls to the curb in front of Jake's

house—the very same spot where it waited all those weeks ago. The snow has long since melted; the path to the front door is clear. Jake climbs out, collects his backpack. Can't quite bring himself to say goodbye yet.

"You could come with me," he says.

They both know this isn't true. Not right now, anyway.

Kmart shakes his head. "Nah, I'm good."

"You could try things out here for a while. Go see your family."

"I could," Kmart admits. It's not a commitment, but it's not a no, either.

He pulls the roll of cash from his pocket, but Jake refuses.

"At least give it back to your brother," Kmart insists.

Now Jake shuts the door. He cups his hand to his ear, then shrugs, pretending he didn't hear. He knows that Kmart will need the money, and that Luke is way too generous to want the gift returned, in any case. He's a good kid like that. The best kid.

As the truck rolls away from the house, Jake takes a paper from Daphne's stack—the one she's marked up the most. At the top she's drawn a bold, dark star next to the words "works best for Jake."

Jake studies the words. Maybe rehab didn't work for his dad because he didn't work for himself. But Jake is willing to work. Always has been.

With shaking hands, he dials the number, and with a shaking voice, he answers a woman's questions about what he needs.

"We have an open bed," she says. "Can you come in tonight?"

Jake looks through the front window, sees the outline of his mom and Luke asleep on the couch. He rests his hand on the glass, half hoping to see their eyes flutter open.

But they don't, and he knows it's probably better this way. He has to take this next step while he's still got the courage. Walk away now so he can be with them again.

"Yes," he says quietly. "I can come in tonight."

After he hangs up, Jake programs the address from the paper into his phone. He finds a pen on the floor of his truck and writes his own words beneath Daphne's, then slides the paper through the crack below the door.

I love you. I'm okay. This is where I'll be
for a while but then I'm coming home.

This time he knows the ink is real, and the promise will be kept.

Jake goes to his truck, takes the key from the ashtray, and drives.

Loose Earth

The whole world has woken up. Crocuses bloom, then tulips and daffodils hurry to catch up. The stream runs, muddy and strong. And one blade at a time, the dry, yellowed grass of last autumn is replaced by this season's green.

Across the town, four phones vibrate as one, coming to life with the same message.

> **Rehab going well. Visiting hours on website.**
> **Will text more when I can.**

Daphne reads it as she fills out her housing application for the university. She'll show it to Seth later, before they staff the table for summer basketball sign-ups. He'll want to know.

Kolt will share the message too, both with his parents and with Jenna. He still waits for the day when his brother will reach out to him, but somehow just knowing what he knows now has already helped the old wounds begin to heal.

Luke reads the text as he rides his bike to his very first day at his very first job. Before he puts his phone away, he looks back at the thread. All these messages to the same four people, but he still isn't sure who the fourth is.

Across town, Coach B stops at the end of his driveway to gather the mail. There are two packages: one from a small college hours away where he used to take the boys for a summer tournament, and the other without a return address. He drives the old Jeep into the carport and takes them both to his kitchen table to open.

Mrs. B brings him a glass of water and his medication. She sets his phone next to them.

"Someday you'll actually remember to take that with you when you go out," she says, kissing him on the thin waves of his gray hair.

Coach B grabs her hand and gives it a squeeze. The best he can, anyway, with his arthritis. He's never quite gotten the hang of cellular telephones. Maybe his new employee will show him how to use it as more than just a telephone. He turns back to the packages, opening the larger one, which has the name of one of his former players—now a successful coach himself—in the top corner.

"Oh." The sound escapes him as soon as he sees the sign, its paint worn off along the bottom edge by the good-luck taps of decades of his players: HEAD, HANDS, HEART. All those boys, for all those years. *They gave it all, didn't they?*

He thinks he'll return the sign to the school, but then he thinks again. On the one hand, the team was certainly successful without it last season.

But on the other, that success came at great cost.

Which reminds him—he has a poem to write and a visit to make today, to a former player who is working toward a fresh start from inside a prison cell. *If you want somebody to do what's right, let them see you believing that they can.* He's said this for years, and he's believed it every time.

Coach B sets the sign aside and looks out at the buds on his maple tree. He knows the team will need a new tradition to go along with their new coach, whoever it ends up being. But he'll keep the sign safe somewhere, just in case.

The second package is more of a puzzle. All it contains is an old notebook he doesn't recognize. But tucked inside the front cover, he finds a note with his name scrawled across the top.

Coach B,

I wanted you to know that I finally took your advice and wrote a poem. It's not very long or very good, but I've written more, and they're getting better. It's actually for Luke, but I wanted you to be the first to read it. Will you read the back page and give him this notebook when you're done? Will you keep an eye on him too? And tell him I said to keep an eye on you?

Thank you for everything, always.

Jake

Coach B reads the cover of the notebook: *The Book of Luke and Jake.* He's curious about what's inside, but he is also an unfailingly honest man, so he turns only to the back page and reads the poem.

a haiku for my brother

Baller and Jedi
May the force be with you, Luke.
Someday I will too.

It isn't long before Coach B hears someone humming his way up the path.

"Ah," he says as Luke comes to the screen door. "My

new employee. Are you sure you don't mind getting paid in raspberry lemonade and basketball lessons?"

Luke shrugs. "If that's what you paid Jake, that's what I want you to pay me."

Coach B can tell he means it. But more important, he can tell Luke's not just saying it to be nice but because he still truly wants to be like his big brother. And even after all that has happened, this is a very good thing.

"Do you want me to mow the lawn?" he asks.

Coach B shakes his head. "It's still a little early for that. I was actually hoping you could show me how to operate this contraption."

He holds out his phone, knowing it's capable of so much more than he's ever used it for. He's spent decades doing what Luke is about to do—helping someone see the potential in the palm of their hand. There's something nice about being on the other end of that today.

They sit together in the crackling wicker chairs on the front porch. Coach B demonstrates that, yes, he knows how to turn the phone on.

"This is your text app," Luke says, tapping on something that looks like a speech bubble.

Then Luke's jaw drops. "It was you. It was you!" He stands up, still staring at the phone.

He turns the screen to face the old man. "These are your texts," he says. "You have three of them."

Coach B reads the messages.

It's not your fault.

I'm so sorry I wish I would have done
everything differently maybe when this is all
over you will find a way to forgive me

Rehab going well. Visiting hours on website.
Will text more when I can.

"These are from Jake?" Coach asks, already knowing the answer.

Luke nods.

"Can you show me how to write him back?"

Luke shrugs. "He can't really text very much right now. But I'll show you how to text me."

After that, it's Coach B's turn to teach Luke something. He shows him how to till the garden, loosening the soil so things can grow. It's hard, slow work, and the boy begins to sweat after only a few turns of the handle.

"Are there machines that can do this faster?" he asks.

"I'm sure there are," Coach B says, afraid the boy will give up before he's really begun. But Luke just pushes harder against the tiller.

"If there wasn't, I'd invent one. I'm very interested in inventing lately. I have forty-seven ideas in my invention notebook. I can bring it next time and show you. Or my poetry notebook. I have one of those too."

Coach B takes a moment to marvel at this fascinating, confident kid. He can't help but feel that it's Jake who has helped shape him this way.

And then the mention of a notebook reminds him. "Ah," says the old man. "Don't let me forget. I have something for you. Come in when you get thirsty, and I'll give it to you."

Inside, Coach B sits at the table with his eyes closed, willing himself not to get dizzy today. And then, because there's still something of the stubborn kid he once was inside him, he tries sending Jake a text.

Proud of you. Call me anytime.

He's not sure how to determine whether it worked. Probably it didn't. And it's just as well—the arthritis makes it hard for him to text anyway. It's certainly no way to write poetry.

He's about to go ask Luke if he needs a drink yet when the phone rings on the table.

"Hello?" he answers.

"Coach" comes the voice.

Coach B swallows. Blinks back the tears that have sprung so suddenly.

"Jake."

"I probably shouldn't have called," Jake says, but Coach B protests.

"You call me anytime."

"Well, not anytime. They're kind of strict about that here." He clears his throat. "I stole from you."

"I wondered about that."

"I'm sorry."

"I know, son."

There's a long pause, and the boy's next words are choked. "What do you think of me now?"

"Now?" Coach B stops to consider this. "I think, or I suppose I hope, that you're starting to see the worth I saw in you all along. Not on the court but the real worth of your soul." He closes his eyes. "I think you're facing an opponent as tough as any I ever did, and you're conquering it, day by day."

Jake starts to protest, but Coach B won't have it.

"It's true," he says. "How many soldiers face the enemy on the battlefield with great courage, only to fall to the very same foe you're facing now?

"And why?" he asks. "Because we treat it like a shameful, secret battle. We make each other face it alone." He thinks of all the friends he has lost, in one way or another, to this same shadowy opponent. "Please know you're not alone, son. That you're never alone. And please know how proud I am of you."

They both have a hard time saying anything after that. Coach B clears his throat and looks out the window to where Luke still toils away at the tilling.

"This brother of yours," Coach says. "He writes poetry. Did you know that?"

"Some of my favorite people do," Jake says. "I'm starting to write some too."

"I know. I read one today. It's a fine poem, son. Have you called your mother?"

"I can't."

"I know. But you'd better do it anyway."

Jake only hesitates a moment. "Okay."

"You don't have to talk about the hard things yet, if that helps."

Another pause. "There's a cooking group here. I could ask her how to make pad thai."

"I think that would be an excellent idea. I might ask her that myself. I'll get off the line so you can give her a call now. But you take care, son. And if you happen to hear from Kade again, tell him I said hello."

"I will."

Coach B waits for Jake to end the call, then tucks the phone into the pocket of his sweater. He looks out the window and sees the tiller lying across the loose earth, the task completed and its master gone. Then a smile breaks across his face as he hears a familiar rhythm: three dribbles, pause, then the clang of the ball off the rim. If he didn't know better, he'd swear it was Jake out there shooting foul shots.

He opens the screen door and watches.

Three dribbles, pause, and this time, only the *chunk* of the ball through the net.

All at once, Coach B is transported back to the first time he watched Jake shoot at this very same hoop.

"That's nice," he says. "Foul shots are important. Fundamental. I can see somebody's been working with you on those."

Luke nods. Dribbles three times, exhales, shoots again.

Makes it again.

"Has anybody ever taught you the fadeaway?" he asks.

Luke nods again. Dribbles once, pulls up to shoot, fades it away.

Misses badly.

But the form is there. His head is in it, hands are soft. No doubt the heart is there too.

"Good, good," Coach B says. "Should we work on that for a bit?"

And they do.

Big Bang: Part 2

Luke

Once upon a time there was
Nothing
and then there was
Something.

No brother,
then
Brother.

But before that
galaxies
planets
oceans
mountains

grass and trees
seasons
whales
birds
cows
spiders
people.

And it was good.

Mostly.

Because as soon as there were people,
they could hurt each other,
but they could help each other too.
And they did.
And it hasn't stopped.

The opposite of a big bang
is a fadeaway,
but the opposite of a fadeaway
is something else,
I think.

Something that disappears
and you wait

and you wait
and you hope
and you wait
and just when you're about to give up
it comes back again.

Like leaves on bare branches.

Like spring.

Author's Note

Even though the events of this story are fictional, they are far too real for so many in America. In 2019, overdose deaths in the United States surpassed 700,000, with over 50,000 of those deaths involving opioids. Tragically, these numbers will likely continue to rise along with the usage of other drugs, such as methamphetamine, cocaine, and heroin, and a drastic increase in illicitly manufactured fentanyl analogs—all of which has been complicated and exacerbated by the COVID pandemic. Although a lot of smart and dedicated people are fighting the problem from a lot of angles, it isn't going away anytime soon, and our tendency as a society to shame and other those who suffer from addiction only makes the problem worse.

The national addiction crisis is as devastating as it is

far-reaching, and whether the struggle is our own or that of a friend or loved one, it affects us all, regardless of age or ethnicity or socioeconomic status. It affects our communities, urban and rural, regardless of geography.

It has certainly affected my own hometown. The first seed of this story came from a youth night in response to this problem that I attended years ago with my son. The scheduled speaker had nearly lost everything—including his life—to painkillers. I knew he would be a powerful speaker, but I naively assumed his message might not be directly relevant for me and my family. My son has a supportive network of friends, teachers, coaches, church leaders, and immediate and extended family. He's a great student who excels at a lot of things. He has grown up with three pharmacists in the family, including his father, and a grandfather who was a judge for thirty-two years. As a result, he's been made very aware throughout his life of the heartbreaking and dangerous impact of drugs. He knows there may be a genetic propensity for addiction within him and has made a promise to himself and to me that he'll never cross—or even approach—that line. But above all, he's a kid who genuinely tries to do what's right, who aims for perfection in all he does.

We were only moments into the speaker's presentation that night when I realized that none of these things made my son immune. In fact, some of the very things I had always loved about him—his drive, his desire to be the best he could possibly be—were the very things that could make him vulnerable. The speaker described his own successes, athletic and academic and professional, and the tempting and temporary comfort that came from the painkillers he was given after an injury. For the first time in his life, he had found something that took the edge off the depressing and debilitating thought that, in spite of his successes, he had never been, and could never be, enough.

I wept as I saw my son in him.

So even though writers are not supposed to be obvious about the message within a novel, I want to state it here, for any reader who needs it:

You are enough.

Your worth doesn't come from the court, or your paycheck, or your number of likes or followers or whatever society seems to be telling you is important. It comes from the beating, bleeding heart inside you. Head, hands, heart. That's it.

In contrast to the events that occur in this book, addiction of any type is not a problem any of us should feel we have to take on without the help and support of the people who care about us most. When families are involved in the recovery process, people (and especially kids) do better, not worse.

All people and events in this story are fictional, except one: Coach Braithwaite is based on my own great-uncle

Wilbur Braithwaite, whose life and example formed the heart of this story and served as the heart of the town of Manti, Utah, throughout his life. With his wife, Jane, by his side, Wilbur coached basketball and tennis at Manti High School for fifty-one years, guiding his teams to eleven state championships—and earning himself a spot in the National High School Hall of Fame—without ever receiving a single technical foul! Wilbur's résumé is impressive, even beyond his coaching record: he held a master's degree from the University of Michigan and received a Purple Heart for wounds sustained in World War II. He played the piano and clarinet and wrote music and poetry.

A wise and thoughtful friend of mine, Conrad Wesselhoeft, once described to me his love for literature that explores "the cross-pollination of wisdom across the generations." He spoke those words right as I was wondering whether I could have the points of view of an eleven-year-old and an eighty-five-year-old in a young adult novel. I was so grateful for these words every time Luke's and Coach B's voices found their way into the book.

Because, of course, none of what happens in this story—or, indeed, in life—happens in isolation. If you or somebody you care about is struggling with addiction, please know that you're not alone, and that you are enough. And please, please, reach out for help.

Here are a few places you could start:

Substance Abuse and Mental Health Services Administration: SAMHSA offers a twenty-four-hour national helpline that provides free and confidential treatment referral and information about mental and/or substance use disorders, prevention, and recovery. Its website has a treatment program locator, where patients can find authorized programs across the country that treat addiction and dependence on opioids, such as heroin or prescription pain relievers. Call 1-800-662-HELP (4357) or visit samhsa.gov/find-help.

Partnership for Drug-Free Kids: This organization's helpline makes bilingual support specialists available (Monday to Friday, 9 a.m. to midnight, and Saturday to Sunday, noon to 5 p.m., Eastern time) to those concerned about a young person. Call 1-855-DRUGFREE (1-855-378-4373) or visit drugfree.org/get-help/helpline.

National Institute on Drug Abuse: NIDA's website offers general information about opioids and published research articles about opioid abuse and treatment. drugabuse.gov/drugs-abuse/opioids

Narcotics Anonymous: NA's website offers information about support for people with addiction who wish to maintain a drug-free lifestyle and about where to find local meetings. na.org

American Academy of Addiction Psychiatry: AAAP's website offers resources for patients and their families. aaap.org/patient-resources /helpful-links

(List adapted from abcnews.go.com/Health /resources-heroin-opioid-addiction -treatment-support/story?id=37352500.)

Acknowledgments

It's hard to express my gratitude for the championship team that helped bring this book into the world, but I'll try:

Ammi-Joan Paquette, thank you for your endless wisdom, your fierce advocacy, your unflagging confidence in me and my work, and your genuine friendship.

Michelle Frey, thank you for believing in me and in this story and for shaping it into something far better than I could have dreamed. Huge thanks to Nancee Adams, Jim Armstrong, Artie Bennett, Jake Eldred, Arely Guzmán, Amy Schroeder, Ray Shappell, Neil Swaab, and the entire team at Knopf.

I'm doubly lucky to have the input and expertise of two incredible writing groups. Jenn Bertman, Helen

Boswell, Ann Braden, Tara Dairman, Rosalyn Eves, Tasha Seegmiller, and Erin Shakespear: Your friendship means the world to me, and you make every page better, every time.

To my EMLA family, your emotional and enthusiastic response to the first pages of this book kept me going every single time I started to doubt myself or this story.

Heaps of gratitude to the expert readers who helped me get it right in terms of everything from astronomy to police procedure to painkiller addiction to recruiting practices to poetry: Todd Brown, Tracy Fails, Kari Ann Holt, Sharon Levy, Justin Ludlow, Carter Miller, Cameron Pace, Nick Parson, and Chloe Seegmiller. Any mistakes are my own, and sometimes I chose to have my characters make decisions that were not exercising their best judgment or applying first-line treatment.

And to the home team:

Mom and Dad, thank you for showing me what it looks like to be hardworking, kind, and honest—and what it feels like to be loved unconditionally.

Robbie, you made a difference in every aspect of this book, from the smallest pharmaceutical detail to the very soul of the story. How lucky I am that you have made such a difference in my life too.

Jack, thank you for saying *Fadeaway* was the best book you ever read. You are, now and always, my favorite son. I am so very proud of you.

Halle, you shine in every role you play in life. Thank you for being the kind of person who shows me every day how to dream big dreams.

Lucy, you are strong and smart and good and not only funny but—to use your own word—the most "hilariest" person I know. Thank you for making me smile and laugh and keep going, even when things are tough.

To all the extended family of both Braithwaite and Vickers branches, thank you for your endless love and support all along this journey.

And finally, thank you to the readers. It's all just words on a page until you bring it to life through the lens of your own thoughts and experiences. Please know how much that matters, and how much your voice matters to the world.

About the Author

E. B. Vickers grew up in a small town in the Utah desert, where she spent her time reading, playing basketball, and exploring. Several years and one PhD later, she found her way back to her hometown, where she now spends her time writing, teaching college chemistry, and exploring with her husband and three kids. This is her first novel for young adults. Visit her online at ebvickers.com.